DEAD ON TARGET

STEPHEN JOHNSON

Clan Destine
PRESS

First published by Clan Destine Press in 2025

Clan Destine Press

PO Box 121, Bittern

Victoria, 3918 Australia

Copyright © Stephen Johnson 2025

All rights reserved. No part of this book may be reproduced or transmitted in any form or by any means, including internet search engines and retailers, electronic or mechanical, photocopying (except under the provisions of the Australian Copyright Act 1968), recording or by any information storage and retrieval system, or for any form or use of AI, without prior permission in writing from the publisher.

National Library of Australia Cataloguing-In-Publication data:

Johnson, Stephen

TITLE: Dead on Target

ISBN: 978-1-922904-91-1 (paperback)

ISBN: 978-1-922904-92-8 (eBook)

Cover Design by © Willsin Rowe

Design & Typesetting by Clan Destine Press

Clan Destine
PRESS

www.clandestinepress.net

Dead on Target is dedicated to my editing angels,
Lindy, Ruth and Wendy – who gave my story its wings.

CHAPTER 1

APOLLO BAY, MAY

Morgan estimated he had 15 minutes to enjoy the fiery spectacle.
'Burn, you fucker.'
Sweat beaded his brow and arms, as flames spiralled into the night. He enjoyed the sensation, although technically he didn't consider himself a pyromaniac. Morgan believed he was an arsonist; his main pleasure came from the destruction, not from starting or watching the fire.

The ancient weatherboards ignited easily; the tin roof had peeled which aided combustion. The corrugated iron sheets and a pot belly stove would be among the few items likely to survive the inferno. Kitchen chairs, a table, cupboards, shelves and a bed were well ablaze.

It had been called a weekender by the last owner; a shack would have been an apt description. It was tucked into a gully at the end of a dirt track on the fringe of the Great Otway National Park. The first report of a glow in the hills would initiate a klaxon at the fire brigade headquarters in nearby Apollo Bay. Volunteers would scurry from homes, pubs, backyard barbecues. Most were likely to be within a few minutes of the station, about five kilometres from the inferno as a crow would fly. The narrow, winding access road would give the arsonist extra minutes to flee his crime scene before the truck arrived.

A side wall crumbled. Morgan watched sparks float towards the trees; he had waited for an evening with a sea breeze. Any collateral damage from the mission would blow away from his escape route down the creek. He picked up an empty plastic container; five litres of petrol and neglected timber had been enough to turn the rustic setting into a bonfire. He would have preferred the owner was inside to make it a funeral pyre, but that bastard was already burning in hell.

He biffed the red container into the flaming ruins where it melted swiftly. Investigators would know the fire was deliberate, he had even left a cryptic clue to taunt them because he knew the cops would never trace anything back to him. The preparations had been excruciatingly long, which meant the final plan was meticulous; no clever cop or forensics expert was going to spoil his mission. Any evidence of his time at the shack would soon be ashes.

A piercing wail from the sea heralded the approaching firefighters. He hoisted an empty daypack that had carried the fuel and sundries. His dark jacket, black jeans and hiking boots were tainted by the smell of petrol and smoke. He needed them as protection against the scrub and any startled snakes during the trek down the creek. The clothing would be changed at the car by the beach, then discarded in various bins on the drive back to Melbourne.

Morgan took a final look at his flaming handiwork. The shack's destruction hadn't been necessary. It had been empty, the real estate agent unable to find a buyer since the final occupant's car had been shunted over a cliff on the Great Ocean Road near Lorne. A bushfire or the forest might have consumed the shack within a few years. The blaze was symbolic for Morgan; it removed one of the last traces of the evil that had destroyed so many lives.

'The mission has started, Amy. You will have justice.'

Morgan turned his back on the blaze and disappeared into the bush.

CHAPTER 2

'I'm going to *kill* Stephanie.'

A flail.

'Sodding… Grant.'

Another wild swing.

Kim Prescott strangled the club, hands and fingers awkwardly interlaced around the skinny shaft.

A third swing. A clump of turf was hoiked 10 metres.

'Damn it.'

Jo Trescowthick yawned and reached into the coolpack at her feet for a juice bottle. It was three-quarters freshly squeezed oranges on a vodka base.

'I think Stephanie's safe. Unless you run across to the fifth fairway and clobber her with your iron.' Jo sipped.

Kim swung harder and connected. The fluorescent yellow ball dribbled 30 metres off the tee and rolled to a stop; taunting her: *come and smack me again – if you can.*

The other members of the golfing foursome, *Melbourne Spotlight* senior producers, David 'Mac' McKenzie and Christopher 'Curly' Rogers struggled to smother their laughter.

'I love these team building exercises. Does wonders–' Mac choked the cliché when Kim pointed a loaded 5-iron at him. 'Um, I think it's your turn Jo.'

The program's production manager hopped from the golf cart and teed up her ball; it was hot pink. The Big Bertha driver almost reached her chin. She swung it with the lethality of a headhunter and sent her ball 100 metres past her friend's effort.

'That was hardly elegant.' Kim said.

'It's not about style. Off you go, princess. Mac and I will have another cocktail while we wait for you to hack your way to the green.'

Jo resumed her seat in the cart where Mac was behind the wheel. Curly was on his phone a dozen metres away.

'Isn't that bad etiquette on a golf course?'

'Yeah. But we're journos – rules can be broken for a good story on a Sunday afternoon.'

'Who is it?'

'Don't know. But Curly was excited when he saw the contact's name. I'll forgive his bad manners for a program lead tomorrow.'

Mac pressed the accelerator and the cart rolled forward. Kim's next five swings progressed her yellow tormenter another 70 metres.

'I know Kim's not a golfer, but why is she so grumpy with Stephanie? I thought they were on friendlier terms.' Mac watched Kim's latest effort soar a mighty…not far. They would all get a second shot soon.

Jo pointed to Stephanie's foursome. 'Look who Steph's playing with.'

'Richard, Dugal and Hackett. They're all reasonable golfers; it makes sense to put them together.'

Jo shook her head. 'You're missing the obvious – as usual.'

'What? I know that Dugal and Stephanie are shagging. Why would that upset Kim?'

Jo rolled her eys. 'It's nothing to do with Dugal. That's over anyway. It's The Hatchet.'

Mac shrugged. 'I'm lost. He's been almost human the last few months. No cutbacks. Our booze budget hasn't been threatened. He's even found a cunning way to fund a Channel 5 correspondent in London.'

'Exactly. And who is on the committee to make the appointment?'

'The CEO, Richard Hackett.'

'And who have applied for the position?'

'Mike Berry, Pete Benson, Kim and – oh.' Mac nodded. Stephanie was the fourth candidate.

Jo shook her head. 'Kim's been watching Steph smash golf balls down the middle of the fairway – in between flirting outrageously with The Hatchet. This golf day, which was Steph's idea, was never about staff morale. It was an extended job interview, according to Kim's paranoia.'

Mac watched Stephanie step into a bunker. She looked like a LPGA professional: blonde ponytail, blue polo shirt, white skirt, tanned legs. Her shot landed close to the flag. He turned to Kim who was waiting for the cart; her glowing face wasn't from sunburn. He laughed.

'Maybe you should share some of your special juice to help her chill.'

Jo returned her bottle to the coolpack and snapped the lid. 'There's 15 holes to go. Some sacrifices can't be made.'

Mac stepped on the accelerator as Curly jumped onto the bag platform, another faux pas.

'Was that a good call or a bad call?' Mac didn't slow down.

'I'd say it was excellent. Scoot up to Kim and I'll tell everyone.'

They huddled on the side of the fairway and waved the final foursome through.

'That was Jim Laidlaw from Lorne on the phone.'

Two sets of eyebrows arched; Jo frowned. 'Who?'

'The cop who gave us the scoop on Tugga Tancred's car doing the swan dive over the cliff at Lorne.'

Jo bristled at the memory of the story they'd all covered five years before about the violent fallout of what Tugga and his awful mates had done 30 years ago.

Spotlight led the media pack for weeks on that story and it boosted the program's ratings, and kick-started Kim Prescott's reporting career.

'Do we have another gem from Lorne?'

'Apollo Bay, actually. Tugga's shack has been destroyed by fire.'

'Was it arson?' Kim asked.

'The fire crew reported a strong smell of petrol when they arrived, so probably.'

Mac scratched his ginger beard. 'Did anyone buy the property after Tugga died?'

'Never sold. Tugga had no family in Australia, his Kiwi relatives didn't want to touch it, so it's been empty. It's rough and hilly country, not likely to appeal to farmers. A couple of investors had a look but were spooked when they learned about Tugga's history. It's not considered haunted, just tainted.'

Mac folded his arms. 'It could be kids having a lark.'

'I doubt it,' Kim said. 'Most people know they could lose everything in a bushfire. My gut's telling me there's something sinister there. I think it's worth a look.'

'When did it happen?'

'Last night.'

'Do any other media know about it?'

'No. Apparently the Apollo Bay cop is new and and there was no other damage. Luckily it didn't set off a bushfire. But Jim saw the report this morning and recognised as Tugga's shack. So, we've got a headstart.'

Mac looked at Kim. 'Do you fancy escaping this golf purgatory?'

She shrugged.

'I thought you'd be in the cart and halfway to the office. What's wrong?'

'It's a worthy story, Mac. It's just that there are other things to consider.'

Jo stated the obvious. 'Kim's London job interviews are tomorrow and Tuesday. An old Tugga story isn't worth much compared to that'

Mac clicked his fingers. 'Don't worry about the inteview, Kim. We'll make sure you get a chance to impress the panel. But we do need to check this story out. I'm afraid you'll have to drive because the chopper is getting serviced this week. You'll be at Tugga's place first thing in the morning. Dugal or Kenny can bash a rough edit together. You might even get back in time to do some tweaks.'

'Curly can produce a retrospective on the Tugga's Mob saga,' Mac said. He turned to Jo, the office linchpin. 'Do you fancy some overtime to get them all organised?'

Jo grinned. 'Triple-time might pay the deposit for my Oxford canal boat trip.'

'Oh yeah, I forgot about your long service leave.' Mac shook his head. 'Go find Kenny or Dugal and see who can drive down the coast now.'

'Make it Kenny,' Kim said. 'I'll need Dugal to look after Sexy Rexy.' Kim's pet greyhound was used to shuttling around the *Spotlight* family for emergency accommodation.

Jo climbed into the golf cart. 'Jump in, Kim, we'll kidnap Kenny and head for the carpark. You guys can haul your own bags.'

Mac had barely unstrapped his Callaway clubs when Jo accelerated. She couldn't tell by the painful cry whether she had clipped Mac's toes or shin.

'Can I get one of these carts for the office?' she said.

CHAPTER 3

A Cast iron stove, charred timber, ash, roofing iron and scorched earth were all that remained of Tugga Tancred's shack by Monday afternoon. The *Spotlight* crew had the crime scene to themselves. The local cop declined to accompany them for an interview. He had more important police work; ticketing speeding drivers on the Great Ocean Road.

Kim, and her cameraman Kenny Withers, had hoped to send a rough-cut story to the studio by 1pm, then drive back to Melbourne. But thanks to the real estate agent running late were now likely to get stuck in rush-hour traffic on the way back. It had been a frustrating day all around. Nobody in Apollo Bay wanted to talk about a vendetta against the late Tugga Tancred; he was dead news on the coast these days.

Kim sniffed. There was a faint smell of fuel, whether or not it had cause the blaze remained to be seen. But the stench of burnt timber and melted plastic and metal would linger for weeks. She watched Kenny kneel with his camera for a low-angle shot. He would need all his creativity to make the limited debris look interesting on television.

Kenny grunted as he stood. 'Have you prepared a piece to camera yet?'

'No. It's not the most inspiring scene.'

He hoisted the camera to his shoulder, and filmed the blackened ground that stretched to the trees. 'It would've been a different story if the fire crew arrived 20 minutes later. This could've burned through to Colac.'

Kenny methodically worked the site, milking every angle and

shot while they waited for the real estate agent, the only person prepared to talk on camera.

Kim doodled on her notepad unable to find any interesting to say about this fire. 'Did you film any stories here after Tugga died?' she asked.

'Yeah,' Kenny said looking around the ruins. 'The shack was kinda appealing. Well, to guys like me who enjoy the outdoors, a few beers, a bit of isolation – and the occasional puff.'

Kim grinned. 'Where was his crop?'

'He had plants scattered through there.' Kenny pointed up the scrub-clad gully. 'The cops had ripped them out by the time we got here though.' He looked wistful. 'Hmmm. I wonder if any have seeded since then.'

'Don't even think about it.'

'You're so easy to wind up.' Kenny framed a close-up of the charred potbelly stove.

'Did you get a look inside the shack back then?'

'Yeah. But his porn collection had already been souvenired by the cops.'

'Until they realised it was evidence.'

Kenny looked puzzled. 'Why all the questions about what the shack used to look like? Shouldn't the story be about who wanted to burn it down?'

Kim jotted a note. 'I'm trying to get a feel for Tugga's bolthole. Was it a haven from city life, or a twisted shrine to the horrors he was involved in?'

A car horn announced the estate agent's arrival; a dust cloud followed the BMW sedan up the track.

'G'day, I'm Jonny Hayle.' The silk-suited, mid-30s salesman offered his hand. 'Can I interest you in a bush retreat?'

Kenny laughed and Kim smirked and they both shook the guy's hand. 'Never waste a sales opportunity, eh?' Kim said.

'Just practicing the patter – your story might attract some buyer interest. It was a shithole last week.' He surveyed the ruins. 'Run a bulldozer through that for five minutes and voila – you've got paradise in the Otways.'

Kenny chuckled and set the camera on his tripod for the

interview, while Kim followed Jonny's circuit of the blackened earth.

'If you keep talking like that, the local cop might suspect you've created a sales opportunity,' she said.

Jonny laughed and prodded a broken teacup with his boot. 'Nah. It would cause him too much paperwork to investigate. Not that I torched the shack. It was out of sight, out of mind for everyone in town – and our business. All our work is along the coast. We can't find enough holiday homes for city folk. The Melburnians come down for sun, surf and seafood. They don't want to waste time working on a bush block.'

'Have you had any interest at all in the property since Tugga's death?'

'I've brought six people here. Nobody lasted longer than my spiel about the glorious Otways.' Jonny pointed to the hills. 'That is spectacular.' His arm swung to Tugga's landholding. 'This is a waste of money. It would cost too much to clear the gully, and there wouldn't be any benefit. It's too small to graze stock, not worth planting anything legal and has no views. The only person who would want to build here is another hermit. Like Tugga.'

'Did you know him?'

'By sight and reputation. He had some fights at pubs along the coast road, but kept his nose clean in Apollo Bay. He always looked menacing and never encouraged conversation when he dropped into the pub to watch the All Blacks and the Wallabies matches. Most people avoided him.'

Kim made another note as she guided Jonny towards the camera. 'What's your theory about who started the fire? Was it a firebug? Kids? Someone with a belated grudge against Tugga?'

Jonny looked at the ashes. 'Nobody local would be silly enough to light a fire in the bush. No, this has to be the work of an outsider, and it was well-planned.'

Kim look surpised. 'What makes you think say that?'

Jonny waved at the whole scene.' Someone cleared the low scrub all around the shack. When I was last here that vegetation was encroaching on the bush back there. But as you can see, it's been cleared down to the dirt.

'Talk at the pub last night was the fire was started by someone who still had stupid grudge against Tugga; or it was us trying to make the land saleable.'

Kim nodded. 'Brilliant. Now, we'll get that on camera, and you can go prepare a new sales pitch.'

Jonny was a natural on camera. He repeated all the important comments on cue and even accented the arsonist's likely retribution against Tugga. It gave Kim's story some legs, although there were no clues about the culprit.

'Thanks for time Jonny,' Kim said.

'Happy to help. I wonder if you can do me a favour. Would you mind including a shot of the For Sale sign by the entrance in your footage? The fire truck must have knocked it over. I've fixed it. I'm hoping an investor watching your program will smell a bargain. No pun intended. We don't care about the price anymore – we just want the property sold.'

'Sure. We'll do that on the way out,' Kim said.

Jonny departed with a smile and another dust trail.

'Do you really want to record a real estate sign?' Kenny asked.

'No. I'll put the company name on his baseline key. No sense sending him away grumpy.'

'What about a piece to camera? Any inspiration yet?'

'I've got an idea for a walking shot along the track. Let's go down to the gate and set up.'

'Okay. No sense packing away the camera then.' Kenny threw her the SUV keys and got in the passenger seat. 'Don't hurt my baby.'

Kim climbed in behind the wheel and they headed down the drive. Thirty seconds later Kim slammed on the brakes and skidded to a stop. Even Kenny didn't complain as they both stared open mouthed at the back of the For Sale sign.

Handwritten in charcoal and in large letters were two words:
For Amy.

'Holy shit!' Kim said. 'Now we've got a real story.'

Chapter 4

Spotlight's producer, 'Mac' McKenzie, was on the phone to Kim who was talking at a million miles an hour. His phone was on speaker so Jo could listen in.

'That's brilliant, Kim. How long before Kenny can send us the rough cut?'

'We'll send it through in half an hour. What do you want us to do in the meantime?

'I think it's worth spending a night on the coast,' Mac said, swivelling his chair to the office maven. 'What do you think, Jo?'

Jo nodded and said, 'I'll sort hotel rooms for you, Kim.'

Mac gave Jo the thumbs up, and said to Kim, 'The local plod might get a rocket up his arse after our story airs. Let's see if he calls in the arson squad or other detectives in the morning. It'd be good to have you on the spot.'

'What about my interview for the London job?'

'You won't miss out, mate. I'll talk to them upstairs. And now, it's time for me and Curly to bash the background of this story into shape, while we wait for your footage. Cheers.'

He hung up and glanced across The Dungeon, the crew's nickname for their subterranean Channel 5 office. 'What's going on there?' he asked Jo. 'Steph is almost floating around the editing suite with Dugal. I thought you said they weren't shagging anymore.'

'They weren't, but I heard they left the golf club together last night. So who knows? But I doubt that's why she's excited. Steph's just finished her London job interview. It looks like she's seriously happy with how it went.'

'A bit bloody premature for her to be so confident when Kim hasn't even had her interview yet,' Mac said. He swivelled to glance at Richard Templeton's office. The executive producer hadn't returned from the top floor yet. 'I need to know if they've offered already Steph the job. Can you wheedle it out of Richard when he gets back?'

'Why?'

'Kim would kill me if she missed her chance to present to the panel because I sent her on a job.'

'Okay – but judging by Steph's excitement, you might need to start running.' Jo rolled her chair to the kitchen for a caffeine fix.

Andrew Hackett was in a buoyant mood when he arrived at his luxury Southbank apartment. Channel 5's chief financial officer barely glanced at the breathtaking views of the city and Port Phillip Bay, that only mattered to him because it made his ex-wife, Marianne, jealous. His pleasure had peaked with her instant envy and the knowledge her boyfriend, the ex-SAS wanker, could never afford to buy anything this extravagant.

Hackett went straight to the oak-panelled office on the south side. It was a masculine room: business books, travel mementos, golf trophies lined the shelves behind the large desk which faced the bay. He regretted allowing the interior designer to hang a two-metre by two-metre modernist painting on a side wall. It was crap. But he couldn't bin it because Marianne had told him it was crap. Hackett never surrendered post-divorce points easily.

He had walked to and from the TV studios, that short exercise merited a generous gin and tonic. A panel beside the shelves opened to reveal a mini fridge and half a dozen gin bottles. He reached for the Hendrick's and poured. He wanted to continue working, but the housekeeper hadn't filled the ice tray or left any lemons. A tart note would be left for her in the morning.

The views were ignored again as he walked through the extended gallery and living room before hooking through the formal dining room to reach the north-facing kitchen. The apartment occupied the whole floor. It was too large for his requirements: he had not remarried, the kids were living overseas, he travelled often.

Its purchase was more than a "Fuck You, Marianne." It was a

secure haven in the sky. Crazy daughters – that he didn't know he'd sired – could never get at him 60 floors above the street.

Hackett glanced at his watch: spreadsheets, or turn on the TV to see if Stephanie Grant had a story on *Melbourne Spotlight* this evening? The thought of Steph made him smile. He was looking forward to some gratitude sex with Channel 5's new London correspondent on his next UK trip.

It wasn't official; chief executive Reg Bradley wanted to hear from the final candidate before deciding. It was clear that Richard Templeton favoured Kim Prescott, the ambitious younger reporter who had taken a bullet in the back while solving a double murder. Hackett gave Kim credit for creating ratings-winning stories; she and the team had a knack for finding bodies, earning them a weird nickname as The Cadaver Crew. Journalists have a sick sense of humour.

But, in an even contest between the abilities – and attributes – of the females, there would be no thank you benefits from Kim. Stephanie's flirtations on the golf course indicated she knew how the corporate game should be played. The executives were tied at one-all until Reg cast his vote. Hackett was considered heir apparent to the studio throne and recokoned he could sway Bradley's vote.

He rejected work and retired to his formal lounge room with the plush sofa and the biggest of his five televisions. His mobile pinged and he reached for it, hoping the call would save him from saturation coverage of the weekend footy matches. Bugger. It was Marianne.

She'd been texting more frequently since SAS Mitch had taken an overseas bodyguard contract. Their contact caused mixed emotions for Hackett; the iciness and silly gamesmanship had softened. He was never going to forgive Marianne's treachery, but his bitterness was easier to manage. Sometimes. He decided to ignore his ex until after Stephanie's stint on *Spotlight*.

And besides, he had an idea why Marianne's was texting. She suspected Mitch was cheating with his new client, an oligarch's daughter. Six months ago, Hackett's response would've been brutal: *betrayal's a bitch*. He'd since tempered his tone, but still enjoyed some of the pain Mitch's alleged duplicity had inflicted.

Hackett reached for his gin as the news anchor introduced Richard Templeton in the *Spotlight* set.

'Who wants justice for a dead killer? A mysterious fire in Apollo Bay reopens the Tugga's Mob saga that left a trail of bodies throughout Australia and New Zealand five years ago. All for a crime that went unpunished for three decades. Join me for a Melbourne Spotlight exclusive, after the weather report.

Hackett spat gin all over himself and the ottoman. 'What the fuck?'

The intercom buzzed. The nearest was in the kitchen, where he picked up a tea towel to mop up his drink. 'And fuck again!' he said when he saw his ex-wife's face in the screen.

He pressed the button. 'What?'

'Didn't you get my text that I was coming over Andrew?'

'I was watching the news. Didn't hear the phone. What's wrong?'

'I–' Marianne looked over her shoulder. 'I can't talk down here. There are people in the atrium.'

Hackett sighed. 'Okay, I'll send the lift for you.'

He was torn. Good manners demanded he greet Marianne at the lift, but that might mean missing the program start. The television won. What further pain was Tugga going to cause him from the grave. He left the front door open and dashed for the sofa. The program titles arrived at the same time as Marianne.

'Andrew? Where are you?'

'In the lounge!'

She entered as Templeton read the introduction.

'I know my visit was short notice, Andrew, but I expected a bit more courtesy than an open door–'

Hackett waved her to silence.

'What's so important that you couldn't–'

'Shh. You'll find out.'

Hackett focused on the television as the screen changed to the charred ruins of a humble shack at Apollo Bay, and Kim's voiceover.

'This is all that's left of Tugga Tancred's bolthole in the bush near Apollo Bay–'

'Oh God,' said Marianne as she slumped onto the other end sofa. 'Why would someone want to destroy it after all this time?'.

Hackett shrugged. 'Let's just listen,' he said as a local real estate agent appeared on the screen.

> *'We don't think it was anyone from the coast who started the fire. They hardly knew Mr Tancred and a bushfire in the Great Otway National Park would be devastating.'*

The camera cut away to Kim.

> *'Do you have any theories, Mr Hayle?'*

> *'If you go by the gossip in the pub last night, it was someone who really hated Tugga. My own opinion, having followed your program's original stories about him and his awful mates, is that the police should be looking for someone who's stilll out for payback. I think anyone who still has anything to do with Tugga's Mob should be very worried.'*

'Oh fuck!' Hackett's head drooped.

Marianne's hand covered her gaping mouth.

The camera angle changed to a dusty track. Kim walked into frame.

> *'At first we thought Jonny Hayle was being dramatic, until we were about to leave the property.'*

The camera stayed with Kim as she walked towards a country gate.

> *'Mr Hayle had told us he'd fixed the fallen For Sale at the entrance to the property, believing it had been knocked over by the fire crews on Saturday night. Mr Hayle did not realise in doing so he had revealed a vital clue to the motive for his fire.'*

The camera now revealed two words written in charcoal on the back of the sign:

For Amy

Hackett and Marianne gasped. Kim's voiceover continued.

> 'We believe this refers to Amy Stewart, who had targeted the members of Tugga's Mob for raping her mother during a European bus tour in the 1980s.
>
> Ms Stewart murdered four members of the group, and the tour driver, Eddie Malone, as payback. Mr Malone was not involved in the sexual attack on Judy Williams in a Dutch campsite, but Ms Stewart blamed him for failing to protect her mother when she'd complained about sexual harassment.
>
> 'The fifth member of Tugga's Mob was Andrew Hackett, currently a Channel 5 executive. Ms Williams had been his girlfriend during the bus tour. Hackett denied knowledge of the rape but Ms Stewart clearly didn't believe him. She attacked Hackett with a crossbow at his home in South Yarra. He was saved when a security guard shot Ms Stewart. DNA testing later revealed that Amy Stewart was Andrew Hackett's daughter.'

Hackett downed the rest of his gin, as he watched Kim walk to the side of the track.

> 'We have alerted police about the implications of this message. Detectives will return tomorrow to look for more clues. This sign could be vital. Amy's only living relatives have been in prison for the last five years for helping her commit the murders.
>
> 'This fire now appears to be much more than an arson attack on a rapist's empty shack. Someone is seeking justice for a killer; for Amy Stewart.
>
> 'We cannot yet explain what that might involve.'

'Fuck, fuck, fuck!' Hackett raked fingers through his grey hair. 'Why didn't those bastards in The Dungeon warn me?'

Marianne stared at the TV which was now showing a package on the original *Spotlight* invesitagion and the past sins of Tugga and Amy.

'I need another drink.' Hackett stood. 'Do you want anything?'

Marianne shook her head as if to shake off memories of the

nightmare that had torn their marriage apart. He picked up the remote and killed the program. 'You don't need to see that again.'

The spell was broken. 'Maybe I'll have a whisky.'

He returned with their drinks and sagged into the soft leather.

'Who the hell wrote that on the sign? And what does it mean?'

'Are you in danger, Andrew?'

Hackett raised an arm, then let it fall. 'I don't know.'

'Do you need protection again?'

Hackett closed his eyes and pursed his lips. He wanted to yell at Marianne. That worked really well last time!

He breathed heavily. Her warm hand found his.

Chapter 5

Kenny drank deeply from his pint as he browsed the pub menu. Kim had claimed the seat in front of the brick and glass decagon fireplace. It was a cool autumn night so the heat from the burning logs was welcome. Kim scanned a list she'd compiled while watching the *Spotlight* program in her Apollo Bay hotel room.

Tugga Tancred – Dead
Drew Harvey – Dead
Gerry Daley – Dead
Helen Franks – Dead
Eddie Malone – Dead
Amy Stewart – Dead
Heather Langer – Prison
Jason Langer – Prison

Kim sipped her sauvignon blanc before adding the final name.

Andrew Hackett – Alive.

'For how long?' Kenny had learned an essential journalistic skill: reading upside down writing. 'I wonder if he saw the story. Hope he's shitting himself.'

'It doesn't make sense. The Langers have at least another decade behind bars – who's left to carry on Amy's vendetta?'

'Maybe they hired a hitman in gaol but had to wait for him – or her – to get out.'

Kim tapped the table with her pen. 'Possibly, but I don't think it's likely. The Langers were a broken family. Heather and Jason pleaded guilty – they wanted to forget about the whole Tugga thing.' Kim made a note. 'I'll check with the Corrections Department in New Zealand in case they've turned into prison thugs.'

Kenny snorted. 'I'm hungry. Can you order me the surf 'n' turf?' He looked over Kim's shoulder at the pool tables. 'I'll see if I can hustle some beer money while we wait.'

Kim rolled her eyes and searched her purse for the company credit card as she walked to the bar.

'Didn't I just see you on the TV?' slurred the short, bald man in grease-stained blue overalls swaying next her with a beer in one hand and a slice of pizza in the other.

'Yeah,' he added. 'You just done that story on Tugga.'

Baldy and Kim were the only people at the bar. Brilliant. Most drinkers tuned out the television, unless it was sport, or a story from their backyard, which admittedly applied to anyone in this pub. She was almost saved by the barman returning from the cellar.

'Riley, this lovely lass is a TV star. She knows all about Tugga's drunken orgies in the hills.'

'Oh really?'

Kim winced, and then saw the bewliderment on the barman's face. Maybe he was the only person in Apollo Bay who didn't know about Tugga. Kim didn't want to encourage the drunk, but ignoring him wouldn't work either.

'I was doing a story on the fire. I don't know much else.' She turned to the barman. He was rather handsome: mid 30s, tall, fit, dirty blonde hair and designer stubble. 'Can I order two meals please – a surf 'n' turf and the calamari?'

While the barman was logging her order Kim's new fan kept talking.

'Come on, love, you must have some juicy gossip.' He took another swig from his pot as an olive fell from his pizza. 'Tugga and his mates are all dead. Who else is left?'

'Bryan. She's off duty. Go finish your dinner and leave her in peace.'

Kim mouthed a thank you as Bryan grumbled back to his seat under the television. He didn't take his dismissal easily.

He collected the rest of his pizza moved to a table closer to the fireplace where Kim had been sitting.

Kim decided to stay at the bar until Kenny came back. The barman could be a nice distraction until the meals arrived.

'You don't sound local, Riley.'

'No. I'm English,' he said, stacking glasses in trays for the dish washer.

'Then Tugga doesn't hold any interest for you.'

Riley laughed. 'The first time I even heard the name was Sunday, when everyone was talking about the idiot who lit the fire at his shack. I heard bits and pieces about him since.' He shrugged. 'Wasn't really paying attention. No offence–'

'Kim,' she said.

'Pleased to meet you, Kim. News in general doesn't interest me much, it's really not my circus.'

'Weren't you curious when all the firefighters ran out of the pub on Sunday night?'

'I missed the excitement. Wasn't working on that night. I went to Geelong to watch the Cats game.'

Kim smiled; it was good to meet an English convert to Aussie Rules footy.

'Are you here for a while, or doing a working Aussie pub crawl?

'I've done a bit of that.' Riley's smile was enigmatic.

Their conversation was interrupted by an empty glass being thumped onto the bar.

'Take it easy there Bryan, if you want another beer.'

'Sorry, Riley. I thought you were going to spend all night chatt'n up this TV star.'

Kim ignored Bryan as Riley poured him a fresh one.

'This is your last. Okay? I don't want the boss to lose his licence.'

Bryan shrugged, then slouched against the bar. 'Say, what do you call an avenger for an avenger?'

Kim refused to take the bait.

Riley looked at her, then took Bryan's money. 'What do you mean?

'Well, the media,' Bryan jerked a thumb at Kim. 'They reckoned

25

the woman who killed Tugga and his mates was an avenging angel. She died trying to get payback for her Mum. If someone is trying to get justice for Amy, what do you call *that* killer? Can you have a double avenger?'

Bryan chortled. 'Maybe I'm not that pissed. I know more than people give me credit for.' He winked as he swayed back to the table for his last slice of pizza.

Chapter 6

Morgan, logged in to the Channel 5 website, was watching the *Spotlight* story for the third time.

'Look at that, Amy. They got the message I left them, even though the bloody firies nearly ruined it by knocking the sign down.'

He'd never doubted *Melbourne Spotlight* would investigate the fire. The current affairs team had been an integral part of the original investigation; pride wouldn't allow them to be eclipsed by another news channel.

He felt safe. There was nothing in the news report to connect to him. Even any bootprints he'd left would be mingled among the firefighters. And cops, camera crew and the estate agent had also tromped through the ashes. Morgan was sure the detectives didn't have the budget or inclination to make plaster casts of every footprint. Besides, he'd already dumped his boots a long way from Apollo Bay. Checking tyre tracks would be a bigger waste of time and money. Investigators would focus on the sign and possibly more closely on the fire now.

'They won't identify me from that.'

Morgan wanted the message to stand out, and wanted it written in ash. So before he'd set the fire he filled a ziplock bag with ash from Tugga's own potbelly stove, and found some linseed oil in a cupboard to bind it. He wrote *For Amy* with a steady, gloved hand. There was no DNA to trace, and he'd burnt the gloves. It was ironic that his careful work was almost ruined by a zealous firefighter with poor driving skills.

He poured another red wine as he thought about the sign hiccup.

It would have been frustrating; bruising for his ego, but not damaging to his mission. It didn't change what he would achieve in the coming weeks. The system had let Amy down; her quest for justice had been brutally cut short. He would make amends for that. The Aussies and Kiwis would come to understand the significance of the crimes he was about to commit. And all thanks to the *Spotlight* crew. He knew they wouldn't drop this. They were already playing their part.

Chapter 7

Police tape now blocked the track entrance to Tugga's shack when the *Spotlight* crew arrived on Tuesday morning.

'I didn't think the detectives would move that fast,' Kim said. A forensic officer was examining the For Sale sign while a man and a woman in suits watched.

'I guess that's another surprise,' Kenny said.

Three heads turned their way; one of them was Detective Sergeant Nathan Potter. He'd been Kim's occasional lover since they met at a murder scene during the first Tugga investigation. Busy careers and the pandemic had scuppered a permanent relationship. They were still friends, although hadn't caught up for several months. Nathan smiled as Kim exited the vehicle. The female investigator scowled.

'Hi Nathan. I didn't know you had been banished to the bush. What have you done wrong?'

'It's your fault,' he said, smiling. 'The boss saw your story and told me to get my arse down here before you found a new body. This is DC Baines.'

Everyone except Baines laughed.

'How are you, Kenny? If I had known you were with Kim, I would have brought down the whole homicide team. What's your cadaver count?'

The forensic officer and Baines shared an incredulous look.

Kenny retrieved the camera from its case. 'I've got three with Kim. But she found another body in New Zealand.'

'But he wasn't dead.' Kim enjoyed the discomfort of the other two officers.

'He would have been if you and Jo kept him locked up in your van for a few more hours,' Kenny said, grabbing his camera from the SUV. 'Don't forget the Queenscliff victim at the murder mystery weekend.'

'Oh yeah, he almost slipped my mind,' Kim said.

Nathan glanced at his colleague and laughed. 'Don't worry, I'll fill you in on the drive back.'

Kim pointed at the forensics team near the sign. 'Are you okay if we record this part, Nathan?'

'No probs. But you can't go back up to the shack. We're obviously taking a closer look at the site. And I'm sure you got all the good stuff yesterday.'

Kenny moved closer to the taped area around the sign, and chatted quietly to DC Baines between shots. His professional charm worked as usual; she smiled and shuffled aside for him.

Nathan and Kim withdrew to the side of the *Spotlight* car. 'I see Kenny hasn't lost his crime scene skills. What's happening with him and Jo – is it an on or off again month?'

Kim sniggered. 'Who knows? Jo's flying to Europe soon for long service leave. She's booked a canal boat holiday in England – but keeping quiet about who her crewmates are. Anyway, what about you – any new romances?'

'Um.' Nathan glanced towards DC Baines who, it seemed, had positioned herself to watch both Kenny and her boss/boyfriend.

'Oh.' Kim blushed. 'Sorry, I shouldn't pry.' She supressed a pang of jealousy; their third parting had obviously been the last. 'We've only been out a couple of times. You know, drinks – a meal.'

'What did you say her name was?'

'Cheryl Baines.'

'She looks nice.' Cheryl's dark bob, high cheekbones, almond eyes and athletic body warranted more than a half-hearted assessment. Kim changed the subject to safer territory.

'What's your assessment of the fire? Who did it – and how does it involve Amy?'

Nathan scuffed the gravel. 'On camera, all I can say is that we're making inquiries.' He turned his back on the trio around the sign.

'Off the record, we've got no leads and yeah – I'm worried. It's a stark warning.'

'But who would want to avenge Amy – and why?' Kim asked. 'She killed all of Tugga's rapist mates. I can sort of understand her twisted logic in going after Eddie Malone too, because he didn't protect her mother from Tugga's sexual harassment.' Kim shivered at the memory of finding the former tour bus driver stabbed to death on his own doorstep.

'So who is this arsonist warning?' she asked.

Nathan shrugged. 'Your own program suggested Andrew Hackett – for the same reason, that he didn't protect Amy's mum.'

Kim rolled her eyes. 'Yeah, we said that. But who could still be angry enough to target *him* after all these years.'

'There's no statute of limitations on revenge.'

Kim leaned on the bonnet of the SUV. 'Again, who? Amy has no relatives outside of prison. Did she have a boyfriend or girlfriend that we never found?'

'We checked. She'd been single for a while. Her Kiwi teaching colleagues said Amy had dropped out of the dating scene.'

'So, you've got a mystery man or woman chasing justice for Amy. And you don't know what that might involve. I'm glad you're the cop.'

Nathan smiled ruefully.

'Sarge.' DC Baines was approaching. 'Jacobs wants to know if we should fingerprint the reporter.'

Kim raised an eyebrow at Nathan.

'Kim has been around a few crime scenes. We already have her prints on file.'

The constable frowned while Kim choked a laugh.

'Take the car up to the shack, Cheryl. I'll be along in a few minutes.'

'Yes Sarge.' Cheryl returned to the car, waited while the technician loaded his gear, then drove up to the remains of the shack.

Nathan and Kim joined Kenny who had set up his tripod.

'Come on. Let's record my noncommittal responses and get you out of here before you clutter things up with another body.'

Kenny handed Kim a microphone but addressed Nathan. 'Do you reckon Hackett will get police protection this time? I don't think he'll trust a private bodyguard again – not since his wife fucked the last one.'

'You're cruel, Kenny.' Nathan smiled as he straightened his tie and jacket. 'To be honest, I really don't know. My bosses will want hard evidence Hackett's in danger before they commit to the expense. It could be someone having a lark, or a business rival trying to distract him. It's bizarre, but crazier things have happened.'

'But you don't think that's the case,' Kim said.

'No. My instincts tell me this is serious.'

CHAPTER 8

Mac stood in front of the floor-to-ceiling window of Channel 5's boardroom. News and current affairs producers rarely enjoyed these city views. Few left the 10th floor with their job intact. *Spotlight*'s senior producer knew he was in for a confrontation; the summons had been from The Hatchet. His own executive producer, Richard Templeton, had intervened and demanded to be part of the meeting, along with the chief executive. Mac was confident he would be sent back to the dungeon after a few minutes ranting.

Andrew Hackett was a veteran of executive skirmishes. He entered the boardroom alone and slammed the door. Mac grimaced; he'd been ambushed.

'Don't think Reg or Richard are going to save you. They're under the impression the meeting has been delayed half an hour.'

Mac folded his arms. He was half a head taller and carried an extra 20 kilos than the angry finance boss; there was no physical danger. Fuck him.

'Okay. Have your say – I've got a program to produce.'

Hackett paused half a beat. 'Why the fuck didn't you call me about what the crew found at Apollo Bay.'

'I did,' Mac glared.

'No, you didn't.' Hackett held out his iPhone. 'There's nothing on there from anybody in *Spotlight*.'

'I sent you a text.'

'When?'

'Yesterday afternoon.' Mac retrieved his phone from a back pocket. He flicked through to his message service and showed Hackett. 'I sent that at 3.43pm.'

Evidence someone has restarted Amy's vendetta. You might be in danger. Call me or watch program tonight.

Mac watched the executive hissy fit fizzle.

'I don't understand it.' Hackett held out his own screen. 'These messages came in while I was doing the London job interviews. But nothing from you.'

Mac could understand the anger, but he had no explanation for the missed text. 'It's a company phone and we're both with the same service. You can check with them but, really, that horse is well down the road. More importantly, do you think this might be a fair dinkum threat, or someone playing mind games with you?'

Hackett threw the phone on the table. 'I don't bloody know.'

'My team have been digging all day. They've confirmed that Amy's collaborators are still in prison. The Langers deny any connection to the fire. The New Zealand corrections department says Heather and Jason are model prisoners; eager to serve their time and get back to their Waikato farm.'

'Then who else is left to come after me? And why? I wasn't involved with Judy's rape.' Hackett slumped into a chair and pivoted to the window. 'Your program made that clear when Amy's campaign was uncovered. I shouldn't be a target for another twisted nutter.'

'Do you think you are?'

Hackett threw up his hands in frustration. 'You told me I was. There's the fire, the Amy reference. You don't think they're going to stop at burning a shack.'

'Probably not. But I'm wondering if you're likely to be the primary target?'

Hackett frowned. 'Amy got everyone but me. Who else is there left to kill?'

'The person who killed Amy.'

'Oh.' Hackett leaned forward. 'I hadn't thought about that. Mitch Stevens shot her. It would make sense to go after him – if there's any sense attached to this. But the killer's not likely to find him. He's out of the country.'

'Where?'

'Somewhere in the UK. He's got a lucrative job babysitting

a filthy rich Russian oligarch's daughter. He's been gone for a couple of weeks.'

Mac understood the conversation might be entering awkward territory. Everyone and their dog knew about the scandal of the bodyguard and Hackett's wife. Mac wondered if Hackett was thinking the former soldier was already screwing his new client; he let a lengthy pause twist that knife.

'Perhaps Mitch should be given the heads-up.'

Hackett grunted.

Mac shrugged but understand why Hackett didn't give a shit about Mitch. 'This does leave you as the only local target.'

Hackett flinched.

Mac didn't feel guilty. 'Have you made any security plans?'

'I spoke to the cops an hour ago. They said there hasn't been a specific threat against me. If I want protection, I'll have to pay for it.'

'Will you?'

Hackett looked Mac in the eye. 'After what happened last time?' A long pause. 'I don't know.'

Mac knew about Hackett's current luxury nest. A highrise apartment was more secure than the South Yarra backyard where everyone thought the case had ended.

'Have you got any business trips planned?'

Hackett nodded. 'Europe.'

'Can you bring that forward – and make it last longer than you originally planned? The pandemic has shown that businesses can be run from anywhere with an internet connection. It would give the cops – and my crew – time to see if there is any substance to this story, or if someone's yanking your chain.'

'Fucking bizarre tactic to spook me.'

'It's working. Normally, I'd be asking you to sit down for an interview with Kim or Steph. This time, I think it's safer for you to keep a lower profile. We won't badger you – unless we find evidence that might explain why this arsonist has picked up Amy's torch.'

Hackett leaned on the table. 'I have some business to sort out in France. I could go there earlier' He ran shaky fingers through his thinning hair. 'My son and daughter and their kids have been begging me to visit. Plus, there are a few details to sort before the London correspondent can start.'

'You're still going to interview Kim,' Mac said pointedly. 'It was bad timing I had to send her out of town. She deserves a chance to be considered.'

Hackett shrugged. 'Yeah. Reg booked a slot for tomorrow morning. The girls will know our decision by lunchtime.'

Mac didn't know whether to be relieved or disheartened. Whether it was Kim or Stephanie, he was going to be short a good reporter for his roster.

Chapter 9

Kim texted her producer as Kenny filled the SUV's petrol tank in Apollo Bay.

    Leaving in 5. Unless chopper back in service

She didn't expect a reply. Curly Rogers would be busy with an editor fine-tuning their rough-cut story. She closed her eyes. A knock on the window startled her. It was Bryan, the pub drunk, still in the same dirty overalls. Kenny had gone inside the servo to pay. She reluctantly opened the window.

'What did the cops tell you about the fire? They got a suspect?'

The beer smell overwhelmed the petrol fumes.

'No. Nothing new to report, Bryan. We're going back to Melbourne.' Kim reached for the window button.

'Do they know about the car on the beach on Saturday night?'

'What car?'

'Little Jap car.'

Kim remembered Bryan's pub boast about knowing more than people gave him credit for. Was he grandstanding, or did he know something important? 'Why did it make you suspicious?'

'I saw it on my way to the pub late arvo – and it was leaving, with the lights off, as I was walkin home. Same time the trucks were screaming up the main road to deal with the fire.'

'It's a holiday resort, Bryan. The car could've belonged to someone at one of the beach houses.'

'No beach houses there. And it was one of them shady carparks. You know, a bit hidden.'

'Maybe someone had a picnic or a walk on the beach.'

'Nah, the beach is shitty there. Even local fishermen avoid it. So who would park there for four hours – at night.' Bryan tapped his nose. 'And it's getting cold on the coast now.'

That was true; Kim had used the heater in her hotel room last night. She shrugged at Bryan. 'So a hidden carpark? What beach?'

Bryan pulled what he seemed to think was a secretive face. 'Not telling ya everything at once.'

'We need something, Bryan,' Kim said. 'A random car on a random beach is bugger all news.'

Bryan shrugged an okay. 'One of the many beaches between Tugga's road and the one to my place.'

Now Kim was interested. 'Okay. What kind of car? What colour?'

'White Corolla. Didn't look like a local; it was too clean inside.'

'Inside? You had a look inside?'

Bryan shrugged.

'Was it a rental?'

'Dunno. Could've been.'

The pandemic had reduced rental stocks, but there were still hundreds of tourists on the Great Ocean Road every day. Kim would need to pass this info, and Bryan's details, on to Nathan. Should she also get Bryan on camera?

Kenny returned, arms loaded with sugary treats. 'Everything okay, Kim?'

'Yep. Bryan was telling me he saw a suspicious car on a beach near Tugga's road on Sundday.'

'Oh yeah?' Kenny nodded. 'Did you see anyone, or just a car?' Kenny dumped his junk food stash on the seat.

Bryan grinned and tapped his nose again.

Kim sighed. 'Does that mean yes or no?'

'Might've seen someone.'

'Male or female?'

'What's it worth?'

'Oh. You want money to talk?'

'Yeah. You TV people pay a fortune for news.'

Kenny shook his head. 'Wrong channel, mate.'

Kim pointed at the lollies. 'You can help yourself to the Twisties or Jaffas. But we don't have money for interviews.'

Bryan's grin faded. 'I might really know something.'

'It's still just a car and maybe a person,' Kenny said.

'On the passenger seat...' Bryan began.

'What?' Kim said impatiently.

'There might've been one of them glossy real estate pamphlets of land for sale. Is that worth anything?'

'It might be to the cops, Bryan. I'll call the detective on our way back to Melbourne. What's your phone number?'

Bryan shuffled nervously. 'Don't have one.'

'What's your surname, Bryan.'

'Don't need to tell you.' He backed away from the car.

'The cops will find you. All they have to do is walk into the pub any night.'

'Shit.' Bryan turned and fled as a BMW pulled into a pump beside them and Jonny Hayle emerged.

'G'day guys. Looks like you've got the town drunk running scared. Maybe he'll keep going to Warrnambool.' They all watched Bryan disappear around the corner. 'What did you say to him?'

'That we wouldn't pay him for an interview,' Kenny said.

The estate agent was gobsmacked. 'What would Bryan Cowan know that would be worth anyone listening to?'

Bingo! They had his full name, but Kim didn't want a gabby salesman knowing about a possible suspicious car. She realised she should've handled Bryan more delicately.

'Bryan thinks he saw something on the beach on Saturday night. He was vague,' Kim said, also being vague. 'We reckon he was bullshitting to get some beer money. We suggested he talk to the detectives, that's when he ran off.'

Jonny nodded and turned to fill his car. 'Hey. Great story last night. We've had a couple of inquiries about Tugga's property. Showing our sign worked well for all of us.'

Kenny moved his snacks so he could get in and start the car. 'Does that mean we split the commission three ways?'

They could see Jonny still laughing in the rear vision mirror as they merged with traffic onto the Great Ocean Road.

'Was I too dismissive with Bryan?'

'Don't think so,' Kenny said. 'Can you open the Jaffas?'

'He was too vague,' Kim agreed. 'Let's kick it to Nathan and he can decide if Bryan's an attention seeker.

CHAPTER 10

Nathan and Cheryl had just returned to their car with takeaway coffees when Kim called. Nathan noticed Cheryl frown when she saw Kim's name on his screen. 'Looks like your ex has another tip, *Sarge*.'

Cheryl's reaction bemused him so he'd have to sort that quick smart. He and Kim were ex-lovers who chatted occasionally; nothing more than that.

'Hey Kim,' he answered. 'You're on speaker. Say hi to Cheryl.'

'Hi guys, I might have some info for you. Or a wild goose chase.'

Kim filled them in on her chat with Bryan. Nathan admitted the town drunk didn't inspire him as a reliable witness. He thanked her for the lead and hung up.

With so few other leads, they couldn't afford to ignore Bryan Cowan. Nathan called the local cop as Cheryl drove and a file search didn't improve the credibility of him as an informant. Bryan had several DUI convictions and half a dozen minor theft charges. He still had a job at a marine shop near the port despite his workplace being listed as the crime scene in two police reports.

'The locals are very forgiving. Cowan seems to help himself to anything that's not tied down.'

'Yes, Sarge.' Cheryl kept her eyes on the road.

Nathan raised his eyebrows and stared out the window, enjoying the rugged coast and pounding surf until they got to the pub. It was logical to start there; Cowan was a heavy boozer, and it was after business hours.

There were about two dozen men chugging beers in the bar. The babble died instantly; punters could always pick cops from a mile off. Nathan knew from the police report and Kim's info what Cowan looked like: bald, 50s, greasy overalls, usually drunk. Nobody fitted that description. He went to the bar; no need to play it cool.

'We're looking for Bryan Cowan. Has he been in tonight?'

The barman's name tag said: Riley.

'He was here for a few hours after lunch. It was bit of surprise when he took off. He usually has an early meal before he gets sent on his way.' Riley smiled. 'We have to obey the licencing laws.'

Cheryl stood behind Nathan. He could tell she was giving all the drinkers the stare: there wasn't a squeak from the patrons.

'Does he ever go to another bar or club?'

'Unlikely,' Riley said. 'This is the last place in town that hasn't banned him.'

'Yet.'

The comment came from an anonymous wit around the decagon fire. It drew a few chuckles, and encouraged some bravado.

'What's Bryan done this time?' asked a man in a suit.

'Nothing that we know about. We just want a chat with him.'

Nathan had a home address and nodded Cheryl towards the door.

'Is he involved in that fire up at Tugga's place?'

That question came from someone at a table by the fireplace. It caused an uneasy murmur.

Nathan understood a blaze close to the Great Otway National Park would have spooked Apollo Bay. The firebug would not be shown any mercy. Obviously many had watched the *Spotlight* story on Monday, not to mention local goss. They would now make random connections because there were new cops in town. Nathan had to protect Cowan.

'No, he's definitely not responsible,' Nathan said, with his fingers crossed. He actually had no idea what the the guys's involvement might be, beyond reporting a mystery car on the beach. But the greater risk could be angry drinkers seeking their own justice.

'He's got some outstanding fines. Our boss asked us to give him a reminder while we were in town. That's all.'

A laugh eased the tension. 'You'll have to stand in line. The little bugger owes everyone money.'

Nathan waved and ushered Cheryl outside as the drinkers began calculating how much the absent barfly owed them.

'Where to next, Nate?'

Nathan smiled, and checked his notepad. 'There's an address in Marengo. It's away from the beach, probably one of the original homes.' Nathan looked at the sun sinking behind the Otways. 'Let's hope he's home giving his liver a rest. Otherwise, we'll have to drive back tomorrow. There's no budget for motel rooms.'

Cheryl pursed her lips and headed for the car. There was no conversation in the few minutes it took them to reach the outer suburb that held the town cemetery.

'Take the next right. We're looking for number 53.'

The Otways side of the road was covered with trees. They had to backtrack to confirm Cowan's property as only the 3 survived on the letterbox. It looked like it had been rescued from the tip, along with most of the house.

'No wonder he spends his time at the pub,' Cheryl said. 'Tugga's shack looked more inviting.'

The corrugated iron and weatherboard hovel looked empty and weeds grew under the Ford sedan in the driveway.

Nathan opened his car door. 'Let's knock and have a look around. Stay alert.'

Twenty minutes later they were back in the car; a business card left under the door. With any luck, Cowan would call and save them another trip down the coast.

'We might still be in time for a meal at the pub. I'll shout.'

'Last of the big spenders,' Cheryl said, starting the engine.

It was dark on the Great Ocean Road when Nathan's phone rang. He checked the ID: Kim again.

'Hey Kim. You're on speaker. Are you checking if we've spoken to Cowan? You know I can't share any info.'

'*We* found him,' Kim said. 'He's been bashed.'

'Where? How bad is he?'

'A head wound. Lots of blood. We found him in the carpark behind the pub. I've called the ambos.'

'We're already on our way there. About two minutes away.'

Nathan shouldn't have been shocked that Kim and Kenny found Cowan. Kim had an uncanny knack for finding victims; although usually they were already dead. He was surprised they were still in Apollo Bay, as he thought they'd be back at the studio by now for tonight's show.

His thoughts turned back to Cowan as he realised the bloke might have genuine intel. The old bastard getting bashed could not be a coincidence.

As Cheryl turned the car into Moore Street approaching the pub carpark he was horrified to see the crime scene was already a circus.

Every drinker from the pub was outside with beers in hand. And it seem that half of Apollo Bay's residents were spilling from their nearby homes all with their smartphones.

And in the centre of it all, the two professionals: Kim with a mic and Kenny with his camera on his shoulder.

Wonderful!

CHAPTER 11

Hackett looked at the uninspiring fridge contents: broccoli, kale, tomatoes, and a steak that wouldn't cover the palm of his hand. He needed to sack his housekeeper. Southbank had restaurants, cafes and bars within metres of his apartment building. Could he risk going out alone?

He slammed the fridge door and reached for a takeaway menu for the Asian kitchen that delivered downstairs. The concierge would put his dinner in the lift. That was a safer bet. He rang and ordered mixed entrees, Tom Yum soup and a Pad Thai. It was more than he needed, but Hackett wanted comfort food. At least he didn't have Marianne here to nag him about his divorce diet.

Hackett pinched his gut as he stood in the kitchen and looked at the city lights. His wealth, career and social standing were still aphrodisiacs for women willing to overlook a bit of middle-age flab. These women were poor substitutes for the life he had enjoyed with Marianne.

Then his skin crawled at the sudden recall of his naked wife beside the security guard in the bedroom window. Hackett shook his head, snatched a beer from the fridge and headed to the lounge. It was almost time for tonight's *Spotlight*.

This program shouldn't contain any shocks. His bollocking of Mac hadn't gone as planned, as his producer had proof he'd sent a warning text. And Mac had surprisingly sympathetic even though he'd been shouted at.

Mac's suggestion that Mitch Stevens, the bodyguard, was a more likely target this time, as *he'd* pulled the trigger, was reassuring.

But, Hackett still wondered, was Mitch the only target? Mac had agreed to copy Hackett's executive assistant, Zara Hennessy, into any future warnings. Hackett always responded to texts from the glamourous Zara.

The intercom buzzed. 'Your dinner is on the way up Mr Hackett,' said the concierge.

'Thanks, Raymond.'

Hackett slouched against the wall until the lift doors direct to his apartment opened.

Damn. His food wasn't alone.

The weather at the end of the news was on the pub TV. The *Spotlight* program was next, just a few minutes away. Kim was waiting anxiously for Nathan to finish taking statements from the pub patrons.

The top of their program had been rearranged to go live with her breaking story. Mac and Curly had thrashed out a loose running order that would leave most of the talking to Kim, as she was in the middle of the action.

It was both thrilling and nerve-wracking to have that trust from her producers. Although they'd be disappointed she hadn't yet talked Detective Sergeant Nathan Potter into appearing on camera.

She headed back outside to the carpark where Kenny had the camera set up to do their live cross – close enough to catch Nathan or Cheryl in a broad shot at least.

'Hey Nathan,' she called out. 'Still no chance I can change your mind about doing a live interview?'

'Is Mac on his knees in the control room?'

'Yep.'

'Tell him I got a warning from the DI – I can't talk to you live on camera. He almost busted a fufu valve when he learned it was you guys, again, who found a victim. He thinks you're secretly creating these cases for me to solve.'

Kim grinned. 'But I usually solve them.'

'Touché.'

'What about Detective Chatty?'

Nathan faked a cough to smother his laugh.

'She's been giving me killer looks all day.'

Nathan's coughing turned real. Kim resisted patting him on the back in case his partner reached for her Glock.

'Kim!' Kenny stuck his head through the open door and held up a finger. 'One minute to broadcast'.

She scooted outside and took the microphone. They were set to go live in the pub's carpark.

'Sorry Mac. No luck with Nathan. We're good to go.'

She glanced over her shoulder. The crime scene was now two cop cars, a couple of lights and half the residents of Apollo Bay on the fringes.

Bryan had already been taken to hospital. That didn't matter – the setting looked dramatic. And they still had the exclusive on the assault that seemed to be latest episode in the resurrected Tugga's Mob saga. She raised a thumb when Curly, back in the studio, gave her a 30 second warning in her earpiece.

If this performance didn't get her the London gig, nothing would.

Hackett's surprise at finding his ex-wife holding his dinner in his private lift had been hijacked by the *Spotlight* promo at the end of the news.

The show's host, Richard Templeton, had announced a breaking story in Apollo Bay. He'd be crossing live to Kim Prescott.

'That bastard was supposed to warn me if anything else came up,' Hackett said, as the *Melbourne Spotlight* theme filled the room. 'Where's my fucking phone?'

Marianne felt around the couch and pulled it out from between the cushions. 'Where it normally is.'

Hackett began thumbing through dozens of messages. Bugger. There were two in the last half hour: Mac telling him a witness had been attacked, Zara urging him to watch *Spotlight*. But there was no text from Marianne.

Hackett grunted. 'There's no message from you.'

'I told you I texted. I had a very upsetting call with Mitch and needed to talk.' Marianne stood and snatched her handbag.

Hackett placed a hand gently on her wrist. 'Don't go. I believe you.' He pointed at the phone. 'It's been playing up. Yours is the second text, at least, I've missed in two days. I'll have to get a new phone.'

They sat in silence as the *Spotlight* titles rolled to a close and Templeton's face filled the screen.

'Is this going to be more bad news,' Marianne asked.

Hackett nodded. 'Probably. Let's watch, then we'll talk.'

> *'Good evening. Thank you for joining us on Melbourne Spotlight where we have a breaking story. Last night we revealed that the infamous Tugga Tancred's shack near Apollo Bay had been torched.*
>
> *Our search of the crime scene yesterday revealed the arsonist may have left a taunting message for police. The blaze was allegedly dedicated to Amy Stewart, the woman who killed five people as part of a twisted campaign to avenge her dead mother five years ago.*
>
> *'Late this afternoon, a witness who might be able to identify the arsonist, was brutally attacked here in the carpark of this hotel in Apollo Bay.*
>
> *Our reporter, Kim Prescott, found the victim close to death. We cross now to Kim, live at the scene.'*

The setting changed from the bright studio to the gaudy lights and police tape of a crime scene. Kim was wearing a waterproof *Melbourne Spotlight* jacket, her hair in a ponytail against a strong sea breeze.

> *'Thank you, Richard. Behind me is the pub carpark where we discovered the victim about an hour ago. We cannot name the man at this time until family have been informed, but can say he is a local, in his late 50s. He was unconscious and bleeding severely from head wounds.*
>
> *My camera operator called an ambulance while I notified the police. The victim was taken to hospital only a few minutes ago. Paramedics and detectives are too busy to speak to us on camera, but we understand the man is in a critical condition.'*

Prerecorded vision of the victim, in dark overalls lying facedown on concrete near an overturned beer barrels, played as Kim continued her report. The victim's head, in all shots, was pixelated.

> 'We're showing you the scene as we found it. Our first impression was that he was likely ambushed and struck by the barrel you can see on the ground.'

The program returned to Kim live on camera.

> 'While, obviously, the police investigation has only just started, our sources indicate that this assault and the arson attack on Mr Tancred's shack are connected.'

Kim walked slowly to her left, the pub and dozens of drinkers in the shot behind her. A couple shied away from the camera light.

> 'I first met the assault victim last night in this pub where he's a regular. We chatted very briefly about the fire, which naturally was a hot topic with all the patrons.'

A few more steps and Kim was standing with her back to the sea.

> 'Late this afternoon the man approached me again and hinted he had information about the arson. He claimed to have seen a suspcious vehicle in the vicinity of the blaze. We have given details of this to the two detectives who are in Apollo Bay investigating the fire.'

Kenny's camera slowly zoomed in for a close-up on Kim.

> 'Given the bloody revenge meted out to Tugga Tancred and his mates, it's not overreaching to suggest that crime spree has direct links the events here in the last two days.
>   An arson followed by a vicious assault on a possible witness cannot be ignored. A man who is currently fighting for life in hospital could have vital information for police. Back to you, Richard.'

'Bloody hell, Andrew! Who's doing this? Are they after you again? Or Mitch?'

'I guess I'm likely to be the first target as your toyboy is safely out of the country.'

'That's a cheap shot.' Marianne stomped to the fridge and helped herself to a white wine.

'Sorry,' Hackett said, as he followed her to the kitchen and flopped onto a stool at the bench. 'I thought everything stopped with Amy. That night.'

He unconsciously rubbed the scar on his shoulder. It still ached when he was under stress, even five years later.

'Have you warned Mitch we might have another lunatic?'

Marianne nodded, took a large gulp of wine. 'He didn't take it seriously. He laughed and went all macho, said any death threat is like a badge of honour; let the new avenger come after him.'

'Dickhead.'

'He's a bastard.'

'What else happened?'

'I heard giggling in the background. A young woman.'

'Oh.'

'I asked who was with him and the call was cut. I couldn't reach him again and he hasn't responded to my texts.'

Hackett felt conflicted. His hopes about the randy bastard might be true. Hackett wanted to do a fist pump because now Marianne would finally feel the pain of betrayal. Until he watched her slouch over the bench, eyes red, her world in turmoil again. He felt a smidgen of sympathy, but couldn't bring himself to console her. He swivelled on his stool and grabbed a beer from the fridge.

'Okay,' he said. 'Mitch has been given the heads-up. He's got the skills and enough mates to look after his own back. Unless the oligarch finds out the expensive bodyguard is fucking his daughter.' Hackett watched his wife flinch. 'The question is – what can I do about security?'

Marianne waved an arm at the window. 'You've got an eagle's nest; 60 floors above the hoi polloi and a private lift. That's a good start,' she snapped.

'We have a rule that former spouses can only be admitted by apartment owners. How much did you pay Raymond to get in the lift with the takeaways?'

'Twenty bucks.'

'That's all my life is worth, is it? I should have him sacked. But the next concierge might let a hitman up here for a tenner.'

.'Will the police offer protection after the assault in Apollo Bay?'

'There's no specific threat to me. So no. And the securty wankers in this building, it seems, would probably watch my assassination on camera, then post it on YouTube before the killer left.'

Marianne smirked.

Hackett knew it was facetious, but possibly too close to the truth.

'This is your most vulnerable point when you're at home. You've got the lifts and the emergency stairs. You would only need one or two security people on shifts.'

'No bodyguards.'

'How do you travel to work?'

'I've been walking – until today.'

'How often do you use the bars and restaurants downstairs?'

Hackett waggled his hand. 'A few nights a week.'

'That leaves you vulnerable in many places,' Marianne said.

'Have you been getting security lessons from Mitch?'

'You can be such a contrary prick, Andrew. I'm trying to help.'

Hackett expected her to have the Mercedes keys in hand and ready to depart. Instead, she was pouring more wine.

'No cops. No bodyguards. Unreliable building staff. Although don't be too hard on Raymond, he *does* know me. By the way, have you made Ferdy executor of your will?'

'Oh ha. But I do think Ferdy can help me.'

'How? Are you going to move in with him and this month's chick?'

'No. We have some business deals in France. I was intending make that part of an official Channel 5 trip to England. We're setting up an office for a London correspondent. So, it might be safer for me to go to Paris sooner. Like tomorrow instead of next week.'

'That's hypocritical. You always complain that news and current affairs haemorrhage company money.'

Hackett smiled. 'They do. But I've stitched up a deal with independent stations around Australia. They're chipping in for the occasional story that might involve their city or town.'

Marianne laughed. 'You're such a shark. They don't know they're going to pay for most of your running costs.'

Hackett shrugged. 'That's business.'

CHAPTER 12

Bashing Bryan Cowan with an empty beer barrel had never been part of Morgan's plan.

'He was a nosy, greedy bastard, Amy. He should've kept his mouth shut.'

Amy couldn't hear the frustration, of course. Morgan was an only child who'd never learned to internalise his thoughts. A smiling smartphone selfie of the beautiful Amy kept her real and ever-present whenever he needed a chat.

Violence was Morgan's instinctive reaction to being cornered. So when Bryan approached him as he was taking a short cut through the pub's carpark and tried to blackmail him, Morgan had lashed out.

With a barrel.

'I've invested too much in this plan for a stupid drunk to jeopardise it.'

Morgan hoped the fact that Bryan was always stumbling into tables and chairs inside the pub, would make the cops believe he'd done the same outside and crashed into the stack.

It had been dark, and the luckily the hotel carpark, only six metres away, was empty of people. Morgan had stared at the unconcious man on the ground and decided one more blow would finish him off and still look accidental.

Morgan had grabbed Bryan by his greasy overalls and flipped him onto his stomach. He then lifted and smashed the man's forehead into the concrete. Just once. It needed to look like he'd fallen face first after being struck by a falling barrel. Morgan placed the one he'd hit Bryan with nearby.

In the end the scene looked convincing. Bryan's bald dome was a bloodied mess; his skull was probably fractured. There was fluid leaking from his ear and blood pooling around his smashed face.

Morgan was about to check for a pulse when headlights swept into the carpark. He'd dived for the shadows behind a nearby Holden, as an SUV pulled up 20 metres away under a gum tree.

It was the bloody TV crew. They couldn't see him, but they weren't going to miss the dead guy on the ground. Morgan had slipped away along the fence and took the long way back to his car. He'd then driven around the block, waited for the ambulance to turn up, then followed it into the carpark like a regular patron.

Morgan had mingled with the crowd, keeping out of the way as the TV crew filmed the scene. His concern that the prick was still breathing was allayed when he heard one of the paramedics saying, 'bells and whistles, mate, although it'll be a miracle–' as he slid the door shut.

That comment flashed around the carpark and then the patrons inside at lightspeed. The pub had filled with dozens of amateur sleuths once the TV crew had left. Morgan was pissed off his accident set-up had already been questioned, as most of the drinkers were already sucked in by the reporter's version. They all also knew the kegs had never tumbled even in the fiercest southerly gales, so a flyweight like Bryan couldn't tip them with a drunken stumble. The opinion was unanimous: Bryan had been bashed.

By the time last drinks were called conversation had segued to anecdotes about 'the light-fingered bastard' and how he'd never get elevated to sainthood. Despite that most agreed Bryan didn't deserve a cracked skull.

Morgan had smashed the steering wheel in frustration all the way back to his flat but resisted the urge to wreck everything inside. It was a rental and, as his job here was done, he'd already given notice to the landlord that he was leaving. So it wouldn't be smart to draw attention to himself by trashing the furniture. It took him 10 minutes of deep breathing exercises to regain his equilibrium.

'Bryan has a hard noggin, but he's going to at least be a vegetable, Amy. But I need to reassess.'

He grabbed his laptop and external hard drive from the safe in the wardrobe. The computer was vital for his ongoing surveillance, but only the hard drive contained his Amy file.

The spyware he'd developed was functioning well. He'd spent countless hours at the keyboard, creating the program that would help him attain justice for Amy.

He stroked his chest the way she had done on those few precious nights time had given them, when their hearts were beating in sync. Theirs was a union both had been seeking. Amy had drawn him out of the lost years after a promising career had been derailed. They'd shared a blissful experience – until a bullet in the back shattered their perfect future.

Now wasn't the time to lament stolen dreams. He needed to readjust his plan to ensure no suspicion fell upon him for Bryan's bashing.

'We're lucky no names were thrown around at the pub, Amy. And nobody gave me a second look .'

He'd already planned to leave Apollo Bay the following weekend, but now worried that might raise suspicions. Hopefully, Bryan would die, but while that solved one problem it would create another. There'd be hordes of cops in town; and everyone in spitting distance of the pub tonight would be grilled. Morgan couldn't afford to be the only person missing during a murder investigation. And then there was his fire at Tugga's shack. That reporter, Kim, had already linked the two crimes.

'I need an excuse to stay, Amy. Something to keep me at least another week, or two.'

Morgan clicked on the *Melbourne Spotlight* website. He'd watched the live reporting at the pub, so knew what Bryan had been going to blackmail him about. Perhaps the whole program might give him more clues about what Bryan knew.

Morgan had been certain nobody had seen him last night. Before heading to Tugga's with his arson kit, he'd disabled the car's interior light, and hidden a change of clothes behind a tree.

On his return he'd sheltered in the scrub by the beach for 10 minutes after changing out of his smoky clothes, to ensure no one was around. The only thing moving was the surf.

He couldn't work out how Bryan could possibly have seen him anywhere between Tugga's shack and the beach.

Annoyingly if Bryan did die or remain a vegetable, Morgan would never know what the old bastard had seen.

There was nothing more in the *Spotlight* program itself. Morgan watched Kim Prescott's performance a couple of times. She was impressive on camera and with her analysis.

It seemed Bryan had simply tried to sell his information but not told her anything except that he'd seen a car.

Morgan bore Kim no grudges for doing her job; it was her boss who was still in trouble.

Chapter 13

Kim was close to tears. The wave of euphoria she'd ridden after breaking two exclusive news stories had crashed at the oak-panelled door of Channel 5's Executive Boardroom.

She and Kenny had been driving home from Apollo Bay last night when Hackett called. It was almost 9.30 pm and he sounded slightly drunk. She'd only answered because she figured he was fishing for background info. But she couldn't have been more wrong.

'You know applications for the London correspondent's job closed today, Kimberley,' he'd said. 'But given the circumstances, we're prepard to offer you an extension. It'll be 8 am tomorrow.'

Kenny, who was in the throes of a sugar rush, if the now empty lolly stash was anything to go by, had ranted for the next hour.

'It's 9.30 and we're still 90 minutes from home and that prick wants you to turn up when?'

Kim had somehow made it and rocked to the CEO's personal assistant at 7.55 this morning after managing only three hours sleep. As she was ushered into the boardroom she was greeted by the chief, Reg Bradley, and said hello to the Hatchet who barely nodded in response.

'Don't tell me I beat Richard here,' Kim joked to cover her nerves.

'He's not available.' Hackett's smirk was as ugly as his lime and yellow tie.

Kim felt it in her gut. Then as Hackett launched into his so-called interview questions, she knew this was an ambush.

'You went off the rails after the greyhound trainer deaths,' he said.

'I'd been shot in the back running from a killer.' Kim bristled. She was sleep deprived and there was no way she was going to put up with The Hatchet's barbs.

'I don't recall seeing you back at work the day after your daughter shot you.'

Hackett glared at her. 'I spent appropriate time restoring my physical and mental health. I didn't go bashing cops while denying I had stress-related issues.'

Kim wanted to slap the smugness from his face.

Reg Bradley had the grace to look embarrassed as he fiddled with a pen. He was the boss yet had so far contributed nothing.

Kim addressed him. 'Mr Bradley, I can assure you those issues are long behind me. I was young and still learning the job. I think my work in Apollo Bay this week speaks for itself. I broke two exclusive stories for *Spotlight* and we've left the opposition scrambling to catch up. Our ratings are through the roof.'

'They were a coup, Kim, Bradley agreed. 'Very impressive.'

'But you blew it,' said Hackett.

'How? We broke the news about the fire. We had the exlusive on the assualt of Bryan Cowan–'

'That's my point.' Hackett stabbed his finger on the table. 'You could've identified the attacker if you hadn't messed things up at the service station. That arsonist thug would be in custody now.'

And you wouldn't have to look over your shoulder every day! Kim swallowed the retort.

Hackett continued, 'And that bloke would not have been bashed.'

The bastard picked the guilt scab that was still tormenting her since finding Bryan behind the pub, even though she'd talked it over with Kenny on the drive home. He'd tried to reassure her she'd done the right thing at the servo, and that Bryan still might've been bashed before the cops had a chance to pick up the arsonist.

'We were accosted by a man who is a petty thief and scam artist. He ran off the second we told him the police would have to be informed.'

Hackett glanced at Bradley. 'A more experienced reporter – and might I say level-headed reporter– would have made sure they recorded the exchange; then let their producer decide if it had merit.' He shrugged. 'To me, it was a bad judgement call. You were on your own, away from the support of seasoned journalists. You had the key to the mystery – and you couldn't deliver.'

'I'm not the one who makes the policies that we don't pay random members of the public for dubious tip-offs. Especially if they nick off the moment the cops are mentioned.'

Kim glanced at Bradley who was busy creating swirls in his notebook with his Montblanc fountain pen.

Hackett's ambush had been perfect. Not only did he sideline Templeton, but he'd probably primed the chief executive.

'We're not here to discuss policies or anything else that is way above your pay grade, Ms Prescott. We are interviewing for a journalist who has the capacity to work unsupervised, and who has the skills to follow up on leads. Not someone who runs away from stories that have dropped in their lap.'

Kim wanted to snatch the pen out of Bradley's stubby fingers and stab The Hatchet in the eyeball.

She'd known it from the minute she'd walked into the interview, her dream job was dead in the water.

Fucking Hatchett had drowned it.

Chapter 14

Nobody noticed the office manager, Jo Trescowthick, close the door of Edit Suite 2 during the Wednesday night drinks to celebrate Stephanie Grant's appointment as the station's first London correspondent.

Reporters, producers, editors, studio and road crew were milling around the dungeon making the most of the free booze after The Hatchet had wasted no time announcing who'd they chosen for the job.

Jo liked Steph and knew she'd do a brilliant job, but was also conflicted by the pain management's decision had caused Kim. Rather than watch her friend try to be magnanimous, Jo decided to satisfy a niggle.

Jo placed her wine glass down carefully away from the electronics. It only took a few seconds on the keyboard to bring up the field vision from Kim's story on the bashing the night before. She could've been accessed it from her computer at the command post, but didn't want anyone to see what she was doing.

She ignored images of the victim – who they knew was still in a coma – and slowed the footage as it panned across the lookie-loos at the crime scene. The ambulance turning up had emptied the bar into the carpark: about 30 people, still drinking, were watching the action.

She was searching for one face, belonging to a tall, slender guy, and found him in the background during Kim's on-camera walk along the street. It was just a glimpse. Jo couldn't tell whether he turned from the camera to avoid being seen, or was simply shielding his eyes from Ken's powerful camera light.

Jo rolled back and forth through all the crowd scenes; but found no other sign of him. Jo went back to the clearest image, picked up her wine and saluted the screen.

'That's where you went Simon. Your hair is longer. But that nose, chin and oh, those eyes.' The memories made her flush.

Simon had been a pleasant dalliance between her current fling, Kenny, and previous boyfriends. He was a barista at *Coolio*'s a South Melbourne café nearer to her apartment than the studio. Most of the staff got their brews from the place on the corner, apart from the top floor diva, Zara Hennessy, who also passed *Coolio*'s on her way to work. So, Jo had the café, coffee and Simon to herself – especially on weekends.

Until he disappeared. For the second time.

The first disappearance had been in the Before Times when they'd only been friends. He turned up again after the pandemic and *Coolio*'s owner rehired him without question, resigned to the fact Simon was a wanderer. This time around things had got deliciously intimate, until he pissed off again six months ago. Jo had been disappointed but not devastated; she'd always known Simon's heart belonged to another woman. He could be intense and preoccupied; occasionally he set aside that emotional baggage for casual fun; that had been enough.

Jo rolled her office chair back into the throng, clipping a junior news reporter on his shin. As was her thing, Jo rolled her eyes at him as if the collision was his fault, and swung in beside Curly Rogers at the command post. He was at full stretch in the chair, drink in hand, eyes on an AFL match. 'I thought you'd be watching the game at home,' Jo said.

'I'm here for moral support.'

'For Kim?' Jo looked around the room. No sign of the rejected foreign correspondent.

'More likely Mac.'

'What do you mean?'

Curly pointed to the conference room where Kim and Mac sat huddled at the far end of the table.

'That doesn't look good.'

'Yeah. She came over a couple of minutes ago and asked to talk to Mac – privately. She was holding an envelope.'

'Shit.'

Mac watched Kim twist the paper; he didn't need to read it to know the contents.

'Come on, Kim. We've all suffered kicks in the teeth during our careers. I've been sacked twice. The people that matter understand that most TV executives are clueless. You're not even 30 – there'll be plenty more opportunities. Don't throw everything away.'

Kim slammed the envelope onto the table. 'I'm not Mac. I'm taking time out. I want to go travelling. The bloody pandemic strangled our lives. I want to experience the world.'

Mac sighed. 'Yeah. I can understand that frustration. Two years of Covid stories is enough to drive anyone barmy.'

'I've been working at *Spotlight* since I left university. It's been a fantastic experience, Mac. I've loved everything that you, Curly and the crew have done for me. But missing out on the London job has been a wake-up call. I need to enjoy life more.'

Mac had a full roster an hour ago; now he was losing his two best reporters. Steph's posting was for two years. Would Kim be lost permanently?

He tried a professional tack. 'What about the new angle on Tugga's Mob? Surely you want to solve that mystery. Who burned his shack and bashed the Apollo Bay guy? Is Hackett a target again? I can't believe you want to walk away from that story.'

Kim shrugged. 'I've given a month's notice. If the detectives can't solve the case in that time, chances are they never will. And I don't know if Bryan is ever going to come out of that coma.'

Mac scratched his thick beard furiously.

'I won't be hard to replace. Mike Berry has been champing at the bit to get a permanent role with *Spotlight*.'

Mac grunted. 'I got an email from him two minutes after Steph's appointment was announced.'

'I bet he wasn't the only one. How many from news want Steph's job?'

'Half the department.'

They laughed, which eased the tension.

'I know I'm bloody brilliant, Mac. But you understand that journalists are nomadic. There's always an ambitious reporter knocking at the door.'

Mac sipped his beer; time to weigh the options: accept the resignation or deflect Kim's pique.

'Have you thought about where you're going? Will it be all travel, or do you plan to broaden your work experience?'

Kim brightened. 'I want to go to Europe for the summer. I've never spent more than a week in France, Britain – or anywhere – at a time. I'll make a showreel and send it to the BBC and a few other media companies.'

'I think Curly's got a mate who works for the BBC in Manchester or Birmingham. Mac said. 'He might be able to give you some help.'

Mac saw the gratitude in Kim's eyes, but wasn't ready for total surrender. 'Have you considered another possibility: leave without pay?'

'Didn't you do that at the ABC last century?'

Mac frowned. 'Don't be cheeky.' A grin quickly surfaced. Mac had often shared the story about bluffing his news editor into an extended holiday. Like Kim, he'd missed a promotion and grumbled for weeks about leaving. The boss had gone ashen when Mac walked into his office with a empty white envelope in hand. The executive promised anything to keep his best news producer. Mac had sprung his plan for the three months holidays already owed – plus four months without pay. The executive agreed on the spot.

'You know the story. I can make it happen. Come back at Christmas – that will give you a good six months to wander – and start afresh next year.'

Kim sagged in her seat. It was obviously an option she had never considered. Mac was prepared to do anything to keep his media family together. 'Think about it.' He pointed at the untouched letter. 'Hold onto that until Monday. If you want to resubmit it, I'll accept it – reluctantly.'

CHAPTER 15

Ferdy Ackerman nodded to the armed security guard who'd ridden up in the lift with him, as the doors opened into Hackett's penthouse.

'Your guest, Mr Hackett,' the guard said.

Hackett ignored the guard as he waved his best friend and business partner inside.

'How many gunslingers do you have lurking in here?' Ferdy asked.

'None.' Hackett waved at the floor to ceiling windows. 'King Kong would struggle to climb up all that glass.'

Chilled gin and tonics awaited them on the kitchen bench. Ferdy sipped, sighed, and perched his lean butt on a stool, his back to the views.

'That's the problem. It could be Spiderman after you for all you know. How do you keep attracting these loons?'

Hackett slouched. 'I've no idea if there's even a real threat. So far it's the overactive imagination of the *Spotlight* crew.'

'What's the deal with your armed guards then? How many and for how long?'

'Two on 12-hour shifts when I'm home. One escorts me to work and back. I'm safe enough at Channel 5. I'm getting all my meals delivered, you and Marianne are the only visitors allowed in. I should be safe until we go to Europe. Let's hope 10 weeks away is long enough for the cops to track this bastard.'

'What about the housekeeper?'

'I sacked her. Security risk. But don't tell Marianne.'

'Why not?'

'She will want to move back in.'

'Why? Has soldier boy been caught fucking a new client.'

Hackett winced.

'Sorry, mate. Marianne rarely has a kind word for any of my girlfriends.'

'Forget her,' Hackett said. 'How soon can you set up this meeting in France? I want to get out of Melbourne.'

Ferdy wobbled a hand. 'June is likely to be the earliest we can present them with our bid. They're keen for cash to build their solar farm, but they have a few European suitors. It would be good to see what offers are on the table first.'

'Damn.' Hackett took his drink to the window. 'I want to get on a plane next week.'

'Have you got any Channel 5 work that might fill the gap?'

'Possibly. We appointed the new London correspondent. I could make a case for being part of the on-site studio setup.' Hackett smiled.

'I've seen that mischievous look before. Did your preferred candidate get the job?'

'Yeah.' The grin broadened. 'Stephanie will be in London within a few weeks.'

'I trust she will be suitably appreciative of your efforts.'

Hackett nodded.

'Any boyfriends to worry about?'

'Not anymore. She tried to get her favourite cameraman included in the deal.'

'What happened?'

'I said there was one vacancy. Take it or leave it.'

'Smart girl.' Ferdy raised his drink. 'To the pleasures ahead. Just watch your back until then.'

Hackett drained his glass and reached for the Hendrick's bottle.

'Will you get a hotel in London, or stay with the kids?' Ferdy asked.

Hackett grunted as he poured generous measures. 'No way. Nick and Tara have got young brats, I'll get a hotel in Oxford. That's about halfway between their homes. It will be a handy refuge when the kids start whining.'

Ferdy laughed; no children cramped his professional or personal lifestyle. 'Do Nick and Tara know about your impending arrival?'

'I'll email them after dinner.'

CHAPTER 16

Morgan washed and dried his hands before settling on the couch with his laptop. It was time to check emails.

Hi Nick & Tara

Morgan shouldn't have been surprised that Hackett didn't write individual messages to his son and daughter.

'Your father is a lazy prick, Amy.'

He continued reading.

> I'm going to arrive sooner than expected. Mum has probably told you about the new drama involving Tugga Tancred. I don't know what it means, or how much danger I'm in, but I'm bringing my trip forward.

Morgan nodded. Hackett fleeing the country earlier still suited his plans. In fact, it would hasten Hackett's execution. He returned to the email.

> You won't have to worry about providing a room for me. I'm going to be travelling between London and Paris on business for a few weeks. I'll book hotels close to you when I can visit. That will cause less disruption. Don't worry, I'll have plenty of time to see the grandkids.

Hackett signed off after a few more impersonal lines: Cheers. Not, Cheers Dad, let alone Love from Dad. Morgan struggled to accept that Amy could have been sired but such a self-centred arsehole.

'He didn't offer any reassurance to your half siblings about their safety. Did he even consider that Nick and Tara, their spouses and children could be targets, or possibly collateral damage?'

Morgan shook his head; he wasn't a threat to Hackett's family. Nick and Tara weren't responsible for their father's sins.

The son and daughter had yet to reply. Tara would be excited, gushing about the grandkid's excitement, but understanding the pressure caused by her father's business schedule. Nick wouldn't waste words; he was a banker who commuted to the capital every day. One apple didn't fall far from the tree.

Morgan knew a lot about Andrew Hackett; every digital communication from before the pandemic had been hoovered into Morgan's program. Most family messages were innocuous. Hackett wasn't a frequent online chatter with his family, the exchanges were usually about birthdays, anniversaries or Christmas, but they were still valuable to Morgan.

Nick and Tara had homes in High Wycombe and near Oxford. The university city was ideally situated for Morgan's mission; Tara lived beside the Oxford Canal, perfect for engineering a showdown with Hackett – and ensuring Morgan's escape. Everything had been planned on that premise.

It had been simple to worm his way into Hackett's personal and business life. Morgan's computer and hacking skills would be legendary if he was a show-off. His coding talent was identified early; secondary school teachers considered him a genius, never suspecting the exam questions were his most lucrative early hacks. Money from rich students seeking Oxbridge places had financed some of his own university studies. Scholarships covered the rest, which brought him to the attention of an elderly professor who steered him towards a career in the Secret Intelligence Service.

The vetting process was long, intrusive and revealed his school indiscretions. Morgan thought he'd be shown the door; and he smiled as he remembered the recruiter's practical philosophy:

'We prefer to keep you as a gamekeeper rather than let you be a poacher.'

Snooping for the Realm had been challenging, interesting and fun – for a few years. Boredom led to the recklessness that cost him his job. Morgan's parents greeted his dismissal with the same indifference they'd given to everything in his life. Aloof was the kindest word to describe the relationship with his stepfather; disconnected would be more accurate.

And Morgan always felt a little disappointed by his Australian-born mother. She'd done the adventurous backpacking trip across South-east Asia followed by the obligatory boozy combivan tour through Europe, before falling for the most boring man in history. She never went home and instead turned into a meek English church-wife. She offered no resistance when his father suggested a boarding school for Morgan at the earliest possible age. Obviously, they preferred a childless house as there had been no other siblings before they divorced.

Only Morgan's mother had watched his graduation from Oxford. His father administered pastoral care to millions from the upper echelons of the Church of England, yet couldn't find enough interest for his son's biggest academic achievement.

Morgan deflected those sour memories by opening the file on Marianne. He knew why she hadn't reverted to her maiden name after the divorce from Hackett; her secrets were contained in texts to her best friend. The ex-husband would be Marianne's fallback plan if the toyboy strayed, which she was now convinced had happened.

Little did she know, however, that it was Morgan remotely thwarting communication between her and her lover in the UK. One of Morgan's many phishing hacks was diverting all their texts and calls to Morgan's computer and he was only allowing some to go through.

'This is fun, Amy. They are half a world away from each other – their anxiety escalating with every message that gets lost. Both thinking the worst.'

But it was time to stop tormenting the lovers and Hackett. Morgan didn't want any of them getting suspicious about the missing texts.

He stood and stretched his arms before turning on the kettle. He did a few shoulder and hip twists to release all the upper body muscles and then made a cup of instant coffee.

Morgan moved on to the next item on his check list: Bryan Cowan's condition. He checked several news sites. Apart from the *Spotlight* progam, most Victorian media had already lost interest in the story. They were no new dramatic visuals of the crime scene, and the victim was still in a coma. Even the local coastal news website only had two paragraphs: no change in the victim's condition, no leads for the cops.

Everyone at the pub around the time of the attack had been interviewed. Morgan had been grilled by the attractive cop who obviously had the hots for her senior detective. And a mere constable was no match for a former intelligence officer. Morgan had been polite and precise with his answers, deflecting suspicion onto drinkers who had muttered threats about Bryan for overdue payments; he even created a fictional tourist who'd been annoyed by Bryan's drunken rants. It gave the cops a few potential suspects.

But if Bryan returned from the twilight zone, the cops would be back and looking for him. If he died those cops would be serious homicide detectives who wouldn't have a clue who they were after.

Morgan could still control his departure. His flight out of Tullamarine had been booked weeks ago and the few locals he mingled with already knew that. So if he had to leave the coast early as least it couldn't be regarded as completely suspicious.

CHAPTER 17

Mitch Stevens suppressed a yawn as he stood at parade rest inside the door of the Chelsea fashion boutique. Natalia's wittering, filtered by a mountain of discarded dresses, indicated she was safe. He should have eyes upon her when in public, but weeks of similar experiences confirmed Natalia faced no dangers from ex-boyfriends, or enemies of Putin's cronies.

Mitch was nothing but a fashion accessory, a status symbol for wealthy expat Russians. His pistol rested snugly under the tailored silk jacket he was wearing, one of three suits Natalia had ordered during his first week. It wasn't enough to have an ex-special forces soldier on the payroll, he had to complement her catwalk elegance.

A prolonged swish preceded an inevitable inquiry. Natalia emerged from the racks in a flowing red evening gown.

'Mitch, do I look beautiful in this?'

It was a trick question.

'It looked stunning when you first tried it on – half an hour ago.'

Natalia arched an eyebrow. 'I like it when you pay attention.' She turned her green eyes towards the shop assistant. 'And how much did this peasant want to charge me – half an hour ago?'

The retailer blushed but bit her tongue.

'A mere £2,500. But she only increased the price 10% to do you a favour. You don't want London peasants thinking you are struggling financially because of the war.'

Natalia's eyes flared – then crinkled. 'Your Australian cheekiness will get you into trouble one day, Mitchell Stevens.' Natalia slipped the gown from her shoulders and let it fall to the floor. 'Iron and wrap it carefully, Sarah. My *SAS* bodyguard approves; this is worthy of a one-time wear.'

Mitch shrugged. Play your games Natalia. You'll be first against the wall come the next revolution. He checked the narrow street for nonexistent threats. There was a smartphone shop less than 20 metres away. His mobile had been doing weird things lately, but 16-hour days left no time to get it fixed or buy a new one.

Mitch's dyslexia meant he hated texting or sending emails, and odd dropouts had disrupted some of his calls to Marianne; either one of them might be able to hear, but not talk. The lack of regular communication was clearly agitating Marianne. He hoped any worry could be soothed with a Greek Islands holiday together after this high-paying contract.

Mitch ditched the idea of asking Natalia's BMW driver, Anatoly, to cover for him while he went to get a new phone. The former Spetsnaz soldier, currently smoking a cigarette while resting his ample butt against the car boot, would regard that as a dereliction of duty and report Mitch to Natalia's father.

Anatoly was yesterday's man, and he hated playing second gun, even though the fat Russian's time in the Special Forces would've been when Gorbachev led the crumbling Soviet Union. Their relationship got off to fine start from day one: Anatoly whipped out a hunting knife when Mitch went to shake hands; Mitch knocked it clear and pinned the old fart face down on the bonnet.

Natalia had been highly amused.

Anatoly laughed off the whole thing as a friendly challenge but Mitch knew it meant he could never trust the Russian to have his back in an emergency. He should've walked away from the contract on the spot and gone home to Marianne. But the contract was worth so much.

And it *was* only the money, because of Marianne's ex – Andrew bloody Hackett – that kept him in London. The filthy-rich executive set the benchmark high for material possessions; like the stunning Southbank penthouse that Marianne so desired. Mitch knew he had to make sacrifices and put up with dinosaurs like Anatoly if wanted to provide even a fraction of the luxury Marianne wanted. And deserved.

'I'm finished here, Mitch,' Natalia said. 'Tell Anatoly to put the bags in the car, we can walk to the wine bar.'

Mitch smirked; *Crystal*'s was 20 metres away.

CHAPTER 18

Mac entered the dungeon on Monday morning with a heavier heart than consecutive Collingwood losses would normally inflict. The Western Bulldogs almost doubled the Magpies' score; it was an omen of darker days ahead.

Curly, who was chatting on his phone at the back of the office, raised a finger in greeting. Jo rolled her office death chariot out of the kitchen with a coffee in hand. She took one look at Mac's face and surrendered it without a word; Mac nodded at the noble gesture. Jo disappeared to start the lifesaving process again as Mac slumped into his seat and sipped. The morning news services offered no cheer – or lead stories.

Jo returned to take the phone call that Mac clearly had no intention of answering. She listened for 10 seconds. 'Please hold while I check if Mac has arrived.' She dropped the receiver loudly enough to cause discomfort on the other end.

'It's Zara. Hackett wants to know if you're here.'

Mac grunted.

Jo thumped the handpiece against the desk as she pivoted away from her boss. 'I'm sorry, Ms Hennessy. I can't see him in the dungeon. I'll pass on your message.'

Mac laughed. 'What am I going to do without you?'

'Wallow in misery for three months.' Jo's fingers reached warp speed on the keyboard in a few seconds. 'I'm guessing you had no luck changing Kim's mind?'

'No. Nor Dugal's.'

The clattering stopped. 'Dugal?' Jo's eyebrows arched. 'He's chasing Steph to London?'

'Yep. Steph couldn't make him part of her deal with Hackett, so Dugal is going to freelance.'

Jo slumped in her seat, then rested a hand on Mac's wrist.

'Please don't make my life any worse,' Mac said, 'by telling me Kenny's going to follow you overseas too. We'll have to change the program name to the Mac and Curly Show.'

Jo blushed and slapped his shoulder. 'No – Kenny's definitely staying. My Mediterranean diet has been lacking lately.'

Mac sipped his coffee and watched as the rest of the crew entered The Dungeon. It would be hard to find a better team of of reporters, camera ops, editors and engineers; and they *were* more like a family than a bunch of co-workers. *Damn*, departures and holidays were going to change the dynamics for a while.

While Steph and Dugal were glowing, excitedly chatting about their London plans, most of the others were a little subdued. Kim had slipped in without any greetings, and now sat across from Curly with her headphones on, even the vision on her computer wasn't moving. And Kenny was quieter than normal, toying with a camera while ignoring everyone.

Mac took a breath, squared up to the day and opened his computer. Dugal had dropped his *off-to-London-too* bombshell on Sunday afternoon but the word had spread like wildfire. Mac's inbox was full of pre-emptive expressions of interest for Dugal's position, from reporters and camera operators, only a quarter of whom currently worked at Channel 5. One *consider-me* message was from a reporter in Perth, another from Darwin. Mac shook his head; he didn't even open the one from Mumbai.

'I see the grapevine still works.' Jo perched at his elbow. She pointed at one name. 'I've heard good things about her work at the ABC.' She reached past Mac's fingers and sent another hopeful to the bin. 'I'm not coming back if you hire him.'

Mac sighed and pushed his chair away from the command post. 'Should I let you cull the pretenders before I commit a cardinal sin?'

'Okey-dokey.' Jo rolled into place. She would create a new *Spotlight* family before departure; one that would be operating efficiently by the end of her holiday.

CHAPTER 19

PARIS, JUNE

The heat at Charles de Gaulle airport was stifling. Andrew Hackett undid another button on his polo shirt and used an A4 pad as a fan. All the passengers in terminal 2A were wilting and grumbling. The heat was another layer of frustration on a trip that had been full of niggles since leaving Melbourne. It was five weeks since the possible new threat to his wellbeing had kicked off with a fire and a bashing and brought his overseas business jaunt forward.

'Maybe you should've booked the Eurostar.' It was Ferdy, on the phone in Greece. They'd parted five days previously; Ferdy, with a new girlfriend half his age, opting for a Santorini stop on his way home. Hackett, the money man, had to finalise details on their French solar farm deal – and stay beyond the reach of any supposed assassin.

'The Chunnel would be as stinky and sweaty as Paris.' Hackett looked up as the departure board finally offered some respite. 'I'm boarding in five minutes. They better have proper aircon and ice for the G & Ts.'

'And a vegan meal to go with it?' Ferdy chuckled.

'Fuck you, Ferdy. I'll rip that travel agent's head off when I get home. He denied booking vegan for every leg of the flight from Melbourne, but the airline sent me a copy of the request in his name. I'll shove that up his arse when I find him.'

Ferdy's laughter rankled, but Hackett let it slide. 'I wonder if the prick has a grudge against me. I definitely booked a car from the hotel to the airport. But the Paris company has no record.'

'The gremlins are dicking you around. You've got time now to relax in England. Go to Wimbledon and catch up with the grandkids. If you get sick of them, you can fly back to Greece in a couple of hours. Lots of sunshine, seafood, cold drinks and hot ladies.'

Hackett was sorely tempted to follow his mate to stunning Greek Islands especially as the gratitude romp with Steph Grant was obviously off the agenda. 'I still can't believe she talked the bloody cameraman into following her,' he moaned. 'She understood the quid pro quo–'

An incoming call distracted Hackett. 'Shit.'

'You have another call?'

'Yeah. Marianne.'

Ferdy laughed. 'I'll go back to the pool and let you sort out your tangled domestic life.'

'She can wait. Probably wants to have another moan about Mitch. Why the fuck should I care that her boyfriend is fucking away from home?'

'Is he though? Didn't he deny the allegations?'

'Well, he would, wouldn't he. Anyway Marianne flew to London, where he calmed her down – until she found naked photos of the oligarch's daughter on his phone.'

'Which he denied taking.'

'He's ex-SAS, Ferdy. He'd die before confessing.'

Hackett's phone vibrated. Marianne again.

'Maybe you should talk to her,' said Ferdy. 'At least get the latest drama out in the open.'

Hackett looked up as the PA system announced his London flight. It was about an hour to Heathrow, plus the time to board, disembark and crawl through customs. Probably almost three hours before he could speak to Marianne, if he ignored the call.

'I'll call her at Christmas,' he said.

Ferdy snorted. 'Any updates on the saga back in Apollo Bay?'

'It flared and fizzled within a fortnight,' Hackett said. 'Probably an idiot yanking our chain. Or my chain. I wouldn't put it past one of the *Spotlight* weasels to have faked the For Amy message.'

Ferdy laughed. 'They're your weasels, mate. And I doubt they'd bash a bloke with a beer keg to support their story.'

Hackett repacked his brief case with one hand; the plane queue was thinning. 'Anyone could've thumped that pisshead, and be happy to get away with it because a TV crew provided a bigger conspiracy for the locals and cops.'

'Last I heard he was still in a coma. Any change?'

'Semiconscious apparently; and likely to be a vegetable. The cops won't get anything out of him.'

Hackett stood and joined the business class boarding queue. 'I've got to go. I'll talk to you from Oxford in a couple of days.'

'Have fun with the grandkids.'

Hackett disconnected halfway through Ferdy's chortle. He was about to switch the phone to flight mode when it rang again. Marianne, for the third time.

She could still wait until he got Heathrow. Maybe even the hotel in Oxford.

Chapter 20

'I seen him – the *barsh*tard – on the road to the shack.' Bryan Cowan's voice was raspy, his words barely a whisper.

Detective Sergeant Nathan Potter, sitting beside the hospital bed in the intensive care ward had to lean closer.

'Whose shack, Bryan?' His tone was gentle. 'You mean Tugga's shack?'

'Yeah.'

Nathan glanced at DC Cheryl Baines who'd re-entered the room.

Every word from this bashing victim was important. Up until a week ago, the doctors at Geelong Hospital still gave Bryan little hope of surviving. Then two days ago, when his vitals were improving, they remained convinced that, even if he did wake, the damage to his brain would make it unlikely he'd be able to talk.

The tough little bastard had proved the experts wrong. His head was still swathed in bandages, the bruises around his eyes and nose were fading to a sickly yellow, and he still had many weeks, possibly months, of rehabilitation before he could leave hospital, but Bryan Cowan had already beaten the odds.

His first words, heard by a sharp-eared nurse, had been to mumble something about the footy. She'd told him about the Cats' win the day before, and then called Nathan.

'Water, pl...'

Nathan reached for a plastic cup and held the straw to Bryan's lips. He took a sip and closed his eyes. It had been like that for the past hour, a few mumbled words, then off to dreamland again.

'Did Bryan say it was the same guy near Tugga's property?'

When Nathan nodded, Cheryl settled into the chair next to him. It was early evening; the ward was quiet as most visitors had left.

The two cops were prepared to wait hours if necessary for Bryan to fill in the blanks; if the nurses let them stay. They might not get much more information, but they already had the most important detail – the name of the person who had assaulted him.

And now, confirmation the same man was most likely their arsonist.

CHAPTER 21

Morgan wanted to share the moment with Amy, to articulate the thrill and power he felt again with a holstered gun nuzzled against his ribs.

Focus. There would be time later to relive this long-awaited retribution. It had taken years to get here, and the execution would be over in seconds.

Breathe slowly. Remember the range rituals. Finger off the trigger. No early discharge!

He knew all this. It was part of his MI6 training.

But this was so personal, he knew it was important to control his adrenalin. It could spoil his aim.

His jacket was loose; all he had to do was reach, draw and point, and squeeze, just like he'd been rehearsing at the cottage.

Make it smooth.

Six bullets straight into the target.

Mitch fucking Stevens – the murdering bastard – would be a bloody mess on the street.

Morgan checked his watch; two minutes to wait. Cars lined this narrow and leafy Hampstead street, with its footpath a good metre above the road. All this was to his advantage: height, vehicles, street trees, and gardens. The two girls in the distance, walking their Pomeranians towards the heath, would be out of range before the car arrived. The rest of the street was empty of witnesses.

'All is good, Amy.'

Morgan waited, dressed in running gear, beside a huge tree on the footpath, about 12 metres from a parking space in front of a monument to some 17th century philanthropist who'd donated a well to the poor. Beside the well, now dry and useless, were the steps up to the house occupied by a friend of the Russian girl Stevens was protecting.

The unecessary squeal of cornering tyres at speed was Morgan's warning.

Home again, home again, Amy.

The driver of the black BMW swung dramatically into the empty parking space and stomped on the brakes. Morgan contemplated taking out the stupid Russian too, just for being a dick.

He leant casually on the tree, lifting his right leg as if to stretch a hamstring and then, as the car door opened, he made his move.

This is it, Amy.

He slipped his right hand inside the jacket, drew the pistol and lowered it beside his leg as he walked silently on the higher path towards the vehicle on the road below.

Within seconds he was standing above the target who was facing away from him.

Should he shout? Let the prick know why he was about to die?

You weren't given the chance to surrender, Amy.

Morgan lifted the gun and fired.

Chapter 22

Jo shielded her eyes from the glare as she pushed aside the grey bedroom drapes to reveal a sunny London afternoon. Chelsea bar-hopping made the mornings redundant. The view from the basement bedroom wasn't inspiring: parked cars, pasty legs, electric scooters at bone-breaking speeds. Jo didn't care; she was living in the heart of London – for free.

She yawned and turned to the crumpled bed. Eduardo had left before dawn, or was it midday? She'd found him in the second bar on Kings Road. He was handsome, charming and ludicrously rich, or must've been to pay for so many expensive drinks. Jo wondered if her long service leave could be extended to six months. Maybe a year?

She was alone in the flat, but still dragged on a t-shirt and a pair of shorts. Modesty was required in the reception rooms on the first floor above, where pedestrians could see everything inside. That was the only negative Jo could find in her digs. The flat was chic, had three large bedrooms, two bathrooms, and a stylish kitchen she'd only used for toast and coffee. The tube station was three minutes walk, if she didn't stop to drool at every window display.

So far the free accommodation and her generous one-night stands had stretched Jo's budget a long way, but she couldn't afford to shop anywhere except the cafes.

She headed for the kitchen and her charging phone, where she found a text from Kim.

> Call me when you wake

Kim had gone to Paris for four days to visit the Louvre and other famous galleries. Initially, Jo had been annoyed by Kim's sudden urge to see the world, knowing her own travel plans would become entwined with Kim's.

Jo wanted a private adventure this time; with nobody from home looking over her shoulder in Barcelona, Rome, Istanbul or anywhere else she cared to wander. Flights around Europe were so cheap compared to the long haul from Australia and Jo wanted to go where she wanted, when she wanted.

The inevitable coming together happened the moment Jo got an offer she couldn't refuse. She told herself off again for being such a selfish bitch for complaining about not being a solo traveller. Kim's father had bought this modest London flat for his regular business trips, and said Jo was welcome to use it as a travel base.

Modest! Jo marvelled again at the elegant furnishings, the spaciousness, and the postcode which meant it had to be worth more than £3 million. She'd only bumped into her generous host once, over brunch in the kitchen, since her arrival. Even Kim hadn't managed much conversation with her father, after a late night in the West End. John Prescott had laughed at them and announced he was going to Helsinki.

Jo's spine tingled as she turned on the espresso machine. Life in the *Spotlight* dungeon was usually fun, often exciting and occasionally dramatic. But London felt like the centre of the universe. Her next adventure would be a postponed narrowboat trip down the Oxford Canal. The original trip had been scuttled by crew desertions. The three old schoolfriends she'd press-ganged into helping with the canal locks for an extended river pub crawl cancelled at the last minute. Two of them – *two!* – discovered they were pregnant; the other was suffering from long Covid and didn't have enough energy to swat a fly.

Jo organised a new departure date and engaged a hopefully more reliable crew. Kim eagerly claimed one berth as the navigator; and Steph Grant and Dugal Cameron were recruited as the deckhands.

The canal trip would be Steph's first days off since she took up her post 21 days ago, with barely a fortnight to organise her relocation across the world. And Dugal already needed a break from discovering his camera skills were in demand with local news services. Jo and Dugal were relieved Kim and Steph, the duelling reporters, were back to being friends instead of rivals. Steph was the Channel 5 foreign correspondent; and Kim was an international traveller – for the summer.

Jo checked the fridge: milk, leftover Thai takeaway, butter, two crusts. She shut the door and took her phone and coffee through to the sofa. Her phone rang.

'Hey, Kim, I was just about to call. I had to prepare my first infusion for the day.'

Jo was surprised by the responding chuckle. Melbourne Kim would have ticked her off for drinking too much coffee. She preferred footloose Kim. 'Where are you?'

'Heathrow. Heading for the Piccadilly Line.'

'Cool. Home in time for drinks and dinner.'

'Are you up for it? It's four o'clock and you've only just surfaced.'

'I'm on holiday, Kim. I can't waste any nightlife. Speaking of which, did you get up to any mischief in Paris?'

'Let's see, two cute French guys tried to chat me up at the Moulin Rouge, there was an eager Pom at the Musée d'Orsay and a Kiwi tried his luck at Notre Dame.'

'Let me guess – they all struck out because you were in culture vulture mode.'

'Yeah.' Her giggles were interrupted by an underground announcement.

'Hey, you'll never guess who was on the plane with me.'

Jo sipped more coffee. Kim would crack.

'Oh, you're a spoilsport.' A laugh. 'Hackett was at the back of the plane.'

'What? In the poor people's section?'

'Yep. And he was so pissed off. Kept claiming someone must've made a mistake with his business class ticket. They must have double-booked and some French woman was probably in his seat and wouldn't move. The stewards told him to take the last row or catch the next flight.'

'Karma is a bitch. Did he see you?'

'I stuck my head in a magazine.'

'You wasted a chance for payback, Kim. I would've told him to stop whining and go sit with the peasants.'

'Nah, I'll wait for something more painful to get him. But his troubles didn't end there. As I was breezing through Immigration at Heathrow, the lovely guys in uniforms were demanding Hackett open all his bags. He was really agitated. There's a chance he's in lockup for being a pain in the arse.'

'That makes my day.' Jo's phone vibrated with a message.

You guys free for a drink to plan the canal trip?

'Dugal just texted. He and Steph want a planning session for the boat.'

'I'm sure you've got everything under control. How many wine bottles do we need?

'An even dozen should get us there.'

'For the whole trip?'

'Noooo! That's just getting to Oxford. We'll need to restock for the return leg.'

'Oh. Silly me. Okay, I'll see you soon. I wonder if we should share Hackett's drama with Mac or Curly?'

'I'll let you brighten Mac's day. He'll only beg me to go home sooner.'

Chapter 23

A steaming coffee in his favourite Collingwood mug awaited Mac at the *Spotlight* command post.

'Thanks, Carla.'

'You're welcome, Mac.'

The fill-in Office Manager beamed and returned to typing the production meeting agenda, which wouldn't take long. He stood at the desk, sipped and flicked through the newspapers. They were hours old, ready to wrap fish and chips. The diary was equally bare of inspiring stories. He glanced at the breakfast news services; frippery and fuck-all use to him.

Mac was heartened to see most of the reporters were on their phones, and hoped they were chasing stories, not organising restaurants or weekend dates. Mike Berry lounged in Kim's chair.

Mac couldn't shake the hope Kim would return at the end of the year. Berry was a solid reporter, and Mac would ensure he didn't get bumped back to the news department if Kim did come back. After all, a producer could never have enough good reporters.

Pete Benson hovered at Curly Rogers' shoulder as he listened to a phone call. That was encouraging. The office energy had been flat since half his workforce flew to London. He almost missed The Hatchet. The chief financial tsar's meanness always injected a spark into Channel 5 workers.

Hackett's absence also removed him as a possible target for whoever was seeking justice for Amy. If that was ever really a thing. The Tugga Tancred reboot had fizzled even before Kim and the others left for the UK. The beer keg victim was still non-compus; and the detectives had no fresh clues. Mac was starting to believe the assault and arson were random and maybe unrelated incidents.

An excited Pete interrupted the brooding. 'Mac!' He waved him to the rear desk. 'We've got something.'

'Hallelujah!' Mac brushed aside chairs to reach Curly, as he ended the call.

'That was Nathan Potter. You know, the detective. Beer keg man is awake and has given them a name.'

'Christ. Is it credible? I thought his brain was mush.'

'He's mumbled it a few times. That was enough to make the cops curious.' Curly stood and stretched his arms.

'Have they arrested the guy? Or does Nathan want the cameras there?'

'That's the problem. They have a suspect – but the guy's left.'

'Apollo Bay?'

'Australia.'

'Shit. Who is it? One of the pub drinkers?'

'A barman.'

'What's his name?'

'Riley Hawkins. He's a Pom.'

'He should be easy enough to track down then.' Mac's eyes lit up as he scratchd his beard. 'We can get Steph and a camera there for the arrest. A perp walk at the least. When do they expect to nab him?'

'Yeah, well, Nathan's now convinced Riley Hawkins was not at all who he claimed to be. He landed at Heathrow as Hawkins, but the Brits reckon his was a very good fake passport.'

Mac nodded. 'So, I'm guessing Nathan wants our help to flush him out.'

'Yep. He thinks we might have footage of the barman from Kim's story. The British media might pick it up if we go big. Especially with Steph on hand in the London Bureau.'

'Brilliant. Here's hoping Kim spoke to the guy or at least met him one of the times she was in the pub. We can get her to do a personal perspective.' Mac turned to look for Mike Berry who shrugged from Kim's seat.

'Shit!' He turned to the old railway clock over the edit suites.

'What's the time in London? We'll get Steph and a camera to Kim's flat.' Mac swung back to Pete. 'You've followed the story from the beginning. You wrap it together with whatever Steph can send.' Mac turned to Curly. 'Will Nathan talk on camera?'

'Yes, and he'll give us a head start, but can't make it exclusive.'

Mac waved away the threat of sharing the day's best story. 'The other current affairs shows don't have the pictures we've got.'

'Speaking of pictures,' Pete said. 'are the cops giving us a photo of this guy?'

'They don't have any,' Curly said. '*Apparently* the cameras inside the pub weren't working. The barman lived alone, rarely mingled with the locals outside work, and has no socials whatsoever. At least not under the name Riley Hawkins. The guy was like quicksilver, sliding between all the cracks.'

'Damn and bugger,' Mac said. 'Okay, on the off chance our Kim *did* speak to the bartender – when that's all he was – and with fervent hope our footage caught him in the background, we'll also get Kim to check it again.'

Kenny's booming voice, preceding him down the corridor, made Mac and Curly lock eyes.

'Ask Kenny if he met this bastard, and drag him into to Edit 1 if he did. Don't let him out until you isolate any frame that might include Riley Hawkins. Carla!'

The Office Manager jumped from her seat, notepad in hand.

'We're going to need Kenny for a couple of hours. Find another camera op for his jobs.'

Carla smiled, sat down, picked up the phone. Mac *almost* missed Jo's bolshie nature. He rubbed his hands together as the team launched into their tasks; Tugga had come to the rescue again.

Mac picked up the landline to call Kim, and was still fumbling through an old-fashioned contact book when the phone rang.

It was Kim. Spooky.

'Kimberley Prescott what wonderful timing. I've got a story to woo you back to the fold.'

'I was just about to offer *you* a new break in the Tugga story.'

Mac paused a full beat. 'What? How do you know already? Have you been talking to Nathan?'

A similar pause from the other side of the world. 'Nathan? No. What's happened? Is he all right?'

Mac shook his head, then remembered she couldn't see him. 'Nathan's fine. But he rang with an update. Or rather a huge lead in the Apollo Bay story. Keg man identified his attacker.'

'Excellent. Who was it? And don't call him keg man.'

Mac huffed. 'Cowan identified the hotel barman, Riley Hawkins. Although that turns out to be a fake name. And he's done a runner. Nathan is pretty sure he's in your part of the world.'

'Oh wow,' Kim said. 'I would never have suspected him. He was a nice, polite English guy. Stood up for me when–'

'When what?'

'When Bryan was annoying me with questions in the pub on the Monday, the night before he got the shit bashed out of him.

'So being British is about all Nathan knows about him. That's why I was about to call. We were hoping you'd met him; we want to get you on camera with Steph–'

'Hang on, Mac. I haven't told you my news.'

'Does it trump a man wanted for arson, assault and a werid vendetta?'

'A shooting always does.'

'Shit. Who?' Mac' stomach dropped. The Hatchett was over there – somewhere.

'Mitch Stevens. Hackett's former bodyguard. Someone gunned him down in London.'

Chapter 24

The train to Oxford glided steadily through the night as Morgan relived the execution. Three bullets in the back. There should have been more, including the coup de grace, but the bloody gun jammed as he aimed for the head shot. That was the risk of buying weapons on the dark web; you ended up with a movie cliche.

The three bullets would've done the job though. Morgan was only two metres away when he fired.

He looked down at his perfectly still hands resting in his lap. There was still a thrilling residual charge from the initial adrenalin spike when he'd pulled the trigger. He stayed long enough to imprint the scene in his memory and then took off like any other runner on the path. By the time he left Paddington Station, his body was buzzing in neutral.

Morgan scratched discreetly at the itchy skin around the fake beard. The tinted glasses, baseball cap, sweatshirt and denims were the third change of clothes before boarding the train. It was impossible to completely avoid the millions of security cameras in London. His intelligence service training went some way to limiting his exposure; so he had to beat facial recognition technology too. The CCTV would struggle to match the bearded disembarking passenger in Oxford with the ponytailed jogger who killed Mitch Stevens in Hampstead.

One down, Amy.

The bodyguard had to be the first to die. And only partly because he had murdered Amy.

Morgan wanted Andrew Hackett to suffer the fear and anxiety of being stalked. If an assassin had taken out an elite soldier on a suburban street, what hope was there for a lumpy middle-aged accountant?

A pistol was the appropriate weapon for Mitch Stevens. And no warning, despite the temptation. Mitch had to die just like Amy, shot in the back, with no chance to surrender.

Laziness made the trap easy to set. Natalia's best friend lived around the corner and up the street from her oligarch father's £20 million Gothic villa on the fringe of Hampstead Heath. Natalia never walked anywhere that wasn't a fashion boutique or a red carpet. And her text messages to Mitch's phone were easily intercepted.

She called, Mitch answered, the fat driver drove.

Morgan was waiting. Mitch went down like a sack of spuds, as the Aussies loved to say. No thrashing, just face-first into the side of the car then splat on the ground.

Morgan's escape was easier than expected. The Russian driver had floored the BMW's accelerator the moment Mitch's body smacked into the car. His loyalty would be to his billionaire boss and his daughter. He left the incompetent dead bodyguard in the street.

Morgan jogged to the heath for the first change of clothes. The gathering dusk made it easier to transition through disguises and dispose of the weapon.

Morgan stared out the carriage window. Paddington Station had been a half hour walk from his crime scene, his bolthole was another 57 miles down the line.

It felt good to finally claim justice for the woman he loved.

Just your father now, Amy.

His isolated cottage near Oxford was stocked with the tools necessary to complete that task: computers, other weapons and plenty of food. He planned to enjoy a weekend of watching the British news services until the strange shooting in Hampstead faded from the headlines due to lack of evidence. Certainly nothing that would lead investigators to his door. That made him smile.

Not as much as the thought of monitoring Hackett's rising panic through his phone and emails.

That would be better than binge-watching a Netflix series.

CHAPTER 25

Kim's stomach churned as she watched the camera crew make their final preparations for the live cross to the *Spotlight* studio half a world away from this Hamstead street.

Dugal Cameron had been drafted to provide a second camera footage in the Hampstead street where Mitch Stevens had been shot. Until the now-former senior Channel 5 operator pulled rank to be the main camera.

Tom Smart, the local freelancer, hadn't grumbled about being relegated even though his vision wouldn't show much. A police cordon was keeping the media 100 metres from anything worth seeing.

Gun crime in London was a rare thing, so a shooting in a posh suburb had natually attracted the full swag of print and TV journos. Most of them, including the big broadcast crews, had already left soon after the forensic experts packed up. This left the makeshift Channel 5 crew in the street with only a couple of newspaper reporters who'd tried to doorknock residents. It seemed no one wanted to talk to the tabloids however.

Kim knew the hacks would return with a vengeance once they learned about Mitch's connection to a series of Australian murders.

In the meantime she waited to be interviewed by the person who'd got the London correspondent's job she hadn't got, and for the life of her couldn't work out if that was ironic, moronic or just laughable.

She stood with Jo, leaning against a van, and watched as a sound engineer momentarily blocked the lights shining in Stephanie Grant's eyes to give her a microphone. 'The lapel mic is crackling. We'll use this. Can you give us another sound level, please.'

Steph brushed a blonde lock behind her ear. 'Hello Melbourne. Testing, one, two, three, four, five, six. I'm pleased to say it's another dry London morning. Are you hearing me, okay?'

'All good, Steph,' Curly answered via her earpiece. 'We're six minutes from you going live.'

Comms between Melbourne and Steph were also shared to Jo's tablet. Because she'd demanded it.

Steph gave a thumbs up to Dugal's camera and adjusted her blue jacket. She was a poised and confident, the epitome of a foreign correspondent.

Kim shook off the envy she'd all but discarded. She was happy for Steph, or rather that it was Steph who got the job and not some random recruit.

Jo sipped her coffee. 'I know what you're thinking.'

'What?'

'That should be you in front of the camera – if it hadn't been for Hackett's personal prefence.'

'I'm working my way over that molehill. It's–'

'At last,' Jo said, distracted by an incoming message.

'Is that an update?' Kim glanced at Steph who was now two minutes away from her most important live cross to *Melbourne Spotlight* since arriving in London. 'Do we need to alert her?'

'It's an email from Mac. I asked him to send a photo of the barman, if Kenny could get one from your original report.'

Kim smirked. 'You think he might return here, to the scene of the crime? If it is him who shot Mitch.'

'Who the hell else would it be?' Jo said.

'Well *I* know what Riley looks like; and he's–'

'Oh my God!' Jo interrupted Kim again.

Kim pushed herself off the van. 'What is it?'

'I *know* him.' Jo held up the grainy image.

'Yeah, that's Riley.'

'No. That's Simon.'

Kim was stunned. 'What? Where did *you* meet him?'

'He was a barista in South Melbourne. Near the studio. We were friendly, as in just friends, before the pandemic. He disappeared one day and then resurfaced a year ago. That's when we got together – until he pissed of again about seven, eight months ago.'

Kim's jaw dropped. 'You and Riley–'

'Simon.' Jo shrugged. 'Yeah. It was casual. I hadn't given him a thought until I checked your footage from Apollo Bay.'

'Why did you check it?'

'I thought I saw a familiar someone in your live cross that night.'

'Why didn't you say anything?'

'Why should I? He was just a guy I had sex with who'd gone walkabout.'

'One minute to program titles, Steph,' Dugal called from behind his camera.

'Shit. This guy's a serial – something. Liar, at the very least.'

'Vigilante. Another one,' Jo said.

'And more connected to *Spotlight* than we thought. This is info nobody else has. We need to get it on air.'

Kim dragged Jo towards Dugal, making sure to keep behind him and the lights. 'Steph, Jo's got a critical update on the shooter. Tell Curly you need to interview both of us.'

Steph looked askance for half a beat, then nodded. 'Get Jo. Wait there. Did you hear that, Curly?'

'Yep. Position them to your right during the video and we'll wing it off the back of the story. About 30 seconds until Richard throws to you. Have a good one.'

'Titles running,' Dugal said, his eye on the viewfinder.

Jo, who'd muted her tablet so they could no longer hear the feed to Steph's earpiece, tugged on Kim's sleeve and whispered, 'Why did you drag me into this?'

'This vigilante is using multiple identities, Jo. He's clever. Your perspective of him might create more leads for the police.'

Dugal raised his hand to demand silence.

Kim and Jo knew the first images being beamed home were from Tom Smart's second camera framed on the crime scene down the street, but with Steph's voiceover.

> 'Thanks, Richard. This is the closest we can get to the scene where an Australian, former SAS soldier Mitch Stevens was shot three times earlier this afternoon.

Dugal raised his hand again to let everyone in the vicinity know his camera on Steph was now live.

'The latest news from the hospital is that Stevens is in a serious condition – but his injuries are not life threatening. The bullets, believed to be 9mm, were fired into Stevens' back from a couple of metres away.

'Police attribute his survival to the body armour he was wearing.

'Detectives here believe the real target was Stevens' client – a Russian oligarch's daughter, who was in the rear seat of the car. The Russian driver reacted quickly, speeding from the scene.

'Police say there was no attempt to ensure Stevens was dead, which supports their suspicion he was collateral damage.

'However – because of recent events back home in Australia – we do not agree with that view. We believe we can link an arson and brutal assault in Apollo Bay last month to the shooting in London today.

'You see, six years ago, Mitch Stevens was in Melbourne working as a bodyguard to Channel 5 executive Andrew Hackett, who was connected to the infamous Tugga's Mob saga.'

Yeah, yeah, Kim thought, I could've done that; but she smiled as her old rival delivered a polished and flawless presentation. Steph continued to stare down the barrel of the camera, until confirmation the original video was playing in Melbourne.

Dugal lifted his head from the camera. 'Back to us in three-and-a-half minutes. Kim, Jo, take your places. Steph, you'll open on my camera, the interview will be on Tom's, then you wrap it up on the single.' He looked around. 'Is Tom back yet?'

'Here, Dugal,' the freelancer said. He'd obviously grabbed his gear and scooted back to them the moment his shots were done.

Steph shepherded them into a tight formation under the lights with Jo in the middle. 'Okay. What's going on? I need something to kick this off.'

'If the Apollo Bay guy is the today's shooter, he's using multiple identities,' said Kim.

'Didn't we already know that?' Steph asked.

'Yeah but we now have two known identities. I met him in Apollo Bay as Riley the barman. But apparently Jo knew him as someone else in South Melbourne.'

'Wow! When did you meet him, Jo–' she raised a finger, then tapped her ear.

'Shit,' she said a moment later. 'Curly says the video's corrupted. They have cameras on Richard now, he's apologising and will throw back to me with our big update in 10 seconds. Start with a recap of your last story.'

And in 10, Steph was live again.

> *'That is disappointing to lose the package, Richard, but I'm pleased to say I'm joined here in London by the journalist who broke the Apollo Bay story last month, along with another Spotlight team member who has vital information about the suspect.'*

Steph pivoted her head to camera two.

> *'Beside me is our Melbourne production manager Jo Trescowthick; and Spotlight's most famous reporter, Kim Prescott. They're both on leave in the UK.'*

Kim blushed but nodded at the accolade, as Steph continued.

> *'Ladies, I understand, that in the last few minutes, you have learned something new about the likely suspect in today's shooting in Hampstead.'*

Steph pointed the microphone at Kim, who was well aware she had to choose her words carefully, in order to thread their way through a legal minefield.

> *'We have, Steph. Viewers familiar with the seemingly never-ending Tugga Tancred story will remember our reports on the torching of his shack at Apollo Bay in May.*
>
> *'That incident was followed by the brutal assault of local man, Bryan Cowan, soon after telling me he might have information about the alleged arsonist. Cowan was hit with a beer keg and was in a coma for many weeks.*
>
> *'However, he was finally able to give police the name of*

the man who attacked him. He identified Riley Hawkins, a barman at the Apollo Bay hotel where Cowan was a regular, and behind which he was attacked.

　'Hawkins had already left town by the time Cowan regained conciousness. Victoria Police believe he flew to London.'

Steph nodded at the implication of that info. She turned the mic to herself, then switched between Kim and Jo.

> Steph: *'You met Riley Hawkins while covering the stories, Kim. What can you tell us about him?'*
>
> Kim: *'He was a charming guy; polite and considerate. I have to admit, Steph, I was stunned when Cowan identified Riley as the guy who bashed him.'*
>
> Steph: *'It seems Riley Hawkins is quite the chameleon. I understand, Jo, that you also knew him – but by a different name.'*

Jo nodded. *'He was Simon when I knew him.'*

> Steph: *'When and where was that?'*
>
> Jo: *'At Coolio's Café near our Channel 5 studios. The first time was about six years ago.'*
>
> Steph: *'First time?'*
>
> Jo smiled. *'Yes. Then sometime, maye a few months before covid hit, he just disappeared–'*

Jo turned to Kim, her eyes wide.

> '*And* that *was soon after the climax of the original Tugga's Mob saga.'*

Jo turned back to Steph.

> 'Sorry, I've only just made that connection. Anyway, he returned to his old job at Coolio's, maybe 18 months ago, then left again without a word back in November. Ish.

Steph: *'So, we have a suspect known variously as Riley Hawkins and Simon–?*

Jo: *'No idea. We never got past first names.'*

Kim swallowed, hoping Steph wouldn't probe too deeply about Jo's relationship.

Steph: *'It's understood he is English, can either of you narrow that down?'*

Jo: *'He told me he was from Cumbria.*

Kim: *'Told me, Devon.'*

Steph: *'Okay. He sounds like a practiced liar. But why should police here in the UK be looking at him for the shooting here in Hampstead Heath?'*

Kim: *'The arsonist in Apollo Bay left a message at Tugga Tancred's shack. He wrote* For Amy *in charcoal on a sign at the gate. To us at Spotlight, it meant someone was resuming Amy Stewart's vendetta against the men she blamed for her mother's rape and death.'*

Steph nodded. *'And the only survivor of that crime spree, and the group known Tugga's Mob, was Channel 5 executive Andrew Hackett. Who, it transpired, was Amy Stewart's biological father.'*

Kim: '*Yes. But to bring that old story full circle back to London today, it was Mitch Stevens acting as Hackett's bodyguard who killed Amy Stewart. And today he was gunned down, quite possibly by a man who fled Melbourne for London last month.*

Kim paused; confident Steph wouldn't fill the gap.

'Because anyone seeking justice for Amy would have to add Mitch Stevens to their hit list. Probably at the top.'

CHAPTER 26

Andrew Hackett wrestled with fear as his ex-wife wept on his shoulder outside the Royal Free Hospital Emergency Department. They were only 10 minutes drive from the crime scene, and the street was narrow, and congested with ambulances, cars and pedestrians. Hackett was a sitting duck if the shooter wanted to finish his blood feud. He also didn't give a fuck about lucky Mitch Stevens because, unlike the bodyguard, Hackett wasn't wearing a state-of-the-art bulletproof vest.

He edged Marianne away from the footpath towards a hospital sign on a concrete pillar. It might protect his back, but the first hint of a gun-wielding lunatic and he'd be inside the hospital in a flash.

Marianne would be fine; she wasn't on a killer's hitlist.

'Oh, Andrew. They say the bruising to Mitch's spine is severe; it could take months for him to recover.'

Hackett shrugged. He had zero interest in her lover's prognosis, especially now the two had put their international communication glitches down to Mitch's dodgy phone. Yeah, right. Marianne had eagerly swallowed Mitch's bullshit about not screwing his client.

'You probably need to get back inside. To Mitch.' He tried to sound sympathetic, but he mostly wanted to get off the street. His phone rang.

'I need to talk to Ferdy,' Hackett said, waggling his ringing phone at Marianne, to suggest she should bugger off now. She sniffed loudly and stalked inside the hospital.

'Andrew, what's the latest on Mitch and where are you?' Ferdy, who was back home in Melbourne, had earlier filled him in on the lastest theories thrown out by the *Spotlight* journos. *And* the fact they'd mentioned his name – *again*. He was going to rip Curly and Mac new arseholes when he got home. If he got home.

'I'm outside the hospital,' Hackett said. He tossed up whether to wait inside but figured he'd miss the next cruising black cab if he wasn't on the street.

'Loverboy is going to survive. But apparently the blunt force trauma or something, shit I sound like TV cop, from the bullets has severely bruised his spine. And fragments from the smashed ceramic plates in his body armour, while saving his life, also caused secondary injuries. Marianne is naturally being melodramatic about the whole thing. Mitch is a prick, but he's a tough bastard. He'll be back fucking my wife in no time.'

'Your ex-wife Andrew.'

Hackett grunted. Ferdy wasn't twisting the knife; it was one of his frequent reminders it was time Hackett moved on from his dead marriage.

'How are the London cops treating the case? Do they accept the *Spotlight* theory it's linked to Tugga's shack in Apollo Bay.'

'No. The Met detectives here aren't convinced. So local TV news is going with their working theory the shooting was politically motivated. There have been several death threats against the Russian oligarch and his family since the Ukraine invasion. The guy is part of Putin's inner circle. That's why Mitch was bodyguard to the daughter.'

'Yeah, *Spotlight* led with that bullshit too. Maybe the local plods don't want a complicated investigation, which I assume means you won't have any cops guarding your door.'

'Not bloody likely.'

'What are you going to do? If the vigilante is there, you could come back to Australia. We can finish the French deal on Zoom.'

Hackett's radar pinged, weirdly sending a crawling sensation to his balls, as he noticed a man, mid-30s man in a long army surplus coat, staring pointedly at him as he walked slowly by.

It was too hot to be dressed like that. What the fuck did he have under that coat? And where were the bloody ubiquitous London cabs when you needed one.

Hackett couldn't run in any direction. A siren blast scared the rest of the shit out of him, as a candy-striped ambulance roared out of the driveway. Coat man watched the vehicle depart, then resumed his, *oh*, innocent walk into the hospital.

Shit. You're getting paranoid.

'Andrew? Are you there?'

'Yeah, yeah. Look, if this psycho is in London, it means he's got money and resources. He could follow me home again and the hiding goes on. I don't want to live like a mole.'

'Have you thought about getting your own investigators?'

'More protection?'

'No, like private detectives. They'd be working for you – one case, no distractions or bureaucracy – to find the shooter and stop him.'

Hackett smiled. The cost benefit of that idea far outweighed paying randy ex-soldiers to protect him while they waited for the vigilante to come to them. Hire experts to go after the bastard instead.

'That's a good idea, Ferdy. I'll get some advice here on who to hire, and get Mac to send me pictures of this Riley-Simon bastard so they know who they're looking for.'

'Speaking of the Simon ID,' Ferdy said, 'did you ever go to *Coolio's Café* where he worked?'

'No, but my PA, Zara, did every morning. I recall their branded takeaway cups on her desk.'

'That's a strange connection, and too close to the studio, though I don't see where it fits the puzzle.'

'Neither do I.' Hackett paused for the diminishing wails of an arriving ambulance.

'At least you've got a whole *Spotlight* crew in London who can keep you updated.'

'What do you mean? It should only be Stephanie Grant.'

'Mate, you obviously didn't register what I was saying earlier. Kim Prescott wasn't reporting from Melbourne. She and your office manager, Jo whatshername, gatecrashed Steph's live cross – here in London, on the street where Mitch was shot.' Ferdy chuckled. 'I suspect the dark-haired little pocket rocket had the hots for the barista and got dumped.'

'Christ – this gets messier by the hour.' Hackett spotted a cab and raised his hand. Finally, this one was his. 'I need time to think – and a bloody big drink.'

'You're in the best place in the world for that. Find an obscure pub and get lost in the shadows. I recommend changing your accommodation as well. Some of the back street B&Bs might take cash.'

'The thought of a grotty hotel is enough to make me puke.'

'Better to be queasy than dead, mate. Play this killer at his own game – use a false name. You'll be harder to track down and it'll give you time to plan your next move.'

'I'll think about it, mate. About to get in a cab. Buggering off now.'

Hackett settled in the back seat, gave the driver the name of the hotel he'd previously checked into. It would do for one night. The bedroom was small and comfortable, the internet was free, and the full English breakfast was part of the deal. The downstairs bar would be a good place to ponder his next move.

So far this trip to England was a complete shitshow, starting with the seat mix-up on the flight from Paris, and the battle with the airport officials at Heathrow. Throw in Marianne's phone call when he landed, so filled with joy that she and Mitch were solid, followed by her hysteria when he got shot.

And now, Ferdy pretty much confirmed the man who shot Mitch – here in the fucking UK – was the same one who torched Tugga's shack.

Why does this excrement keep hitting my fan?

CHAPTER 27

The stupid stone walls of the converted barn made the space feel like a prison. There was not enough room for angry pacing, but Morgan stomped to an fro like his parole had just been declined.

'How did the bastard survive?'

Morgan knew how, but needed to vent. He should've known the bodyguard might wear close-fitting armour.

Morgan had been stupid, *stupid*, to be so intent on copying how Amy died that he hadn't fired a fourth shot into the prick's head.

He kicked the ragged two-seater sofa, releasing a cloud of dust.

'I'm sorry, Amy. I failed you.'

He threw himself into the chair in front of his laptops on the pine table. One laptop was running his surveillance programs; the other was currently on the *Spotlight* website. He slumped onto the timber chair and watched the replay again.

'You fucked me, Jo.'

His Riley and Simon IDs were now known to the whole damn world, so had to be discarded forever. It was down to him that he'd not been quick enough to hide his face from the camera in Apollo Bay. But that nosy bloody reporter had put two and seven together and come up with Riley the barman. And Jo, *fucking Jo*, had matched Riley to Simon.

London cops were so far still going with the oligarch being the target line, but that wouldn't last long. The British press would soon latch on to the 'shooting linked to several Australian murders' story as a much more juicy story. The tabloid hacks would be like sharks for a few days, until the story was bumped by a salacious celebrity sex scandal, or political fuck-up in Downing Street.

Morgan had plenty of caps, jackets and trousers, as well as wigs, beards, makeup and other accessories to change his identity daily if he needed to.

He'd kept to himself since arriving in Oxforshire, and had been a child the last time he had been in the area, so no local was likely to recognise him. He'd arranged the isolated rental property online, using another identity, choosing it partly because even the rear courtyard was surrounded by a brick wall covered in wisteria.

The location too was important for his long-term plan. The once flourishing community had withered before the start of the 21st century as tourists preferred the more tranquil and scenic sections of the county's vast canal system.

The closest villages didn't offer many provisions but it was safer to shop in busy Oxford anyway. And the police there certainly wouldn't have the staff, or motivation, to trawl through thousands of hours of supermarket CCTV footage to look for Riley-Simon-Anonymous. Morgan didn't expect a knock on the door, but planned to stay out of sight during the day until his face disappeared from the news cycle. He had enough food to keep him going for a week.

Morgan sighed and turned to the surveillance computer. He checked Hackett's call log and listened to the conversation with Ferdy, snorting at the amateurish advice about staying off the grid.

Andrew Hackett would never be separated from his smartphone; so Morgan would know his every move.

Digital links to the bodyguard had been terminated. The Met detectives would never find evidence of Mitch's phone being hacked. Marianne would now be his unwitting informant on that cockroach's health as she'd no doubt be giving her ex regular unwanted updates. She was also part of his plan to entrap Hackett.

Morgan considered causing mischief for Jo Trescowthick, as payback for revealing his Simon legend, but decided that'd be churlish. After all he *did* have Jo to thank as the initial conduit to Channel 5 and Hackett. Hers had been the easiest devices to hack.

'No, Amy. Jo's a distraction we don't need. Our focus must be on our prime mission – killing your father.'

Morgan had also ruled out another attempt on Mitch Stevens, at least for the time being. An injured elite soldier wouldn't offer an assassin an easy second chance, even while in hospital. And no doubt he'd already recruited a few SAS mates to have his back. It was enough the bastard had been virtually crippled. News reports suggested it might be months before he walked again. Mitch would wait; cold dishes were still tasty.

Morgan parted the curtain to the poky kitchen and turned on the kettle. The courtyard was in shadow from the summer foliage. Would it be safe to continue his twilight walks along the Oxford Canal? He took the rougher track north of Shipton-on-Cherwell, away from the pubs at Thrupp. There were fewer boaties moored along the quieter stretch of water, and he rarely saw another late-night walker. A hat and spectacles would be disguise enough in case he ran into a drinker returning from the pub.

Mitch had two fake identities ready to use; and could easily make more. In retrospect one of the most useful of his MI6 jobs, before he was sacked, was creating legends for undercover MI6 agents.

His dismissal still rankled. He had infiltrated Downing Street's computers to prove their security was inadequate. The Prime Minister didn't see the altruism, only the unsanctioned intrusion. Morgan was cast adrift, despite his supervisors' worry about losing control over a disgruntled computer genius.

Morgan intensified their fears by dropping so far below the radar, they had no way of tracking him. It was lucky he'd thought to create several uncrackable legends for himself while still working for the spook service.

He was in full Simon persona when he met Amy. The emotional connection with the troubled Kiwi was instant; and he knew Amy could one day be trusted to know about Morgan.

Chapter 28

Dugal Cameron placed two wines and an ale on the small table. The pub was busy, but not at shouting levels. 'Where do you think Hackett's hiding?'

Jo gulped her sav blanc while Kim considered the question. 'One place he won't be hanging around is the hospital consoling Marianne. Has Steph called him?'

'He's not answering any of her messages. She's wondering if he's already left the country. Gone back to France, or even home.'

'That makes it awkward for Steph. Hackett's obviously a target, and she needs to get him on camera to keep the story rolling here.' Kim frowned. 'Well, I guess that's what Mac would want.'

'Yeah,' Dugal agreed. 'Either Hackett or Mitch, but the doctors won't let anyone near him for a few days. Steph's scrambling for a new angle for the next live cross.'

'What about Marianne Hackett? She might shed a few tears on camera.'

Jo sniggered. 'They won't be for her ex-husband.'

'Also not responding to calls or messages.'

Jo's glass rattled on the table, as she reminded them of something much more important. 'Steph's not going to be able to come on the boat trip tomorrow!'

Dugal waggled his hand. 'She won't be with us at the start. She might be able to catch up for the return leg from Oxford.'

'Shit. We need at least two people to work the locks.'

'We'll be right,' Kim said. 'There's not much for a navigator to do on a canal. I was intending to share the winching with Dugal and Steph. We'll be fine, as long as you don't ram another boat.'

'Pfft. Easy peasy.'

'Well, that's the canal trip sorted,' said Dugal. 'But what about the vigilante? What is the possible connection between this Riley dude, or whoever he is now, and Amy?'

Kim paused her glass in front of her mouth. 'It has to be through the café surely. The Melbourne cops back then established Amy was given a temp job by Zara Hennessy. Maybe Amy first latched on to Zara at *Coolio's*'s in order to get close to Hackett.'

Jo nodded. 'Maybe. I still see Zara there every morning. Their coffee is still the best even without their star barista. I, however, don't recall ever seeing Amy at the cafe. Like even in hindsight of later events.'

'But *he* disappeared soon after Amy was shot?'

'Yep. Like, gone the next day. Again, noted only in restrospect, because the two things are only now coming together in my memory.'

Dugal put down his empty pint. 'Do you think they were a couple? Simon and Amy, I mean.'

'That's a likely possibility,' Kim said.

Jo hurrumphed.

'I only mean you'd have to be extra close, in some way, to carry on with someone's very personal idea of vengeance.'

'Ooh,' Dugal said. 'Maybe he was in on everything from the start. An accomplice in the various deaths that got dealt to Tugga and his mates.'

'The cops missed the likelihood of any accomplice, if that's the case,' Jo said.

Kim raised both eyebrows. 'As did we, if that's true. But why the hell wait so long to finish the job. It been over six years.'

Chapter 29

Sweat tricked down Andrew Hackett's back. It was so annoying he was starting to wonder if he was going through male menopause. He was sitting in a quaint phone box in the cool of his hotel's bar, so it was the summer humidity that was making him damp.

Maybe it was the urgent tone of the private investigator he was talking to the landline.

'Get out of that pub now, Mr Hackett. Collect your bags but dump your smartphone. That is the greatest intelligence-gathering device ever invented.'

'Shit, Gary. You think I've been hacked?'

'Everything you've told me indicates someone is messing with your life. The plane tickets, wrong food orders, the strange cancellations. These cannot be coincidences. A smart operator can access your texts, emails, voicemails, and monitor your location. The intelligence services, for instance, have technology that can listen to all your conversations. Like them, all any half-decent hacker needs is a phone number.'

Hackett took a swig of his gin and tonic. 'Shit.'

'You're lucky you left your phone in the room to call me. But, whoever is doing this will know what you been googling. You'll have to get rid of any other devices as well, I'm afraid. They'll have control of your laptop or tablet too.'

'I can't ditch my laptop! There's sensitive information on it.'

'Then ask the hotel manager to put it in the safe. You can arrange to get it flown back to Australia.'

'I can't go home yet. There are things I have to manage here.'

'If there's a gunman hunting you in London, Melbourne will be safer.'

'Christ. I don't know what to do.'

'Get moving, is my best advice, Mr Hackett. And don't use your credit cards. Have you got some cash?'

'A few hundred quid. That won't last long.'

The man sighed. 'It would be best to stay away from family and friends. Have you got any business acquaintances who can accommodate you, lend you money, or buy you an airline ticket?'

Hackett took a slug of gin and coughed. 'Not really. I'll have to think. Do you have any contacts here?'

'I'm an ex-cop in Port Melbourne, Mr Hackett, my beat doesn't extend beyond Victoria. I'm still wondering why Ferdy thought I could help.'

'What about fellow PIs here?'

'I've never been to England.'

Hackett winced. 'Okay, let me think.'

'Don't dally, Mr Hackett. I was still on the force when your daughter went after you. If someone has decided to resume *that* vendetta, I'd be very worried about their mental state.'

Hackett wriggled in his sweaty shirt. 'You're not reassuring, but you're convincing. Send an invoice for the consultation to Channel 5. If I don't make it home, they'll pay regardless.'

'A bit of gallows humour doesn't hurt, Mr Hackett. Good luck.'

Hackett hung up the phone, finished his drink, and pulled out his wallet to count the cash: £365. That would barely cover his accommodation and meals here. He'd have to use his credit card one last time and then piss off quick.

If Gary the PI was right, the vigilante must already know he stayed here last night. Perhaps he was on his way to get him right now. Hackett looked wildly around the bar to see if any of the six other customers were watching him. It helped that he knew what the bastard looked like now, since Mac had sent him a photo. He wasn't in the bar. Didn't mean he wasn't lurking outside to gun him down in the street; like he did Mitch.

Maybe the manager could be persuaded to add a large cash advance to his bill when he paid it. Plus a tip if necessary, to store his laptop and phone.

The best he could hope for was head start. How the hell would he function without his phone?

CHAPTER 30

'Wow!' Dugal Cameron exclaimed, letting the Vauxhall hire car idle so they could admire the dozens of colourful narrowboats tethered, cheek by jowl, along the canal.

'I swear we just stepped back in time,' Kim said, switching her gaze from the quaint, pristine and oh-so-inviting canal boats to the whitewashed Victorian buildings to the Cast iron footbridge at the water entrance to Braunston Marina.

'England is one giant time step,' Jo noted drily. 'Welcome to the meeting place of the Oxford and Grand Union canals.'

'How did you find out about this place?'

'My Dad's cousin has a British mate who rents his boat to trusted tourists,' Jo said. 'I had to sling him a bit extra coz I postponed my first booking, and we are in peak season, but his boat is still way cheaper than going through the boat companies.'

Kim leaned between the passenger and driver seats. 'How do we find the boat?'

'He said he'd meet us outside the shop.' Jo pointed at a building with a blue awning. 'I'll text him now. He lives five minutes away and will take our car back to park at his home.'

A toot from behind prompted Dugal to wave and hook the car into a parking spot. It took them two minutes to unload their three packs, two shopping bags and a box of wine. Jo was content to guard the supplies and wait for their contact.

Kim and Dugal set off to explore.

'Where did Jo get the idea for this tour?' Dugal stopped at a 60-foot blue and yellow narrowboat with dozens of pot plants along the roof.

Kim looked at him askance. 'Weren't you listening to her story about the canal trip her parents took back in the '80s?'

Dugal shrugged. 'I guess not. Was it an interesting story?'

Kim slapped his arm. 'Apparently it was one of their happiest memories – before the divorce.'

'Ah. I can see the appeal of a slow life on the water.' Dugal walked closer to the window of *Fyrefly III*. 'Is it bad manners to look in the windows?'

'I think that's a permanent home, so probably yes,' Kim said. She pointed at the two shorter vessels tied side by side. 'They're for sale though, so I imagine peeking is allowed.'

They wandered for five minutes until they heard a piercing whistle and noticed Jo waving them back.

'You can take the girl out of the... I have no idea what,' Kim admitted. There was a burly, middled-aged man wearing a fair dinkum deerstalker standing beside Jo, smoking a pipe.

Dugal laughed. 'That's either Sherlock Holmes or our host.'

A few minutes later the trio were admiring the *Moriarty* – an elegant 60-foot narrowboat with a black hull, and a long red cabin with rich green trim and roof, and rectangular windows.

Kim was mostly grateful the bow was pointed at the marina exit; less chance of an embarrassing departure for the novice crew.

'This is my pride and joy,' said Robert Peel. 'I'm a Victorian era fan, as you might have guessed from my attire, but you will find all the modern comforts on board.'

He ushered them through the hatch. 'Step below, my friends. There are two single beds at the rear, a bathroom with toilet and shower, a double bed up front, kitchen with full-size fridge and oven, a saloon, central heating, lots of storage and plenty of lounging space amidships. The cruiser stern outside with the tiller, at the back obviously, also has seating space for six.'

The interior of the *Moriarty* was also lined with oak, which created a light and spacious ambience despite the narrow beam of less than two metres. All the beds were ready with crisp white sheets and olive duvets.

Jo stopped at the double bed. 'Dugal, do you think Steph will be able to escape London?'

The new foreign correspondent's boyfriend waggled his hand. 'She's still hopeful of meeting us in Oxford.'

'Cool. That's three days away,' Jo said. 'I'm claiming this berth as skipper's quarters until Steph arrives. You deckhands can snore at the back of the boat.'

Dugal laughed, Kim saluted. 'Aye, aye skipper. But you'll have to find your own way to bed. We didn't sign on for tuck-ins.'

Jo flipped her crew mates the finger as the boat inspection continued. Peel pointed to important features and advised Jo on canal boat and locks etiquette.

'It's surprisingly roomy and comfortable,' Dugal said.

'Yeah.' Kim checked a kitchen cupboard. 'Dawdling through the Oxfordshire sunshine, trailing our fingers in the canal will be so relaxing. Do you really believe that Steph will get away?'

Dugal shrugged. 'Probably not. Mac was on the phone a lot before I left. He wants interviews with Mitch, Hackett and the local cops. Even if she wasn't new to the job, what do you reckon her priority is: the story or a few days on a boat?'

'No contest, Dugal. I guess the skipper will enjoy the double bed all the way.'

CHAPTER 31

Hackett figured he got maybe three hour's sleep in the tacky place he'd walked into after checking out of his first hotel. PI Gary had freaked him out enough that he grabbed his stuff from the room, and had a quiet *mano a mano* with the manager to secure his laptop and phone in the safe and get a £1500 cash advance off his credit card.

He moved two streets away to the *Little Raffles Hotel,* a ramshackle establishment where every floorboard creak and pipe rattle jerked him awake. He could hear snoring from the next room, a fight in the street, and at 4am was woken by ominous heavy breathing – which turned out to be his own.

He'd barricaded the bedroom door with a Scotch dresser, hoping that would slow down any room invasion and, maybe, give him time to jump out the window and probably break his legs in the drop to the footpath.

Morning brought some clarity despite the lack of sleep. He'd come up with a possible solution, a safe place to lay low for long enough to find some way out of London.

He couldn't risk calling ahead, even though his call would, by necessity now, be made from a landline somewhere. Nope, Gary had said not to call anyone on his contact list because they might be monitored.

He snorted. 'What bloody contact list, you dickhead! Your phone is locked in a safe.'

Okay. The plan was to take a walk up the street to the shop he'd passed yesterday and buy a rucksack or duffle bag. Much easier to get around with than a suitcase on wheels. Buy a Myki card, or whatever the Poms called – ah, an Oyster card – to get around later like a peasant on public transport, because even taxi trips could be traced by an expert bloody hacker.

'I hate you, whoever you are,' Hackett said to the empty room.

Once he'd repacked his stuff he'd walk to Marylebone and just turn up unannounced.

Chapter 32

Morgan stared at Hackett's current location on the London map. He was still at the hotel. There'd been no movement overnight understandably, but it was late morning now and *Mr can't go a hour with out using his mobile*, hadn't. Not a single call or text.

'Fuck!' He hadn't used his laptop since yesterday either.

Morgan picked up a timber chair and made to throw it at the stone wall. He stopped himself. He was angry – but still in control.

Besides it was Hackett's head he wanted to smash it on.

He didn't dare glance at Amy's photograph on the table.

This conversation would be addressed to her father.

'You cunning arsehole.'

Morgan didn't want to pay him any credit, but it seemed Hackett had outwitted him. For the moment.

Morgan reset the chair in front of the computer.

'Okay, you fucker. Someone told you to dump your electronics. But you, my man, will not be able to stay off the grid long. You won't last a day without a new mobile. You'll need a place to stay. And transport to get there. You're going to be short of money.'

Morgan smiled. His brain was better equipped than most to understand a panicked male in flight. His fingers danced over the keyboard, bringing up Hackett's bank records.

'That little hotel where you aren't anymore was your last public lifeline. You got a nice little advance on your credit card. Only the manager can approve that.'

Morgan's fingers hovered.

'You want to go off the radar until your big meeting in Paris ,so where would you go, you maggot? You're used to the good life, so I'm guessing you won't stay in a backpacker hostel. Not even to save your life. You'll want reasonable comfort, which will cost. You can't flit everywhere in taxis because, hello, I would find you. Would you slum it on public transport?

'Would you risk going anywhere near your children?

'Maybe, you're a selfish prick. But probably not.'

Morgan stood and stretched. Most of the anger had seeped from his system but he desperately wanted to burn off the residual energy. Going for a run would have to wait. It was hot and sunny; and the lanes and canal path would be full of ramblers.

He sighed, and headed for the kitchen to turn on the kettle. He'd make do, for now, with a cheese and pickle sandwich and a cup of Earl Grey.

Chapter 33

The rucksack felt like it was full of bricks. It had been 35 years since Hackett had hauled his worldly possessions around on his back. Wheeled suitcases and valets were so much more civilised. It also felt weird. He was a middle-aged man in a polo shirt and tan chinos, not the usual young backpacker in shorts and T-shirt. But no one gave him a second look, not even when he'd taken a pitstop on a bench near Marble Arch, beside a sulky skinhead.

Hackett was now heading down Great Cumberland Place, blinking in the brightness and wishing he had a pair of sunnies. He was sure it hadn't been this bright in the '80s.

And it was late afternoon now. He'd make the mistake of reclining on the bed after repacking his stuff and he'd fallen asleep; for five hours!

He was being buffeted by pedestrians every few metres, and each bump fuelled a temptation to head to the nearest 5-star hotel. Secrecy be damned. He could ask the concierge to call Ferdy and arrange for him to cover the bill. Surely that wouldn't be reckless.

Oh yes it would, according to PI Gary. The hacker, who he'd said was either the vigilante or someone working for him, would have programs in place to raise red flags about any strange transactions made by anyone in his life. And right now the creep had better access to his friends and colleagues than he did. Who the hell remembers any phone numbers these days? He couldn't call Ferdy right now, even if he was that stupid.

Fortunately, the Marylebone apartment that was his destination, was only a few hundred metres away on Upper Berkeley Street – if he was reading the paper map properly.

Five minutes later he stood in front of the building which was flanked by a hat shop and a Middle Eastern restaurant. The flat he needed was on the fifth floor, so he prayed the lift was working and someone was home. It was almost 6pm, so fingers crossed.

If he had to, he could wait in the restaurant, and he *was* hungry so that wouldn't be too inconvenient.

He entered the tiled foyer which was modern, clean, utilitarian. A light indicated the lift was on the third floor. Hackett decided to take the stairs anyway, just in case the occupant of Flat 5A wouldn't let him in.

MELBOURNE

Mac twirled his steaming Collingwood coffee mug. 'So, Marianne wasn't happy to be door-stopped at the hospital?'

'I think, "Fuck off you cow," says it all'

Mac laughed. He was sitting with Curly beside the speakerphone in the *Spotlight* conference room.

'How did you get around her?'

'One of the nurses taking a smoko heard Marianne mouth off at me. *Apparently*,' Steph exaggerated, 'she has not endeared herself to the medical staff. The nurse told me Mitch had been moved to her ward; offered to pass him a message.'

Mac chortled. 'And Mitch was up for a chat.'

'Yep. He thinks the London cops are on the wrong track. He believes Riley-Simon-Whoever was definitely after him. Despite what the Met detectives are saying, there have been no serious threats against the Russian or his daughter. Mitch's client is careful not to offend Putin, and all the security is mostly for show. Mitch is naturally taking our theory seriously. He's been wearing the vest ever since Kim's first story last month. He'd be dead, or paralysed, without it.'

'And he says all that on camera, Steph?'

'Yep. He's pure gold. He's still a gorgeous hunk, especially being all vulnerable-looking in a hospital bed. Our female ratings are going to be off the charts.'

'Good stuff. That's a great way to end the week. Any hints on where Hackett might be hiding?'

'He's totally off the radar, Mac. He could lurking in London, pissed in Paris, or on a private jet back to Australia. The latter is what Mitch told him to do.'

'That's on camera as well?'

'Yep.'

Mac did a fist pump; Curly grinned.

'Did you get time to do many noddies? I'd like to run the whole interview.'

'There's only a couple of cutaways. The nurse stood guard on the door, and we didn't want to get her into trouble.'

'Send her a bottle of French champers. I'll make sure Accounts reimburse you. It's a pity Dugal wasn't there as second camera. What was he doing?'

'Those three should be two hours from London on an Oxford Canal by now.'

'Oh, of course – the great longboat adventure. Weren't you supposed to join them?'

'Narrowboat, Mac. Longboats are a Viking thing. Was supposed to but would rather stay on the hunt for the shooter. The story will escalate once we run Mitch's interview. The tabloids here will then follow our lead and the London cops might even take Mitch more seriously.

'I've got a phone number for Hackett's mate, Ferdy Ackerman. He might know how and where Hackett is holding up under the pressure.'

'Great work, Steph. We're about to start the production meeting. The likely plan will be live crosses to you either side of the interview. We'll confirm that in an hour with the rundown.'

'Hang on, Mac – no, keep talking, I can multitask – there's someone at my door.'

'Okay, if you can at least get a Hackett update from Ferdy that will keep the story simmering for the wee–'

.'Well I never,' Steph said. 'You are not going to believe who's here.'

Mac snorted. 'It's Jo, isn't it. She sunk the boat already.'

'No. Andrew Hackett is standing in my hall.'

Chapter 34

It took Morgan too long, for his liking, to figure out where Hackett might hide. After checking the most logical flights out of the country, he returned to his sweep of the bastard's contacts in the UK.

'It looks like your father has taken someone's advice to stay away from the big hotels, Amy. Or at least he's smart enough not to blow his cash budget on luxury digs.'

Morgan tapped his laptop screen to widen the view of the London map.

'Let me see, from the first hotel to… Paddington, maybe? Plenty of smaller hotels to choose from there. And the train nearby. He could buy a ticket to any number of English counties; or, shit, maybe Wales or Scotland.'

And Morgan couldn't trace a cash purchase.

'He could hide out in a B&B anywhere along those lines.'

Morgan knew Hackett had to be in Paris in 10 days, so he'd continue to keep an eye on flight bookings, and the bloody Chunnel, but he really wanted to nail him before then; here in the UK. Killing Hackett in France had never been part of the plan, and he certainly didn't want to chase him back to Melbourne.

He rubbed his chin and stared at the maze of London streets.

'I think he'll stay within easy travel to the airports. And he *will* make a mistake, Amy. Ten days hiding for a man like him will be impossible; he'll get cocky or careless in a few days.'

Morgan glanced at one of his phones, the one with Amy as the screen image.

'Yes,' he nodded. 'He'll get himself a cheap phone, he'll ring… Ferdy probably and boast, like the wanker he is, about *using a burner*, thinking he can't be traced. Which he can't; I can't. But he will blab about where he is or where he's going.'

Morgan thumped his clenched fist on the table. He'd be back in control of things in no time. He glanced at his weapon of choice, racked on the wall beside him, then back at Amy.

'I cannot wait to point that at your father's uncaring heart.'

Morgan returned to his study of the map, and received a delicious flash of adrenalin.

'Fuck yes, Marylebone. You idiot, Morgan.'

He quickly delved into Hackett's Channel 5 emails from May, using the keyword "correspondent" to hasten the search. And there it was. Hackett had been negotiating an apartment lease for Channel 5's new London correspondent. It was a three-bedroom property to use for office and accommodation.

Hackett had been generous, intending the place to be a love nest for his occasional visits to England. Morgan remembered the hackles rising while listening to Hackett talking with his sleazy mate Ferdy about all the gratitude sex he'd get for appointing Stephanie Grant over the other chick.

Morgan laughed. He also recalled how quickly she put Hackett in his place, and in no uncertain terms. Had they been talking in person, and not on the phone, she probably would've stomped on his shrivelled balls with her spiky heels.

'Would he risk swallowing his pride and going to her for help? What do you think, Amy?'

A ping on his surveillance laptop alterted him to a call being made by Stephanie Grant to the *Spotlight* studio in Melbourne. He listened in to the call.

'Bingo! And I am a certified genius, Amy.'

Morgan opened up the real estate page attached to Hackett's May email; it had the address and layout of the apartment.

He could be in London in less than two hours.

CHAPTER 35

Andrew Hackett sat with a gin and tonic in hand. The modular sofa was comfortable, especially after the exertion of lugging a backpack across the city.

And yet he felt trapped. Not by the sofa; by Stephanie Grant

'The price for staying is an interview,' she'd said.

Hackett sloshed his drink as he waved at the compact living room. 'You want me to be a tethered goat to lure this fucking psycho to your door so you can film it for *Spotlight*.

'Don't be melodramatic.'

'I'm paying the bills here, Steph. Well, Channel 5 is; but I organised this cosy bolthole for you; and your *lover*. I should be entitled to stay. My life is in danger – and you're extorting me!'

'Get over yourself, Andrew,' Stephanie snapped. 'No one will know where we're filming from.'

Hackett scowled. This infuriating woman showed no sign of giving in. He'd actually seen the surprise on her face, when she opened the door to him, swiftly morph to calculation.

He needed shelter; Stephanie wanted a scoop.

'Besides, you're a target for a resourceful gunman. Why would I risk my life for your sins?'

'I haven't done anything wrong!' Hackett moaned, slopping gin on his shirt as he waved his arms around. 'Why does everyone still think I brought all this shit on myself?

'I've no idea why this nutter has resumed Amy's twisted vendetta. It's been years. It makes no sense. I did nothing wrong back in the '80s, and nothing six years ago. There's no reason to target me now.'

'I'm not the person you need to convince.' Stephanie sipped a mineral water.

'You're a hard-hearted bitc– woman.' Hackett's negotiation instincts kicked in. 'If I do the interview, I get to stay for the week.'

'One night.'

'That's not fair!'

'Tough. You said you've hidden *your* phone and computer; that doesn't mean he hasn't found other ways to track you through–'

Stephanie's eyes darted to her mobile on the kitchen bench. 'Shit!' She scooped it up and headed into the bathroom. Hackett heard running water before Stephanie returned a few moments later.

'Did you just drown your phone, Steph? Are you crazy? You think the guy can hear us through your mobile? He's not the government – he wouldn't have unlimited resources.'

'Of course I didn't, I was washing my hands.' Stephanie sat in an armchair opposite him. 'But this guy doesn't have to be part of MI5 or 6 or the CI-bloody-A. The things that hackers can do would make your mind boggle. He's probably tapped into the lives of everyone you know. I might be compromised too, and *he* could be on his way here right now.'

'Fuck!' Hackett stood to pace the room. 'Where can I go?'

'You've got cash; there's hundreds of cheap hotels. All you have to do is stay off the grid until you go to Paris. A wiser move would be to do what Mitch said, and fly home to Melbourne. You could surround yourself with security.'

Hackett stopped his prowling. 'You've spoken to him, I take it. The stupid prick was gunned down from behind, Steph, that means someone snuck up on him. And you really think I'd take the advice of the man bonking my wife.'

'There's another thing you should get over,' Steph muttered.

Hackett wished looks could kill because right now his was skewering Steph to the armchair. She was annoyingly unpeturbed.

'I could go home, but I also don't want to be looking over my shoulder forever.'

Stephanie shrugged. 'At least you'll be alive to give the cops more time to catch him.'

Hackett slumped back into the couch.

'Let me get a cameraman here and we'll record the interview.' Stephanie stood. 'You can tell the world you're innocent – again.

It might not convince the vigilante, but the story *will* get picked up by the British tabloids. Once they understand Mitch's shooting has nothing to do with an attempted hit on an oligarch's family, their reports will put pressure on the Met to get off their butts.'

Hackett knew he was out of options. 'Can you get lover boy to do the filming then? The fewer people who know where I am, the better."

Steph had scowled at the personal dig. *Good.*

'I can't ask Dugal. He's currently floating along the Oxford canal on a narrowboat.'

'News story or holiday?'

'Holiday – with Kim Prescott and Jo Trescowthick. I'm going to make a call from the bathroom.'

Hackett stood at the window, staring blankly at the street below, as he considered a new lifeline. Perhaps he could hide on the narrowboat with the holidaying *Spotlight* crew. The vigilante would never think to look for him there.

"Camera guy will be here in 30,' Steph said, returning to the lounge room with her phone in hand.

Hackett helped himself to more gin and a splash of tonic. 'How long is this canal trip they're taking?'

Steph glanced at him as she made another call. 'A week. They're going from Braunston to Oxford. I was supposed to join them for a few days – but here I am.'

'Well, I was think–'

Steph raised a shushing finger. 'Hi Mac. He's agreed to talk. You'll have the full interview in about 90 minutes.' She glanced at her subject. 'No, he's not staying. I've given him a list of cheap hotels, and I expect him to piss off as soon as we've finished recording.' Stephanie held up another warning finger for Hackett.

He nodded, recognising the ploy.

'Of course not,' she said. 'I won't ask him where he's going. I don't need his stalker kicking my door down for info, should he find out about this flat.' She disconnected.

'I take it that was a ruse to keep me safe.'

Steph's expression was incredulous. 'And me, you selfish prick.'

'I feel you should show me a bit more respect, *Stephanie*.'

She raised an eyebrow. 'Respect? You? You gave me this job on the assumption I would be your London fuck buddy, you entitled prick.'

Hackett wisely decided against any comeback.

Steph began rearranging the furniture for the interview.

'And the whole hotel list might have been a ruse for anyone listening in, but I *will* be enacting it. There's no way it's safe for either of us for you to stay here.'

Hackett didn't argue. He realised how true that was. 'Do you have Dugal's itinerary?' he asked.

'Of course. Why?'

Hackett shrugged. 'I thought I might be able to join the crew for a few days.'

'You're joking.'

'No. Hiding out amongst thousands of boats on dozens of canals is a great idea.'

Steph was laughing now. 'You honestly think our Kim – who you humiliated during her interview for my new job – would want to set eyes on you, let alone be confined to a narrowboat with your overgrown ego. Believe me, Andrew, you would not have to worry about your vigilante. Kim would throttle you and dump you overboad. Jo would help her.'

'Oh,' Hackett said. 'Really? She, they–'

'Yes, Andrew. And strange as it may seem, that's how most of the women at Channel 5 regard you.'

Hackett blinked a few times. 'Surely they'd help out a colleague in dire straits. I could cover the cost of their boat.'

'What about their safety, if Riley-Simon tracks you down?'

'They're not in any danger. This guy wants justice for Amy. That means killing Mitch and me. I doubt he'd shoot up a canal boat.'

'For fuck's sake, Andrew. Who knows what he will do? Kim broke the story on Riley; and Jo ID'd him as Simon. You don't think that's gonna get on his goat. Besides, he's probably all tangled up in Jo's devices and knows exactly where she is.'

Hackett sighed heavily. 'So even if they all went dark while I was on board that would also be a clue, as that lot are never off their socials.'

Steph's expression this time was pure squinty bewilderment, accompanied by head shaking. 'Did you not understand me when I said *none* of them would have you on board?'

'What am I going to do?'

Steph rubbed her forehead. 'How about, in the interview, you hint about going home accompanied by a new security team to keep you safe. We could even get Mac, or your mate Ferdy, to make fake arrangements.'

'And in the meantime? I'm back on the streets of London on my own again? Fucking brilliant.'

'It's not even been two days, Andrew. Stop whining. And you're not a total idiot. I'm sure you will think of something.'

CHAPTER 36

Morgan's fingers tapped a regular beat on the daypack in his lap as the train glided towards London. He had opted for the convenience of Chiltern Railways over BritRail; the station at Oxford Parkway was close to his rental, had plenty of parking, and the terminus at London Marylebone was a few streets from his destination. The last evening train to the capital attracted few passengers, which meant Morgan could get away with subtle changes to his appearance, rather than a full disguise. A snug peaked cap, a shabby khaki jacket and thick, dark spectacle frames held together by duct tape were enough to blend in as another loser.

It hadn't taken long to scope the Channel 5 apartment where Hackett was hiding. The challenging part was planning his next move. He could have an opportunity to kill Hackett in the next 12 hours – but should he do that?

Justice would be achieved with Hackett's death, but would killing him on a London street be satisfying? It had been fine for Mitch, being shot in the back, the way he'd shot Amy.

Even though that hadn't gone to plan.

No. The end he had in store for Andrew Hackett was poetic. Unless he had to improvise and then any end would do.

When he'd done a google street view of Upper Berkely Street he'd ruled out a walk-up ambush like he'd done in Hampstead. It was a busy area; no cover whatsover, and any random hero could thwart his escape. There were no convenient cafes or alcoves from which to observe the apartment block, except the restaurant right next door which would be stupidly risky. The homeless look he was wearing would give him street cred and a chance to loiter, but not to stay overnight.

Then there was Stephanie Grant. Hackett was his target, not the Aussie reporter. Even though her program bore some responsibility for Amy's death, Morgan understood the extra danger to himself of killing a foreign journalist on British soil.

If he *did* take Hackett out in her flat or the street, escaping the crime scene without leaving a trace would be almost impossible. The apartment complex itself, and the surrounding streets, were riddled with CCTV.

Unlike the suburbs like Hampstead, where he'd stalked Mitch, there were also more police patrols in central London. Even changing his disguises every time he found a blind spot mightn't be enough this time. Especially with his face being flagged in connection to Mitch.

Most infuriating was his lack of a suitable weapon. He'd ditched the gun he'd used on Mitch almost immediately, in a drain on the far side of Hampstead Heath from where he fired it.

And the death-dealer he'd chosen for Hackett was hanging on the wall back at his barn. It was not the kind of thing he could carry on a train or bus.

I could use a hunting knife, Amy. Just like you did with the tour bus driver. You were so brave to confront him like that.

Morgan stared out the window. *But I don't think I can gut your father and get away unseen.*

Another village flashed by: dark stone cottages, and pubs already spilling light from their windows.

The biggest risk of stabbing Hackett was the need for close quarters and the likelihood of being covered in blood.

The bottom line though was the fact he'd been visualising Hackett's final moments for a long, long time. And they didn't involve a quick death, let alone one he couldn't stay to watch.

He did not want to rush in, all stabby, and then run away.

He wanted to torment Hackett, to remind the bastard why he deserved to die. Morgan wanted to explain why justice had been delayed, though he'd never admit to his hasty exit from Australia after Amy's death. It was enough she understood it wasn't cowardice; that it made sense to distance himself from the investigation into everything she'd done. He had to be free to plot *their* revenge.

Yes, his plan had been years in the making but it was important Hackett understood how numb he'd been after discovering the awful truth about Amy and–

Morgan screwed his eyes shut for a moment.

It was important Hackett knew how long he'd been under electronic surveillance. Him *and* Mitch and *all* the people in their lives.

It was important Hackett knew Morgan's first plan was stymied by the deadly virus that closed international borders and stranded him in New Zealand. And that he should be grateful the pandemic extended his life for a few extra years.

Morgan's smirk was reflected in the carriage window. He'd be able to tell Hackett none of this in a blitz attack on a London street.

No, murder won't be on our agenda tonight, Amy.

Scoping out the Marylebone apartment would simply be the means to get Hackett back in his sights. Maybe plant a tracking device if he could get close enough.

I just need to get eyes on him, Amy. I doubt Ms Grant will want a hunted man in her apartment for long.

Morgan had his basic field surveilance gear in his battered daypack, and planned to check in on the reporter's phone calls again before heading into her street. There his tactic would be shambling circuits of the area, stopping to scratch for imaginary butts and other worthy street detritus.

Morgan pulled an energy drink and chocolate bar from his pack and smiled as his train entered the outer London suburbs.

Chapter 37

Mac and Curly sat shoulder-to-shoulder in the cramped *Spotlight* edit suite while Pete Benson and Mike Berry looked through the doorway; seniority had it its privileges. They were all watching the end of the recording of Steph's interview with Hackett.

'Great stuff, Steph,' Berry said. 'She got the shooting victim *and* the shooter's likely next target. Are you going to run it all?'

'Yep.' Mac stood and stretched his arms and body. Curly instinctively ducked his moving elbow.

'She's given us plenty of back cut questions and we've got lots of overlay to dress it up. Curly will look after that.'

'What about us?' Pete asked, as eager as Berry to get involved. 'Are there any local angles we can chase?'

Mac's fingers explored his beard. 'Actually, there might be. See if you can find a psychologist who can talk about the mindset of a man, a vigilante, like Riley-Simon-Whatever we're calling him. The guy's obviously intelligent and resourceful. What might his background be? We all hold grudges against people who have wronged us; but very few mount elaborate global vendettas. Let's explore the triggers for that kind of revenge. And what this vigilante might do now his identity has been exposed.'

'Identities,' Berry said. 'Which means he could have dozens of aliases to help him stay undercover.'

'Exactly,' Mac beamed. 'Are we dealing with a super brain, or someone with learned skills like an ex-cop? I'll give you 45 minutes to find us an eloquent expert.'

Berry and Pete returned to their desks.

'I'm surprised you didn't tell them to make sure the talent is a blonde who looks good on camera,' Curly said.

Mac arched an eyebrow. 'Have you met me?'

Curly laughed. 'Yeah, I know, that's what the other stations would do. Being serious for a sec. Mitch Stevens *is* fortunate to be alive, but he's a trained bodyguard, who was armed and wearing a vest. What are Hackett's chances of survival if this guy corners him? And if he is a Pom, like Jo and Kim think, then the UK is his home turf.'

Mac worried his beard as he gestured Curly to follow him into the kitchen for a coffee. His Collingwood mug sat ready, cleaned again by Carla. He turned the kettle on.

'Hackett's an arsehole, mate, but he doesn't deserve to die. He *does* possess an instinctive rat cunning, which will serve him well, once he stops whining.' Mac shook his head as Curly pulled a green teabag from the caddy.

'He's ditched his phone, laptop and credit cards, which takes him off the vigilante's digital grid. Steph says he's got enough cash to last him at least a week.

'I'm also wondering if Hackett was bullshitting about needing to complete some deal in Paris. I might ask his mate Ferdy about that; in person, in a noisy bar, with no phones within cooee.'

'Good idea,' Curly grinned. 'Especially the bar bit. I'll come with you.'

Mac rolled his eyes. 'Hackett will probably pop up in his Southbank tower over the weekend, surrounded by the army he implied he was going to employ to protect him.'

The kettle boiled and Mac poured water into both cups.

'Yeah. I *guess* Hackett's smart.' Curly shrugged. 'And he should have an advantage because he knows what the shooter looks like.'

Mac snorted. 'Unless he's also a master of disguises, like the Jackal.'

'Fuck!' the two men said in unison.

There was no getting away from the subtext of their conversation. There was the good chance that one of their next stories could be about the murder of their chief financial officer.

CHAPTER 38

Kim, Jo and Dugal huddled silently over muesli, toast and coffee on *Moriarty*. Their focus was the *Melbourne Spotlight* website and a replay of Steph's interview with Hackett. It was riveting television, even on a laptop screen. Kim quelled envy that she wasn't the reporter asking the questions. Steph looked poised, as if she had been a foreign correspondent for years, not weeks.

> *'The British police have a photo of the person we believe is the alleged shooter. What are you going to do now?'*

Hackett snorted.

> *'Keep running. The London cops wouldn't listen when Mitch Stevens was shot. They think the Russian's daughter was the target. I can't trust them to make the right decisions, let alone protect me.*
>
> *'This shooter has hacked into my phone and emails; my credit cards are useless to me. All my contacts are compromised. I have to stay off the grid until I complete my business in Paris, and find a way back to Australia – with an armed entourage in tow.'*

The camera stayed on Hackett as Steph asked her next question. He looked tired, dishevelled, belligerent.

> *'You're out of your comfort zone of suits and international boardrooms, Andrew. You're trying to outmanoeuvre a man who has extensive resources. How does that affect your mind?'*

Hackett swallowed before answering.

'My life is at stake. Again. For no reason, again. I can't afford to dwell on the injustice of that, which makes me bloody angry, when the very real fear of what he might do is even bigger.

'You know me, Stephanie, so you know I'm a bit of a mess right now. I'll have to stay out of his reach until the cops get off their arses and catch him.'

Hackett wriggled in his seat, then straightened and turned directly towards the camera.

'I'm not going to be a victim again. You'll never find me.'

'Jeezus,' said Jo.

Dugal stood and claimed his phone off the charger. 'I'll give Steph a call. Mac might give her the weekend off after those scoops. She could meet us in Oxford.' He ducked through the doorway into the bow.

Kim glanced out the window. Their boat was currently moored in a bucolic setting. *Bucolic* being a word she'd never had a use for before. It was such an English word, and it perfectly matched the very Englishness of the flat green fields and hedges that stretched into the distance, beyond the towpath that hugged the contours of the waterway they were on. And there was not a ripple disturbing the surface of the canal.

'I feel like I'm in a Famous Five adventure,' she said. 'Except, you know, coz it's us: *Three Go Boating with a Box of Booze*.

Jo snorted with laughter as she leant over the kitchen bench and flicked the kettle on. 'That was bolshie stuff from The Hatchet. I wonder if Simon has seen the interview. Hackett almost threw down a gauntlet – catch me if you can.'

Kim closed the laptop. 'Getting nailed to a fence by your crazy daughter can give you some attitude. Especially when her boyfriend resumes hostilities several years later.'

'Do you reckon he is/was Amy's boyfriend?' Jo asked. 'He could be another long-lost sibling who wants to avenge Amy for avenging their mum. Or aunt. Or distant third cousin.' Jo moved to the other side of the bench to fill the plunger with roasted coffee grounds.

'Man, that *would* be like one of those eternal blood feuds then,'

Kim said. 'Nah, I think it's more likely a twisted love knot thing. I'm more interested in why he's waited until now to finish the job *for* Amy. Does it mean he's better prepared – or more unhinged?'

The brain-wakening aroma of coffee floated through the cabin to the bow, from where Dugal's hand suddenly appeared. Kim passed him a mug. They were already well adjusted to to the handing-things-along life on a narrowboat.

'You can ponder that as you and Dugal tackle the first set of locks. Tell your deckmate we're leaving as soon as we've finished our coffee.'

'Aye, aye skipper.' Kim saluted. They were on a nautical holiday in the English countryside, while the mystery-solving was being done by her former colleagues and the British bobbies.

Was it her imagination, or did the coffee taste a tad bitter?

Dugal stepped back into the cabin brushing rain droplets from his hair. 'Bugger. I left my jacket back in London.'

CHAPTER 39

Andrew Hackett peeped out between the lounge drapes. It was maybe half an hour after dawn, and drizzle had set in while he slept fitfully in the spare bedroom. Steph had finally relented and let him stay. For one night only.

She'd 'retired' to her room early, after a post-interview, slap-dash pasta meal – *okay*, it was delicious – but he hadn't been able to settle. When he finally went to bed at 1.30 he spent an hour staring at the ceiling.

Now he was staring at the street. All this staring at shit was not helping. His thoughts were totally focused on staying ahead of his stalker.

'Not going to call him a killer,' he said aloud. 'Far as I know, he hasn't actually murdered anyone. Not even Mitch. Maybe he'll miss me too. Shit.'

Was there anybody lurking ot there? He'd spotted three black cabs, a few dozen cars, and 12 pedestrians in the last 15 minutes. Half of the latter were using umbrellas, making it impossible to tell if Riley-Simon-Fuckface was prowling the street. But none of those brollies had been tilted as if someone was taking a gander at this building. And all of the walkers were striding like they wanted to get somewhere else and out of the rain.

Hackett grimaced; was he being too paranoid?

'No you are not,' he told the room, as he turned away from the window and sat on the sofa.

Hackett realised Steph was right. He could not stay here.

His bravado was replaced by anxiety as he dashed into the spare bedroom to repack the few things he'd taken out last night. He then unpacked to get to his clean boxers and shirt, and put fresh socks in and out three times. London had suffered a prolonged hot and dry spell so, naturally, he'd left his rain jacket with his suits in the Gucci suitcase at his first hotel.

Damn, getting drenched would be a miserable start to his escape plan. He opened the small wardrobe where, it appeared, Dugal's clothing had been relegated. Hackett flicked through half a dozen shirts until he found a jacket. It was green and, oh, branded with a Channel 5 logo on the left breast. It wasn't ideal but its all-seasons design would keep him dry and warm, and the hoodie would partly hide his face.

Hackett hefted the closed rucksack and returned to the front window. The drizzle had intensified; pedestrian and vehicle traffic had also increased. Hopefully it would be too crowded for the shooter to risk a public execution.

He looked at Steph's door and decided waking her just to say he was leaving would take too much time. And, to be honest, he didn't want to see the look on her face that implied she didn't care he was going out into the wilds of the city alone. To face whatever, alone. Because that would also made him feel like no one, anywhere, gave a rat's about him.

Well, Marianne might; at a pinch. But he couldn't talk to her.

The tide of mostly black umbrellas in the street below looked like a damn funeral procession. That was enough to spur him towards the door. He noticed a notepad and pen on the kitchen bench. Guilt made him stop; he scribbled quickly.

Thanks for the bed.

He dropped the pen, then picked it up again.

Maybe you should move to a hotel for a few nights.
Put it on the Spotlight account.

He felt better. Steph was well aware of the risk of recording the interview with him. And the likelihood all her devices were also compromised. She was never not going to take the scoop but she really should take steps to protect herself.

The pack dangled from Hackett's shoulder as he descended the empty stairwell. He peeked around the corner from the bottom step. There was nobody in the foyer. He edged along the elevator wall to the double front doors. The view was limited; and his stalker could be under any of those umbrellas.

Hackett raised the hood on his jacket and cinched it under his chin. He hoped he looked like a geeky backpacker rather than a TV executive.

He inhaled deeply and exited the building. He'd cross Edgeware Road, a couple of blocks away, then head down Conaught Street and wouldn't stop walking until he got to Paddington Station.

Chapter 40

Morgan almost laughed when he saw his prey hustle out onto the street. The green jacket was bold in the river of black umbrellas. And, *hello dipshit*, the TV Crew logo stencilled on the back wasn't exactly subtle, even if it was partially obscured by the backpack.

Morgan could afford to wait a little before following the tool, because he'd be obvious from a distance whatever direction he took from Edgeware Road.

He yanked a folding umbrella from his daypack and let himself out of the transit van he'd spent the night in. They guy who'd parked it, two doors down from the apartment block, was so drunk when he came home, he'd forgotten to lock it. And so drunk he'd be unlikely to rise before noon.

Hackett, meanwhile, was waiting about 25 yards ahead, at the lights on Edgeware, casting wide-eyed looks left, right and behind himself. He wasn't *seeing* anything though, because he was the cliched startled rabbit.

Morgan figured, in his diguise of blond beard and silver-framed glasses, he could be five feet behind him and still not be noticed.

That sparked a frisson of excitement. He *could* take him out right here on the street. Stick him several times with his knife before anyone noticed. The prick would bleed out on the footpath before any help could reach him.

Morgan had invaded every nook and cranny of Hackett's world, planning how he would kill him slowly... Until right now. Until the reality of having him within reach. The proximity was intoxicating.

No. I will not do that, Amy.

Morgan resisted the urge; this was not the time or place.

Hackett crossed with the green light and headed down Conaught Street. Morgan followed, on the other side. There were enough people out, with umbreallas, to make progress tedious.

Morgan really wanted to laugh when he realised Hackett was using a spy movie-inspired surveillance tactic: stopping at shop windows to check for a tail. He abandoned it after three shops, and simply walked faster.

There was still no reason for Morgan to match his pace; the green jacket was like a neon sign.

Apart from the thrill of shooting Mitch Stevens, his tracking and ambush of him had revived the excitement from his early days serving the Crown. His pursuit of Hackett, though, was the long, open-ended operation. He'd follow him to his next bolthole, then work out from there how to get him to the execution site.

Hackett took the left side of the Hyde Park Square Gardens, and eventually, way ahead now, turned right onto Sussex Place.

Okay. Looks like we are indeed heading for Paddington Station.

As Morgan turned into Sussex Place his stomach dropped. Hackett was nowhere to be seen.

Fuck! Had he gone into one of the shops; or worse, a house? Had he simply ditched the green jacket?

Your dad is proving to be far sneakier than I expected, Amy.

Morgan scanned the street. There was nobody dashing through the sea of umbrellas; and the crawling black cab carried no passengers.

Do not panic. He's mostly likely in one of those cafes.

Morgan struck a nonchalant pose against a pole and waited. There was basically nothing else he could do.

Moments later Hackett in all his green glory emerged from the second cafe carrying a takeaway mug.

Why on earth didn't he wait until the station, or even the train, to get food.

Hackett kept walking. Morgan kept following – getting closer all the time – all the way into Paddington Station and right up to a ticket window where Hackett bought a seat on the next train to

Oxford.

Morgan already had a return ticket to Oxford Parkway, a mere six minutes further along the line.

His daughter lives near Oxford. She's the softest of your step-siblings. He's just going to turn up on her doorstep.

Can you believe it, Amy? He's walking into our kill zone. He's coming to us.

CHAPTER 41

Kim's competition against Dugal for the fastest wincher waned by the fourth lock on the famous Napton Flight; she was puffing heavily, and there were still another five locks to manage in this section. She finished winching and leant on the ancient timber as the water level rose. The stiffness in her shoulder, smashed by a 9mm bullet before the pandemic, reminded her not to waste energy.

Dugal was now chatting on his phone on the other side of the narrow lock; Jo stood at the tiller, hand on the throttle to keep the vessel steady.

Kim frowned, and called out, 'You should really have a line around a bollard, Jo.'

Her friend dismissed the nagging with a wave. 'It's fine. We go up or down slowly, only a Wally can get into trouble.'

Kim let the safety concern slide and took in the view. It was an idyllic summer setting: a meandering waterway, quaint villages, friendly travellers; and life reduced to movement at a couple of knots.

So why did she feel irritable? She huffed at herself. Steph's scoops in the story that had been hers.

The *Moriarty* rose to the winchers' level. Dugal stepped onto the bow still talking, and Kim trotted to the far end of the lock to push open the gate. She was starting to think Dugal had checked a canal map, as so far he'd consistently chosen the bank that required less work.

Jo deftly guided their narrowboat through the opening with minimal scraping. There was no need for Kim to close the gate as another boat waited its turn to transit the locks. She stepped aboard

Moriarty near the stern, and Jo steered the vessel to pass safely on the port side.

'Do you think Dugal is peeved Steph didn't want to leave London?' Jo asked.

His call had finished, yet Dugal remained in the bow. The next lock was only a few hundred metres away.

'Probably, and I can sympathise with him, but I'd never leave the story either if I was a newbie foreign correspondent.'

Jo perched on the rail seat, her legs swinging, and reduced power, there was a boat ahead of them at the lock. 'Were you thinking of volunteering for weekend duty?'

'No! I don't work for *Spotlight* anymore.'

'Technically Mac is holding your job until the end of the year.'

'I'm on holiday.'

'Yeah, right. You're as relaxed as a wound spring.'

Kim's shoulders slumped and she slouched on the cabin roof. 'Am I that obvious?'

'Yep.' Jo eased their boat into the bank. It would take 10 to 15 minutes to navigate the lock, depending on the winching habits of the other crews. Some treated locks as social occasions; time for a chinwag with other boaties or bloody walkers.

'I was doing okay about the whole not-getting-the-job thing until Steph scored the interviews with Mitch and Hackett. It's not just that it was my story to begin with, it's a story on the move. Mitch survived – will the shooter try again? Hackett's running – is the shooter on his tail. Riley-Simon seems to have unlimited resources and expert-level reach. So, yeah, I would love to be a part of it. But Steph's the correspondent; there's no role for me.'

'Are you sure?'

Kim pushed off the cabin. 'What do you mean?'

'You're going to be looking for a reporter job in a few weeks.'

'Yes.'

'You have your Melbourne showreel.'

'Yes.'

'Wouldn't it look better with a British story on it?'

'I can't steal Steph's thunder.'

'No, but you could find a way to work with her. The tabloids here will soon be frothing about a British-born assassin attacking people on opposite sides of the world. Find a fresh angle to give them. As of this moment, you're an international freelancer; you could sell stories in London *and* Melbourne.'

Jo gestured Dugal. 'He's needing extra camera and editing work; you could split the profits. Even Steph might be on board with the *Spotlight* crew – current and temporarily-ex – sharing the story.'

Kim felt her tension shift to excitement. She'd rainchecked the idea of finding a job until the end of summer; mostly because it was too scary to consider how that would be achieved. Turning up at the BBC with an exclusive on a front-page story was a perfect way to get noticed. Mac would gladly take the item too, although there was a niggle.

'I wouldn't feel right charging *Spotlight* a freelance fee.'

'It's not his money. If the story's good enough – he'll break into Hackett's treasury for the gold coins.'

Kim nodded. It was a plan, but it lacked a vital component. 'I need a scoop – something Steph isn't likely to chase, or want.'

The skipper shook her head. 'Your brain has gone foggy since you left the dungeon.'

Kim folded her arms. 'I'm in holiday mode. *They* didn't think I was good enough–'

'Stop being precious.' Jo stood on her toes to see how the lock transits were progressing. 'You know the decision was The Hatchet's.

'You have a major advantage over Steph. You, and I, have met the would-be assassin. Who is Simon-Riley? *We* know what he looks like, how he talks. You could put feelers out to find people who recognise him. He must have a family, friends, work colleagues. Someone might be able to explain why this vendetta was reignited.'

Kim's goosebumps prickled. 'You're right; everyone wants to know the why? What motivates a killer to act. He's obviously well funded; does that mean he comes from money?

A sudden bark from a golden Labrador standing beside the boat wagging its tail made them both jump. The owner, striding ahead with a lead in hand, called back, 'Come on, Windsor.'

Kim felt a sudden pang of longing for her greyhound, Sexy Rexy. She'd left him in her mother's care, for an undetermined stay. The retired racer would receive more attention than the busy reporter could usually offer, but the separation guilt was hard to smother. It also reminded Kim she was out of her comfort zone.

'But how am I going to get that story?' She waved at the Oxford countryside. 'I'm on a canal boat in woop woop.'

Jo shook her head. 'Oh mate, you *are* in holiday mode. You've got a laptop, phone, Wi-Fi. What's different from Channel 5? We're only going to be on the water for a few days. Use the time to kick-start the research and set up a few interviews. You could piggyback on the psych Mac got for the show the other night. I know he won't mind. That man will do *anything* it takes to make sure you come home.'

'Yeah well, that might backfire if I become the BBC's star reporter.'

Chapter 42

Hackett watched the countryside flashing by as the train headed north-west from London. The trip to Oxford would take 90 minutes. Hackett planned to go straight to Tara's place, in the hope she'd give him a bed for at least one night. And that her loud-mouthed husband wouldn't warn her against it, *because of the danger*.

Once there he could work on laying a false trail before catching another to Manchester, and getting Ferdy to organise a last-minute flight from there to Paris.

There was no way his stalker could watch all the routes out of the UK. Well, he could, but he couldn't get to whichever one Hackett decided to use on the spur of the moment.

Morgan, sitting five rows behind Hackett, was watching the same countryside glide past.

He had his earphones on, checking Hackett's children's devices for any recent communication they may have had with their father.

Nada and bupkis.

It looked like daddy-dear was going to turn up unannounced at Tara's place.

Then what, Amy?

CHAPTER 43

Kim's creative juices simmered while the *Moriarty* crew navigated the last few locks of the Napton Flight. Dugal had mistaken her renewed spark for a resumption of the winch competition, rather than a simple desire to finish their crew duties. Which were now done.

The canal map revealed a long stretch of meandering waterway for the next few hours, so Kim settled into the bow with her phone and a notebook. A journo always had pen and paper handy, even on holiday.

Kim checked the time before placing her first call, to DS Nathan Potter. She hoped her one-time boyfriend wasn't out on a job.

'Hey, Kim.' There was a jumble of voices in the background.

'Hi Nathan. Where are you? I hope I haven't caught you at a bad time.'

'Nah, it's okay. I'm at *The Eureka* in Geelong with some mates watching the footy. I'll go outside so we can hear each other.'

A moment later he said, 'Okay, freezing my butt off on the street and the game is close so, you know. If this a social call or have you found another body?'

'We're on the Oxford Canal, stumbling on a murder is unlikely.'

'Unless you chuck Jo overboard,' Nathan laughed. 'And you *are* on a vessel with the Cadaver Crew. I wouldn't put it past you lot to find half a dozen bodies.'

The banter felt comfortable, even from half a world away. Kim wondered why they, *she*, had been so on again, off again.

'So, again Kim, footy! It's half time but–'

'Yeah, sorry. I'm thinking about getting some freelance work here and reckon my own story about Mitch's assailant is the way to go. Is there anything you can share about Riley-Simon?'

'Like what?' he asked.

'Like have you identified him yet? Is either name real?'

'No. They're both bogus. He left here under his forged Riley Hawkins passport to fly to the UK. A week later he flew into and then out of Paris under the name Simon Carter.'

Kim leaned on the roof and scribbled the new surname. 'It'd cost a fortune to get two black market passports, neither of which he can use anymore.'

'Yeah. It's likely he has more,' Nathan said. 'The bureaucrats in England have been slow with their intel; but *we now* know when he made the change from Simon to Riley.'

'When was that?'

There was long pause, during which Kim could hear the Melbourne traffic. She waited.

'Off the record, Kim. This can't get back to bust my balls.'

'I'm in England. The story is for here, and won't be filed anywhere for at least a week. Unless there's a huge break in the case. I can pretend I have a Home Office contact – or something.'

'Or something; funny you should say that.'

'Oh?' Kim waited for Nathan to elaborate, he didn't. She connected a few dots. '*Oh!* Someone has suggested Riley-Simon has, or had, a connection to the Home Office. Is that how he got the extra passports.'

'Not necessarily.' Nathan dragged out the words. 'Could be one of the MIs.'

'Shit – the intelligence services! Is/was Riley a spook?'

'I did not say that.'

'But you're not denying it.'

'It's just a thing everyone is mulling; here and London. Until there's a positive ID, we're all guessing. Or they are not yet being forthcoming.'

'That he's a real James Bond?'

'No, that he was employed by either MI5 or 6.'

'What's the difference?'

'MI5 is the Security Service and MI6 is the Secret Intelligence

Service. MI5 protects the home front; MI6 – the 007 types – look for foreign threats.'

'Do they really have a licence to kill?'

Nathan's laugh drowned out the Melbourne street noise. 'I think MI6 agents are licenced to carry weapons, but the 'to kill' thing is pure Ian Fleming. I think.

'Anyway, no one thinks Riley-Simon was an agent officially dispatched to shoot Mitch Stevens. There is, however, a chance he's using the skills acquired through one of the services.'

'Jeezus. Which is kinda why the Brits would be disinclined to share intel too fast,' Kim said.

'Or at all,' Nathan agreed. 'And *we*, you and me, are totally off the record, Kim. Remember that.'

Kim bit her pen hard, cracking the plastic. 'Yeah, yeah. I'm just taking notes for background. The local hacks might uncover the connection as well. At least I'll be prepared.'

'Okay. As long as the words *Melbourne police sources* never appear in your story.'

'Understood. What are you guys doing to confirm this theory?'

'Us, nothing. It's gone to the higher pay grades than mine now. I'm lucky to know as much as I do.'

'And, to be honest, I can't see the Brits wasting much time on the Riley-Simon thing for us. The worst crime he committed here was bashing Bryan Cowan. Nobody is remotely fussed about Tugga's shack being torched. My bosses are hoping the Met police find him and charge him for shooting Mitch and that'll be the end of it. It certainly won't be worth us extraditing him for the Cowan assault, after the time he'll serve for Mitch.'

'Especially if he also finds Hackett before they catch him,' Kim said.

This was brilliant info, enough to make a British news service salivate, but nobody would run it without knowing her source. She tapped the pen against her teeth.

'What's that noise?'

'The sound of frustration.'

'Nothing to earn you a job at the BBC?'

'Not yet. *Oh–*' Kim was about to close her notebook when she recalled Nathan's earlier statement. 'You said you know when Simon first became Riley.'

'Yeah, at least in terms of how it relates to us. Immigration records show he arrived in Melbourne pre-pandemic – around the time Jo first met him – as Simon Carter. A week after Amy Stewart died, the same Simon flew to New Zealand. Any intention to leave there was stymied for ages by international covid lockdowns.

'Then, about 18 months ago, he flies back into Australia as Riley Hawkins, bailing again under that passport after assaulting Cowan; but before he'd been ID'd.'

'And then he resurrected Simon to fly to France,' Kim said evenly, before being struck by– 'Nathan!'

'Kim!'

'Sorry. Can you find out if Simon Carter was in Paris at the same time as Andrew Hackett?'

'Oh. Yeah. Bright spark you. Perhaps you should consider being a newshound. And now, the game is well and truly calling. Gotta go.' Nathan hung up.

Just like that.

Typical Cats fan.

Kim reviewed her notes. New Zealand. That was an angle she could explore. It was, after all, where Amy Stewart hailed from. She lost herself in those thoughts for a few seconds – until Jo and Dugal screamed.

'Kim!'

Chapter 44

The rain had stopped by the time Hackett left the station in Oxford. He paused on the pavement to scrunch the borrowed jacket into his pack. The extra weight was negligible, and he might need it again.

He hoisted the backpack and headed off in search of food and a map. He'd realised while on the train, with his now useless London one, that he'd need local info. A second later it hit him he couldn't remember the name of Tara's hamlet. He'd only visited once, before the pandemic. Tara always came to him when he was in the UK.

Hackett screwed up his face. *Was that a bad thing?*

The thought lasted a second as he recalled her hamlet as one of hundreds of chocolate box villages in the back of nowhere: a couple of pubs, and a handful of quaint stone houses on the canal north of Oxford. Was it Tupping? Topping? Something with a T.

Hackett could simply follow the towpath from the city; it literally went past her front door. But no, he did remember Tara was a good 10 km from Oxford. There was no way he'd lug his backpack that far. He gave a passing thought to his dear-departed youth, back in the '80s when he'd crossed the world with a backpack. And Indian pants. And bloody traveller's cheques. Fuck he was getting old.

The first shops he came across offered wine, food, homes and haircuts, but no maps. He guessed they were virtually redundant in a world where smartphones could tell you how to walk from areshole to breakfast without getting lost.

He contemplated checking into the *Royal Oxford Hotel* which dominated the junction. It had a Sainsbury's on the ground floor and wouldn't be expensive. He could take a break to work out how to get to Tara's. Correction, how to find Tara's address.

Hackett's attention was suddenly stabbed by the obvious, again: there were small glass domes mounted on every fucking light post and building. CCTV was watching and recording everything. Shit!

There'd be more inside the hotel and the supermarket. If his stalker even guessed he was in this area it wouldn't take much to track him.

Hackett couldn't take the chance. He lowered his chin and walked briskly along Hythe Bridge Street. He had to get what he needed – a cap would be the first thing – and get away from these streets as quickly as possible. He passed mostly office equipment shops and Asian restaurants, until the bridge at Upper Fisher Row where a council information board provided a glimmer of hope: a map.

Hackett impatiently waited for an American couple to read and discuss the entire canal history, all while blocking the view. A third theatrical sigh prompted them to move. Bugger! The map was too small and too local. He didn't give a fuck about ancient university buildings. He just wanted to recognise a place name so he could get a taxi driver to take him closer: to Tara's hamlet, or one nearby.

His exasperation grew as he was stuck behind a geriatrics' walking tour. The traffic was too fast and dangerous to risk using the road, and sighs and grimaces didn't work on these matrons. They eventually bunched around the entrance to the Oxford Canal path, and he managed to get by them and head into George Street.

The positive vibe generated by escaping London had well and truly dissipated. All he wanted now was food, booze, a map to reach Tara's hamlet, and sleep. And then he saw the window display promising "low cost, high quality International & UK calls, text and 4G data." Smartphones galore.

Hackett worried for all of 10 seconds about his stalker tracing him through a new phone. 'How the fuck can he do that?' he wondered, not realising he'd spoken aloud until the woman walking towards him registered surprise.

If he didn't use a new device to contact friends and family, or access his email, bank or business accounts, there was nothing to trace. Calling Tara – even if he knew her number – would give him away, but using Google maps to search for the village would not.

Hackett rubbed his chin as he looked in the window. One display had a phone, sim and data plan for a mere £150. Hackett opened the door and stepped inside.

Morgan loitered in the entranceway to a Thai restaurant as he watched Hackett enter the phone shop.

Your dad is thinking on his feet, Amy. As long as he doesn't call your half-sister.

Morgan still couldn't believe his luck. From the moment he'd learned about Mitch Stevens' London contract, he had changed his plans to finish the whole job right here in Oxfordshire.

Yes, killing Hackett in Melbourne would've been easier but this was Morgan's home. It was supposed to be Amy's home.

She should be snuggled into his shoulder, while they talk about going to a local mareket, seeing a movie together, or taking a late summer holiday in Crete – any one of the everyday joys forever denied them because of Andrew Hackett and his bodyguard.

Morgan's knowledge of Hackett's long-planned trip to France and the UK had become his deadline for both hits.

Now, as luck would have it, he wouldn't have to abduct Hackett off the streets of London and drive him to his rental house. He could snatch him from his daughter's canal-side home and be in hiding with his quarry within minutes.

Morgan didn't want to hurt Tara or her family, or even subject them to the grim sight of Hackett's body sprawled across their lounge floor.

Hackett must die the way Amy had intended.

And perfect justice meant an eye for an eye.

Or four eyes, because he fully intended to finish Mitch Stevens once and for all, before disappearing for good.

CHAPTER 45

'To avoiding decapitation by bridge.' Jo raised her wine glass in *Moriarty*'s bow.

Dugal tapped it with his beer bottle. 'A dramatic, if ignoble way for a journalist to depart this life.'

Jo and Dugal collapsed in giggling fits. Again.

'It wouldn't be this funny if you were rolling around the deck in my blood, watching my headless corpse flapping around the deck.'

'You're not a fish, Kim," Dugal said.

'Or a chook,' Jo added.

Kim scowled and took a hefty swig of wine. 'I missed that bridge by millimetres.'

'We shouted.' Jo reached for the bottle.

'At the last minute. You're the skipper – you're supposed to be looking after your crew.'

Dugal shrugged. 'Again, mate, it was *my* fault. I was showing Jo the text from Steph about meeting us for a night in Oxford. The bridge popped up without warning.'

Kim curled her lip at him, grabbed the empty bottle and ducked inside the cabin to fetch a fresh one. The sliding tinkle of bottle on bottle in the bin proved wine was fuelling their journey towards Oxford. Jo's original estimate of 12 for the trip was going to be short by a few. Who cared; they were on holiday.

She returned to her mocking friends, refilled the glasses, and waved her notebook at them.

'What did Nathan tell you that almost got you scalped?' Dugal asked.

Kim filled them in on her call with Nathan.

'That's a great angle if you can get it verified from another source. *British agent goes rogue – for love,* Jo said.

'I don't have any contacts in the Australian intelligence community, let alone here,' Kim moaned. 'I can't roll up to spook central and ask if Riley–'

'Or Simon.'

Kim glared at Jo. 'They're never going to tell *me* they trained the guy who tried to kill Mitch.'

Dugal drummed fingers on the side of the boat. 'Pete Benson's brother works for ASIS.'

'You mean ASIO.'

'No. ASIS is our overseas secret intelligence agency; our equivalent to MI6. ASIO is our MI5.'

'I really hope Pete's brother is smarter than Pete,' Kim said, then screwed her mouth shut.

'Indeed. He let it slip at the pub one night,' Dugal said.

Jo laughed. 'He's a two-pot screamer. Even if it's true, what use would his brother be to Kim developing her story?'

'Oh it *is* true,' Dugal said. 'I met him, not long before he got posted to London last year.'

Kim tapped her lips in thought. 'First name?'

'Adrian.'

'Can you ask Pete if he'd give me Adrian's contact info? I could approach him to see if he might at least meet. You know. expats together bonding over a pint or three.'

Kim's phone rang. She eyed it suspiciously as if it had been spying on her.

'*Spoooooky.* ' she said. 'It's Pete.' Kim looked at the time before answering. She put the call on speaker.

Dugal and Jo shared their own worried looks about the creepiness of modern tech, but relaxed into the bow cushions with their wines.

'Hey Pete. You're up at sparrow's fart – or just getting home?'

'Early start. I'm off to Mildura for a couple of days filming. I wanted to give you a tip, before I go bush.'

'I hope it's advice on how not to lose your head on a canal boat,' Dugal said. 'Hi Pete. Jo's here too.'

'Hi guys. So, Kim. Berry and I were at the pub last night. With Nathan Potter and a few of his cop mates.'

The trio on the boat stared wide-eyed at each other.

'Yes. And?' Kim's instincts told her to stay quiet, for now.

'We was all, *were* all watching the footy, not together with them but, you know, close. Anyway, Nathan took a call outside for a while and I happened to be at the bar getting my round when he came back.'

Jo was making circular *get on with it, already* hand motions.

'I overheard his, um, companion...'

'It's okay, Pete. He's been seeing Cheryl Baines for a while.'

'Yeah, yeah good. But, she was not happy with Nathan when he mentioned he'd just been talking to you.'

Kim rolled her eyes. Surely she wasn't still jealous.

'She asked Nathan if he'd told *you* about Riley being an English spook. He denied telling you any such thing. Did he?'

Kim's gleeful fist bump banged into the bulkhead. 'No, mate, he didn't. But wow. They think Hackett's being stalked by a spy?'

'No idea, really. Cheryl spotted me lurking and clammed up. Nathan looked sheepish but.'

'It guess it might be true,' Kim said. 'Riley-Simon is a chameleon, works serious surveillance, and stays way below the radar. Should you share this with Steph?'

Pete snorted. 'Nah. It's such a long shot, Kim. I'm only telling you because Nathan's, um, offsider mentioned you. You could chase it down if you want, I guess.'

'You're a good mate, Pete. Thanks. I'll see if I can worm my way into the spy circles in London. Do *not* like my chances, them being such a secretive bunch.'

Kim let the thought hang, while Dugal held his breath, and Jo began finger counting with her right hand. She got to four.

'Um, I might be able to help with that actually.'

'Really? How?' Kim pulled an *I should be so ashamed* face.

'Um, my brother, um, he's in London at the moment. I will see if he might talk to you.'

'Your brother?'

'Yeah, he knows people. And things. I'll call you again tomorrow.'

CHAPTER 46

The taxi stopped beside a row of clothing and recycling bins a few metres from the tranquil canal. The pub on the other side of the bridge was buzzing with late afternoon summer trade. The clatter of glasses and chatter washed over Hackett as he hauled his backpack out after him.

Tara and Sebastian lived within spitting distance of the waterway, and a different ye olde pub. Thrupp – *Thrupp* – was tiny, but canal traffic and tourists supported more than one historic drinking establishment.

Hackett knew his daughter rarely drank since the birth of his grandchildren. Sebastian wasn't so conscientious; but preferred the pub several hundred metres north of this one. It was right behind their back fence so, if necessary, Tara could shout him home from the beer garden. The front of that pub, like this one, faced the canal.

He crossed the bridge to the towpath and tossed up whether to get a meal before turning up at Tara's. A narrowboat glided by, and Hackett wondered vaguely who had right of way when horses powered the vessels, man or beast?

The local patrons were bantering with people who were obviously not, about which activity was more relaxing: drinking or boating. The dozen tables lining the path were full.

Hackett sighed. He so wanted to rest and eat and maybe enjoy this quintessential English scene: flower-adorned stone pub, majestic canal, colourful boats, happy drinkers.

He could hardly ask to join someone's table because he didn't want to engage in any conversations.

Well, hello, why is a mature gent like you backpacking?

Because I'm on the run from a crazy assassin.

The aromas wafting after the waitress who emerged from the pub with two plates loaded with scampi and chips, changed his mind. He could small talk if he had to.

And then–

'Andrew?'

Hackett pivoted left and right. Fuck!

'Andrew, over here.' His son-in-law, alone with an almost empty pint, was waving from a shaded table.

'Well now, hello Sebastian.' Hackett dumped his backpack and took a seat. 'I didn't think this was your local.'

'There's a wedding party at mine. You look like you need a drink.'

'You've no idea. A beer would go down well.'

The tall, blond, former Oxford rowing Blue downed the rest of his ale and stood. 'Back in a jiffy.'

Hackett sagged as some tension leached from his tired muscles, even though he already knew this annoying coincidence would probably not work in his favour. Sebastian was loyal, and absolutely devoted to his wife and their kids. Today that was the problem. Bumping into him before he could talk to Tara might mean he'd have to make new plans.

Bloody hell, why wouldn't anyone help him?

Sebastian returned with two pints and a packet of pork scratchings. Hackett did a quick reassessment of his son-in-law; arrived at the same conclusion as every other time. Sebastian was nice. And wimpy. Born and educated in Oxford, settled within rowing distance of his alma mater, and worked at a local accountancy firm. The most adventurous thing he'd ever done was marry an Australian; and he'd met her in the UK. He'd never once set foot in the Antipodes.

'Cheers, Andrew.' Sebastian raised his pint. 'I'm happy to buy you another drink and a meal. But I can't offer you shelter. It's too perilous for my family.'

Hackett spluttered. Sebastian suddenly had balls. And his tone rankled.

'Tara's father has a killer stalking him – and you're slamming the door in my face?'

Sebastian didn't blink. 'You're being melodramatic. But, even so, that is precisely the point. I won't put Tara and my children at risk. Sorry. We already know this guy's been monitoring our phones and computers. How do we know he's not watching our home; waiting for you. Your ex-bodyguard and the Russian's daughter were lucky to survive. This bastard might be getting desperate now. I can't afford to have you anywhere near my family.'

'How would he know I'm there if nobody says anything? Even Marianne and Nick don't have to know. I just need a a day or two to organise a flight to Paris. Then I'm straight home to Australia.'

'I *am* sorry, Andrew. I know it doesn't seem fair. Or family friendly even, but you know Tara, she can't keep any secrets from her mother.'

Hackett snorted, and took three large swallows. 'Fine. So, I guess you won't even tell her we bumped into each other.'

'No way. Again, she'll be on the phone to Marianne. As I told her, I'm off out for a couple of quiet beers and will be home for supper. Nothing to report.'

'Do you have any suggestions where I *can* go?' Hackett pointed to the lush greenery across the canal. 'Should I bunk down with the hedgehogs for a couple of days?'

Sebastian frowned, and then his eyes lit up with an idea. 'I may have a solution. But only if you promise not to come anywhere near the house.'

'Promise. What is it?'

'A canal boat.'

'Didn't know you'd bought one.'

'We didn't. It belongs to my uncle on Mum's side, so different surname. He's not long retired and is off to the States for a few months. He asked me to keep an eye on it.'

'Where is it?'

Sebastian pointed along the canal. 'Not far from our place; that's why you really have to promise to stay away. But it's got everything you'll need: power, water, heating, bedding, frozen dinners. And Uncle Cedric's a bachelor bibliophile so there enough books to last you a year.'

Perfect! Hackett contained his glee. The canal was full of narrowboats; thousands lived on the waterways, others rented by the day, week or month. The prick chasing him didn't stand a chance.

'There's a set of keys hidden in a lockbox in the bow. Uncle Ced's always losing them, either dropping them in the canal or leaving them at a pub. I'll give you the combination.'

He looked at his watch. 'Tara wanted me to fire up the barbie at 6.30.'

Hackett did not laugh at Sebastian's terrible Aussie accent.

'We'll be in the back garden, so you'll be safe to go past then.'

'I can't thank you enough. And you're right, this is so much better that endangering Tara or the kids. 'What's the name of the boat?'

'It's the *Booksman*.'

Chapter 47

The microwave nuked a lamb korma as Morgan scrolled through messages between Hackett's ex-wife and daughter. They chatted several times a day since Marianne's got to London, especially since the botched attempt to kill her lover.

Tara: I can't believe the hospital wants to push Mitch out the door already.

Marianne: The bullet wounds aren't life-threatening, and – incredibly – he's even taken a few steps. The NHS says it doesn't even have enough beds for the really sick.

Tara: What about his Russian boss? He should be paying for private care. Mitch was wounded on the job.

Marianne: He sacked Mitch.

Morgan's program couldn't factor in human emotions. He wondered if Marianne was crying as she shared details of the oligarch's ruthlessness. Morgan didn't care about her feelings. He was annoyed Mitch bloody Stevens was back on his feet.

'If only the gun hadn't jammed, Amy.'

Marianne: Claimed Mitch getting shot in the back was proof of incompetence. Next time it could be his daughter getting killed. He's a cruel bastard.

Tara: That's awful Mum. What are you going to do? Do you want to come and stay with us?

Marianne: That's kind darling. If you have the room, we'd
   love to stay while Mitch regains his strength. I thought he
   would never walk again a few days ago. Now – we have a
   future.

'A short one, Amy. I'll get him sooner than expected.'

The microwave pinged. Morgan removed the scalding curry and placed it on the table to cool.

'Mitch is walking into the kill zone too. How lucky is that, Amy? Both targets are coming to us.'

The important question was when.

Was daddy already at Tara's? Morgan hadn't bothered following Hackett from Oxford after he'd overhead him directing the taxi driver to Thrupp.

There was nothing so far in the mid-afternoon texts between mother and daughter that suggested Hacket had been dumb enough to let Tara know he was coming.

Marianne: Have you heard from your father?

Tara: Not a peep. Spoke to Nick a few hours ago and he hadn't
   heard from him either. He said Ferdy should be able to funnel
   enough money to Dad to keep him off the radar until he can
   get out of England. He reckons Dad's in a Park Lane hotel
   drinking G & Ts and going mad coz he can't check his stocks.

Marianne: I don't care where he is. But he knows to stay away from
   you and the kids.

'She doesn't know her ex-husband very well, does she Amy. Your father is probably sitting in an armchair at Tara's by now.'

Morgan tried the curry, it passed the blistering test, then returned to the text conversation.

Tara: Has the hospital given you a deadline?

Marianne: Monday.

Tara: Good. I'll tell Seb you're coming.

Marianne: Tell him?

Tara: Yes, tell him. He told me in no uncertain terms Dad
 couldn't come here. But sometimes family must come first.

'You'll be a grieving family very soon, Tara.'

Morgan wiped the kitchen bench as he mulled his next move. In an hour he'd visit quaint little Thrupp to confirm Hackett *was* putting his daughter in danger. He already knew he could approach the house along the towpath. Or he could hang out in Sebastian's favourite watering hole, until last drinks.

Morgan opened the door to his enclosed courtyard to let the balmy night air in, and returned to his meal.

He might not snatch Hackett tonight but he could make a plan. Catch him. Kill him.

The moment he'd decided to finish Amy's vendetta he knew what weapon he was going to use.

'You shot him with a crossbow, my love.'

Morgan closed his eyes against the physical pain of her loss.

'If you had fired a second earlier, or Mitch a half second later.'

Tears rolled down Morgan's cheek. He always choked imagining that moment. Part of him died when Amy was murdered.

Morgan glanced at the pristine crossbow resting in its wall rack. Morgan was proficient with the weapon he'd taken up in Australia. That's how he first met Amy, she'd been his instructor. Although ironically, given all his aliases, she called herself Susie.

Morgan sniffed. She only knew him as Simon.

The years would never dim the memories of the precious weeks they shared.

Chapter 48

Six years earlier

Simon was smitten with Susie from the first day she stepped into *Coolio's Café* a few weeks before Christmas. She was a head turner: blonde, athletic, attractive, poised. Yet it was so much more than her looks that drew him. Simon was captivated by an indefinable quality; as if Susie's soul was seeking a kindred spirit.

It wasn't long before he wanted to rip off the Simon façade and reveal the real him: Morgan, the failed intelligence officer searching for a new purpose.

Flirting with sexy customers was an undeclared part of a barista's duties, but he wanted to make a real connection with this woman, build on the obvious mutual spark, and do way more than simply make her a succession of cappuccinos.

She arrived at the same time each day, stretched her coffee for an hour as she toyed with a smartphone and people-watched. Morgan was chuffed whenever her eyes caught his. A cheeky wink was acknowledged with a smile. Their banter at the counter hadn't extended much beyond friendly greetings – and learning her name – because of the ever-present customer queues.

Morgan was surprised, however, to see Susie develop a rapport with Zara Hennessy, the ice queen from the television station. Zara had resisted *his* charm offensive, and every other male in the café. She existed in her own bubble – until Susie pierced it. Morgan could only watch the two beauties chat companionably over their coffees. They sat with their backs to the brick wall on a long banquette, sharing a small table and nibbling at pastries.

Other patrons occasionally had to shuffle sideways to make room for the new friends.

His special connection with the Kiwi visitor had been disrupted by the haughty bitch. Morgan was tempted to spoil Zara's coffee, but that might've been counterproductive. Zara would take her taste buds to another café, along with Susie.

Morgan didn't show his envy. He learnt patience at a young age, and to trust his instincts. He would find a way to woo the object of his desire away from the bane of his life.

A week before Christmas, he found Susie lingering on a phone call after Zara had returned to work. It was the lull between the morning coffee breakers and the lunch trade. She ended the call as he collected cups and plates.

'Are you making Christmas plans, Susie?'

Her smile was dazzling. 'No, Simon. As a matter of fact I was changing them. I've just picked up some temp work at Channel 5, thanks to Zara.'

'That's sweet of Zara. Does it mean we're going to see more of you this summer?'

'Yes, probably until the end of January. After that – I'll be a free spirit.'

Morgan saw a new glint in her eyes. His own search for meaning had brought him Down Under via a few personas and a dozen countries. Was it fate that brought Susie into his life?

'Maybe I could show you more of Melbourne in the coming weeks. The city can never have enough gorgeous Kiwis.'

Susie blushed; Morgan panicked. He forgot how notoriously shy New Zealanders were about compliments. They were nearly as bad as Canadians.

'That, would be nice, thank you Simon. I'm going to be busy at the station, but I'm sure we could find some time to explore.'

When Susie looked him in the eye and smiled, Morgan lost his heart forever.

Her café visits continued into the holiday season and beyond, but Susie's new duties restricted her to takeaways and short chats. Even the regular get-togethers with Zara petered out. Finally, just after New Year, Susie agreed to a first date.

She was relaxed, although a little guarded with her conversation about life in New Zealand. Susie talked about her teaching career in Auckland, sporting activities, places she had travelled; nothing about her parents. He sensed she carried a deep hurt. Perhaps it was like minds, or spirits connecting.

It was too early to reveal his career-wrecking folly in the secret service. The woman he now wanted to spend the rest of his life with didn't need to know that yet. He would reveal his real identity when the time was right. He had a feeling Susie would understand.

The Italian restaurant date was comfortable enough for Susie to agree to another the following weekend. Morgan suggested a Greek restaurant in Prahran. Susie began taking her daily early morning sit-down coffee at *Coolio's* again. Made expertly, of course, by her favourite barista.

She would, however, only ever go out on a Friday or Saturday night and there were no invitations to her place in between.

Their fourth date ended, unexpectedly, in Morgan's flat. A kiss as they returned to his vehicle unleashed desires within Susie that Morgan thought would take a few more weeks to inflame. Their coupling was passionate, yet Susie chose not to stay the night. Morgan felt a slight aloofness as they waited for an Uber to take her home.

She explained, nervously, over lunch the next day that she'd simply been surprised by her own reactions to how swiftly the intimacy had developed.

That was okay, Morgan hoped. He could be stoical and patient. Susie's temp job at the TV station had less than a month to go though, and he was now terrified she'd go home to New Zealand to look for something permanent.

Morgan decided to escalate the courtship the next day with a surprise visit to her apartment. She was loading a triangular box into the back of a rusty utility, alongside what looked like camping gear.

'Oh, Simon.' Susie pulled a tattered rug over the box. 'What are you doing here?'

It wasn't the welcome that Morgan anticipated. Susie wasn't unfriendly, but she wasn't encouraging.

'It's a lovely day, I thought we could go for a drive in the country.

Explore a little more of Victoria. It looks like you were already planning an adventure.'

Susie ran a hand over her ponytail. 'Um, Yeah. I'm going camping overnight in the Lerderderg State Park.' She gestured at her jeans and khaki top; a tad overdressed for the hot day. 'I'm told there are some good walks.'

'Never been there.' Morgan looked at the rug.

Susie almost looked nervous. 'Can I let you in on a little secret?'

'Sure.'

Susie pulled the rug back and lifted a corner of the box. It revealed a crossbow.

'I wanted to try this. It was given to me by a friend. I've never fired one before. Have you?'

'No.'

She smiled. 'The state park is only an hour from Melbourne. Do you want to go, and have a go, with me? I've watched a few online videos and should be able to handle it competently.'

She nudged Morgan in the ribs. 'I'll make sure you don't shoot yourself in the foot.'

Morgan treasured that day and night. Their unique bond was sealed with laughter, target shooting with a crossbow, eating baked beans over a camp stove, and making love in a really small tent.

There'd been a wonderful glint in Susie's eyes as they parted the next afteroon.

It was the last time Morgan saw her.

A few days later, he fled Melbourne for New Zealand.

Susie had been unmasked as Amy Stewart, serial murderer, shot dead while trying to execute her father with the crossbow.

The weapon had Morgan's fingerprints all over it.

CHAPTER 49

OXFORDSHIRE, JUNE

'I felt like a coward, Amy.'

Morgan took the crossbow down from the wall.

'I didn't know anything about the reasons for your vendetta when I ran. I was simply worried about being swept up in the police investigation.

'Not that I could've done anything for you after the fact. Before, however! Oh my love, if only you confided in me. I would've had your back from day one.'

He hefted the weapon to his shoulder. The weight was comfortable. He sighted, then lowered it to his waist, then repeated the action, before rehanging it on the wall.

He picked up the only photo he had of himself and Susie. Amy. It was a selfie from that last weekend at Lerderderg. They were happy, laughing, ready for a bright future together.

'I know I was slow to avenge you. I had to make sure the Victorian cops couldn't identify me. They found my prints, as I feared, but had nothing to match them to. I had to be careful when monitoring their computers; any hint of a hack might have encouraged them to dig deeper.'

Morgan's lips and chest tightened. He choked up every time he thought about the crime scene photos he'd managed to access, especially the autopsy on poor Amy's body.

He needed a distraction from the brutal images burned into his brain. He retrieved the black plastic case from a shelf above the fireplace, and took out two miniature cameras. He planned to plant them at Tara's place to monitor their comings and goings.

'I know you've forgiven me for sleeping with Jo from the TV station, Amy. I needed full access to Channel 5. She was merely a conduit. Nothing more.'

Morgan had had these conversations with Amy before, but wanted to make sure she understood.

'Okay, going to New Zealand in 2020 was a mistake. I wanted to alert your cousin that vengeance was still on the cards, that Jason's imprisonment wouldn't be in vain. It was going to be a quick trip – then *wham!* the hobbit kingdom, along with the rest of the world, went into lockdown. I had to wait until the borders opened.'

'As you know, Jason's reaction to the news of my quest on your behalf, and his, was bizarre. He screamed "entrapment" and demanded to leave the visiting room.'

Morgan had reluctantly buried Simon at that point. His Riley Hawkins legend was activated and he moved to the South Island to find work for a while. He didn't need the money; it was about keeping himself occupied until international travel was easier, and he'd done enough reseach to know how to proceed.

'Apollo Bay was a convenient base, Amy. It felt so good using Tugga's property to refresh my crossbow skills.'

Morgan laughed. 'The shack walls looked like a giant pincushion. I even used a photo of Tugga's fat ugly face as a target. The cops had no idea. The evidence all went up in flames.'

Morgan twitched the curtains at the front of his house. Boat activity on the canal ended long before the gloaming. Walkers would stagger home after last orders were called at the pub. Morgan would soon be a shadow crossing the fields.

'We're close, Amy.'

CHAPTER 50

Hackett's luck had finally turned. Sebastian had undersold his uncle's narrowboat. *Booksman* was five-star luxury befitting a gentlemen's club in Pall Mall. The 60-foot exterior was green with gold trim; and the elegance continued below deck with timber from stem to stern.

'You like your comforts, Cedric.'

Sebastian was right, there were books everywhere. The single bed was fronted by a wall of fully-stocked shelves, all hardbacks. Cedric's tastes were more highbrow than Hackett's, which didn't extend beyond a paperback thriller. Maybe once a year.

The porcelain loo, marble vanity and an etched glass shower cubicle indicated Cedric truly loved his comforts. The kitchen was high spec, but the pristine nature and fridge full of frozen meals, suggested Cedric dined out often in the many restaurants or canal pubs. More bookshelves blended into the stylish saloon where the oak table appeared to convert to a double bed. Hackett doubted it had ever been used. The main feature was the wingback Chesterfield beside the log burner.

'I thank you, Cedric.' Hackett raised a tumbler of the Macallan double cask single malt he'd found in a cabinet. His son-in-law had said to make himself comfortable, so he had. Bottles of this 15-year-old whisky sold for about $250 in Melbourne.

'I don't think you'll miss a bottle, old chap.'

Hackett nestled into the well-worn wingback. *Booksman* was moored to a power point across the canal from the cruising club, from which there had been a steady flow of walkers all evening. The boat's luxury fittings would attract curious and envious eyes, so Hackett was keeping the curtains drawn. His haven might feel a little claustrophobic, but it was safe. So he preferred to think of it as a cocoon. With great whisky.

And he was safe here unless his stalker tortured his wherabouts out of Sebastian. Hackett knew his son-in-law would not tell Tara. He offered another salute.

'You showed some grit tonight, Sebastian. I didn't know you had it in you.'

He poured a second Macallan and smiled. He didn't have to run any further. He had free digs, food and booze for as long as he needed. He wouldn't have to go above deck until it was time to head for Glasgow and a flight to Paris.

Hmm. Second thoughts, he might go stir crazy if he didn't get fresh air, or stretch his legs. He stood and peeked through the bow curtains. It had a canopy, drinks table, cushioned seats and pull-down blinds for rainy days. Excellent, that changed things.

The whisky emboldened Hackett: it was close to midnight and he'd heard no voices on the path for a while. He opened the door and eased onto a seat. The night air was balmy and invigorating as he faced the canal. It was a rule that all boating stopped before sunset. Pedestrians drifted back to their vessels or homes when the pubs shut.

Maybe he would become a night owl. The path extended for kilometres in both directions; he could enjoy a walk away from Tara's home. He wouldn't have to go far; just enough to stretch his legs.

The sound of a shoe scuffing a stone spooked him. How close was it? There had been no warning chatter. Had people passed while he sat musing – without the blinds down? He scurried for the safety of the saloon and locked the door.

CHAPTER 51

The pub behind Tara's home was about 15 minutes away, less if he followed the rail line. Morgan could walk past St Brendan's Church and take a beeline to the tearooms.

He skirted several farmhouses and followed a public track to the River Cherwell where he passed under the rail bridge. The flattened grass took him to a smaller footbridge over a tributary. The track continued to Shipton where Morgan turned onto the canal path.

The left bank was lined with narrowboats of every colour, length and sophistication. Most appeared to be privately owned; the roofs were cluttered with solar panels, bikes, pot plants and other domestic detritus. Several had business signs: crafts, handyman, electrician; the regular commerce of the canal. Rental boats were interspersed, moored for a night or two. Most likely, their crews had spent the evening at one of the pubs in Thrupp.

Morgan wore dark clothes and a black baseball cap and kept his head down. There was no need for a full disguise after the witching hour. He walked lightly on the stone path, keeping beyond the light spilling from a few narrowboat windows through which he could see late-night readers.

The current mission was to set up cameras facing the rear of Tara's house. He already knew how much time that family spent in their garden. That was where he'd catch Hackett.

He kicked a loose stone and sent it scurrying over the track. He waited for it to plop into the canal. It didn't, probably caught in the grass beside the swanky-looking *Booksman*.

CHAPTER 52

The skipper and crew of the *Moriarty* nursed hangovers and embarrassment as they joined the weekend canal traffic. So many boats were chugging north and south, but fortunately few travellers had been afloat the previous evening to witness the faux pas of boating faux pas.

Less than a metre of water flowed beneath the *Moriarty*; it should be impossible to sink a 20-metre vessel anywhere in the canal system. But it almost happened at the Nell Bridge Lock.

It was a single lock with one gate, the simplest and quickest way to transition to the next level. Yet, overconfidence put *Moriarty* in great peril.

Jo had been at the helm, Kim on gate and winch duty, because Dugal wanted to take photos in the moody twilight. Technically, they should've stopped for the night long before. The skipper had checked the map; it was only a short distance to the *Great Western Arms* which had excellent food, drink and family hospitality reviews. Jo decided it was worth pushing on.

Kim had closed the gate and marched to the front of the lock to release the water. She noticed Jo had finally heeded her advice about looping a rope over a bollard while the engine was in neutral. The mechanisms were well-maintained, and Kim soon shifted her attention to the next stretch of the canal. There was a kink in the watercourse which obscured their destination about a kilometre away. She was busy thinking about her first UK news report when Jo had screamed.

'Fuck, Kim. Stop the water!'

The *Moriarty*'s stern was four feet above the water, the bow pointing to the bottom of the lock. Everyone was shouting and swearing as Jo tried to push their boat away from the rear lock, and Kim raced to stem the outflow. The *Moriarty* drifted back to the gate, the rudder hooking the lip of the upper canal as the lock emptied.

It was only a few frantic few minutes but they avoided a maritime disaster – witnessed by two ramblers, and Dugal with his camera.

Kim had to refill the lock to steady their boat. *Moriarty* appeared to have escaped damage, until Jo pushed the tiller hard to the right as she guided them towards the bank. A water jet blasted up the shaft, soaking the angry skipper. It was puzzling , however, as the boat still responded to her manoeuvres.

The explanation for the near-disaster was laughable, and ultimately embarrassing – for Jo. She had ducked into the cabin to retrieve her phone from the charger. The outflow was quicker than expected, and the rope hitched too tightly to the bollard that was close to the rear gate. Jo had to scramble *uphill* from the interior to alert her oblivious crew to the emergency.

So, they avoided the impossible – sinking a canal boat – but Jo became an overnight legend. Dugal's video was shared with almost every patron in the pub. Jo's embarrassment was drowned in multiple rounds of free drinks; as the locals were impressed the lass was prepared to go down with her ship.

A crew meeting decided against returning to Braunston. *Moriarty* handled properly, most of the time, and it was only Jo who got wet when he spat the dummy.

'Dugal's video is going viral,' Kim told Jo. 'Fifteen hundred viewings – and counting – since last night.'

'I want half the money he makes.'

'Make that 60/40.' Dugal poked his head through the cabin door with his phone in hand. 'It was my camera. Hey, do you mind if we stop at Thrupp tonight? It's only a few km from Oxford.'

'Why?'

'Apparently a few cars have been stolen near the city mooring at night.' He waggled the phone. 'Steph says Thrupp is a cute hamlet with a couple of pubs. She can drive us into Oxford and back tomorrow. There's an easy turning point for the boat near a cruising club. Jo won't get drenched.'

Kim and Jo looked at each other and shrugged.

'Fine by us,' said Kim.

Dugal turned back to his phone. 'We should arrive by mid-afternoon. Let us know which pub you like, and we'll try to find a berth close by.' He disappeared inside the cabin.

'How much information are you going to share with Steph?' Jo smirked.

'Maybe the New Zealand angle. That Simon Carter returned to Melbourne as Riley Hawkins. Do you think he visited Amy's aunt or cousin?'

Jo shrugged and waved to a passing vessel with a middle-aged couple both holding the helm. 'Does it matter?'

'Not really, I guess. Unless he wanted their blessing to resume Amy's vendetta against Hackett. And to let them know Mitch Stevens would be on the hit list because he killed Amy.'

Jo shrugged. 'Meh. That's navel gazing to me. You've already got the best angle that Riley-Simon-Spyface might have been trained as James Bond.'

'That's melodramatic.'

'You're in a new media market Kim. You have to make the story sexy. You've got the scoop this guy might have an intelligence service background. The tabloids will go bananas once that information is broadcast: *Licenced to Kill Aussies. Spook Goes Rogue.*

That's what the British public will remember, not the woman who broke the story. Unless she gets creative. This could be your first television exclusive over here – you need to own the story.'

CHAPTER 53

Morgan's frustration grew with every minute he spent in front of his laptop. He was looking at a split screen; two camera angles from the pub into Tara's backyard. Drizzle had smeared the lens, partially obscuring the conservatory. The droplets couldn't hide the obvious; Tara, her husband and their two children were at home, but Andrew Hackett was not.

'It is possible he's having a sleep-in, Amy.'

Morgan slumped against the seat. 'Or in a room facing the canal, avoiding the grandkids.'

The cameras were showing those kids in all their glory. The bawling baby, strapped in a bouncer, had food all over her pink onesie and the floor. The toddler was flinging toys in every direction. Tara and Sebastian were paying no attention because they were engaged in an animated discussion.

'I wonder what that's all about. Did Sebastian get drunk at the pub last night? Or is it something to do with your father? I'd love to get an audio feed inside.'

Tara was tiny compared to her husband. Her arms were waving, but she didn't seem to be making any impression on him. Sebastian stood, arms folded, shaking his head and shrugging. Big expansive shrugs of the 'what do you expect' kind.

'Tara's not going to win.'

Morgan was right. Tara flounced out of the room, leaving Sebastian to tend the baby.

'Children are a gift, Amy. They're so impressionable. They shouldn't see their parents arguing like that.'

Morgan's chest tightened, he blinked rapidly several times. He wanted to pace, to release the energy but he couldn't drag himself away from the screen. There might be a fleeting glimpse of Hackett. It wouldn't be missed, as both cameras were recording, but didn't want to waste time re-trawling through the footage.

An alert flashed on his screen. Tara had called her mother.
'Shall we listen, Amy?'

Tara: Hi Mum.

Marianne: Hello darling. How are the Seb and the children?

Tara: The kids are grumpy and Sebastian's being an arsehole.

The ambience of the call changed. Morgan guessed Tara had gone outside on the canal tow path.

Marianne: What's he done?

Tara: He says he won't let Mitch stay here after he gets out of hospital. He reckons it's too dangerous for us if the psycho finds out and comes after him again.

Marianne: We don't think there's much risk of that. The assassin failed; no one thinks he'll try again. And even wounded, Mitch will be on alert.

Tara: That's not how Seb sees it. He thinks this guy is crazy. And even though the papers and TV news programs have been showing his photo the police have yet to catch him. Seb won't allow Mitch anywhere near the house until they do.

Morgan was angry about being called a psycho. This was all about justice. An eye for an eye. Hackett and Mitch were culpable, they had to pay.

Marianne: It's okay darling, I understand. We don't want to cause any stress or put the little darlings in danger. We'll stay in a hotel, maybe close to you in Oxford.

Tara: Mum – Seb said Mitch couldn't stay. You can come here. No one is after you.

Marianne: I won't be separated from Mitch again. He's a strong man but he need... I need to be with him. Don't worry about us darling, we'll find a nice hotel or a quiet bed and breakfast.

Tara: Oh. Hang on Mum. I've just had an idea. Let me check it out and call you back.

'Unbelievable, Amy. While Sebastian is convinced I'm going to come after them all, your sibling and her mother have ignored all the warnings about how *this crazy psycho*,' Morgan waved his hand at himself, 'is probably monitoring all their devices and they really shouldn't be talking about all this.

'Thank god for stupid people.'

Morgan stood and stretched his arms and back; the joints responded with satisfying clicks. He pulled a small case from a nook in the stone wall and opened it. It held a Sig Sauer pistol and a 6.7" suppressor. The first weapon had failed him. This one had been daily cleaned daily since his return from Hampstead. He should probably take it out for a test firing.

'Maybe I'll do some target practice behind the church tonight.'

Chapter 54

Hackett gazed through the narrow gap in the curtains at the activity on the opposite bank. He wasn't game to check the view on his own tow path. The rain had stopped, although the clouds threatened more, and walkers and boats had been passing all morning. The cruising club members were chatting, and fussing over their vessels and the vibe on the canal relaxed.

The flow-on effect was obvious. Hackett had slept well for the first time since Mitch was shot, and his mood was boosted by a hearty breakfast of bacon, eggs and baked beans.

The wingback chair beckoned again, and two novels from Cedric's collection sat on a small table. His first selections the previous night, *David Copperfield* and *Ulysses*, held his interest for all of 15 pages. He planned to give some other classics a try: *Kidnapped* and *Kim*; in the hope those ancient tomes held more adventure for an accountant hiding from a deranged assassin.

First things first. He used his new 'burner' to scroll the British news sites; which, it seemed, had already lost interest in the hunt for Mitch's shooter. Not surprising with the news cycles the way they were. Interest in an Aussie being shot beside a Russian's car was old news.

Hackett enlarged the grainy photo lifted from Kim's Apollo Bay story footage. No wonder the cops couldn't find him. The shooter could be any white bloke in his 30s. And the passport photos of Riley and Simon looked like two different men.

Hackett sighed heavily. He was already antsy about being cooped below decks and he hadn't been here a whole day yet. He might have to risk a late-night stroll for some fresh air.

In the meantime he cheered himself by checking the financial news. He was buried in the Australian stock exchange reports when he heard a metallic scratching at the stern.

Hackett froze, eyes on the rear door. Fuck. He hadn't accessed any personal details; it was impossible for the stalker to have found him. Unless he had gone to Tara's and Sebastian had blabbed.

The lock clicked and the door swung inwards before Hackett could find a weapon to defend himself. But he stood and dropped his phone, which clunked on the floor.

'Oh, is there someone on board?'

Jeeezus bloody christ in a cup.

'Tara! What the hell are you doing here?'

'Dad! Wow. Back at you. How are you here?' She ran into his arms and hugged him fiercely. 'I'm so glad you're safe.'

Hackett felt awkward. The embrace was welcome, but he could see walkers on the path through the open door. 'Hello darling.' He disengaged himself. 'I need to shut the door if I'm going to stay that way.'

Tara was wiping tears away when he returned to the saloon.

'We've been so worried about you since Mitch got shot. It's been horrible not knowing where you were.'

Hackett put an arm around Tara's shoulder and guided her to the only dining chair. He turned on the kettle. 'Fancy a tea? Sorry, there's no coffee.' He pointed at the tea set. 'Dear Uncle Cedric is an old-fashioned guy.'

Tara dabbed the final tear and laughed. 'Oh yeah, Uncle Ced's an antiquarian in every respect. But, again Dad, how are you here?'

Tara's eyes narrowed. 'Oh. Bloody Seb! Wouldn't let you stay with us, I bet. And then said Mum and Mitch couldn't stay here.'

Hacket missed the pot with the second spoon of tea leaves.

Mitch fucking Stevens!

'I thought loverboy was going to be in hospital rehab for months.'

'Nah. The shrapnel wounds were mostly painful and debilitating. He's already back on his feet. The hospital is booting him out tomorrow.'

'And they wanted to hide here?' He added hot water to the teapot.

'Hide? No. I asked them to stay with us but Seb got all macho and said it was too risky. Mum could stay but not Mitch. We had a blazing row last night and I stormed out. I was letting Mum know, when I remembered Uncle Ced's boat. It's a perfect hideaway.'

'It is. *Oh, no*, please tell me you didn't talk about this boat in a phone call with your mother. Honestly Tara!'

Tara looked horrified. 'Oh.'

'Oh, is an understatement, darling. Did you?'

Tara thought for a moment. 'Not specifically. I mentioned *a* boat as a possibility but Seb had ruined the idea.'

Hackett did not feel reassured.

'Speaking of my secretive bloody husband, how did Seb get you on here.'

Hackett had the grace to look sheepish. 'I was on my way to your place, hoping if I simply turned up I could stay a day or two and then take a train to Mnchester to fly home. Via Paris. As you know I couldn't *call*, or email. But Sebastian spotted me outside the pub. Wasn't even his local so, you know, *huge* coincidence. He was adamant I could not go to your place. And then he thought of this, told me where the spare key was, and said to make myself at home.'

Hackett added milk to the china cups and poured the tea. He handed one to Tara, then placed some Ginger Nuts on a plate and offered her one.

'Whoa, Dad, domestic much?'

Hackett pulled a face. 'So you told Marianne about *a* boat. How did Sebastian wreck that idea?'

Tara's expression said *oh no*.

'What?'

'I told Mum they couldn't stay here because Seb said there was already someone on board.'

Hackett was ashen. 'And you were talking about this on the phone you shouldn't have been using for such conversations.'

Tara was suddenly angry. 'Fuck you, Dad. All our lives have been uprooted *again* because of the shit you were involved in 30 bloody years ago. So shoot me if I want to have a normal chat with my own mother.'

Hackett raised his hand in surrender. 'Tara, I'm so sorry. I didn't mean – well, yes I did but – It's just if this arsehole is still monitoring your phones to get updates on Mitch let alone me, he will now know to start looking here. He'll be trawling every camera in the area.'

Tara laughed. 'This is Thrupp, Dad. There's no crime here; which means no CCTV. And I did not say where the mystery boat was. It could be on any canal anywhere.'

'But this is where he will start looking. Perhaps you could share another phone call with you mother, and throw him off the scent. Like suggest Marianne and her toyboy go to the Shetland Islands for his rehab.'

Tara laughed, and then, 'You're gonna have to stop being so insulting about Mitch, Dad. I think he's here to stay.'

CHAPTER 55

Morgan was happily thrumming his fingers on the table. He'd returned from a leisurely walk across the fields to catch up with a recording of the latest phone call between the wonderfully-clueless mother and daughter.

He was now convinced that Mitch and Marianne couldn't stay on a particular canal boat because Hackett was already on it. He just didn't know the boat's name, where it was moored, or why Sebastian was looking after it.

'But imagine, Amy, I could've walked right past your daddy on my way to Tara's last night.

Wherever Hackett was along the miles and miles canals, Morgan knew it was a sure bet the boat was stationary. The vessels were difficult to move through the locks without a crew.

'So he's moored, Amy. And if Sebastian is acting as caretaker of sorts, it will be local. That guy never ventures far from home.

'Which leads to the next likelihood that verifies my theory. Sebastian has not been communicating with Hackett by phone or laptop; he doesn't even like his father-in-law. That means they met in person while Hackett was en route to Tara's. It's the only thing that makes sense.'

Morgan couldn't search for Hackett by doorknocking every narrowboat on the canal around Thrupp, so flexed his fingers and began re-trawling Sebastian's life for a clue about the boat.

He'd also check Marianne and Mitch's threads for an idea of where they were going to stay in Oxford from tomorrow.

CHAPTER 56

Moriarty glided at a gentle pace. Dugal frowned at the threatening rain clouds as they motored under the bridge at Shipton-on-Cherwell.

'I should've asked Steph to bring my jacket.' He flicked the hem of the cheap poncho he'd found in a cupboard. 'This won't protect me from a deluge.'

'We'll be inside the pub before the heavens open,' Jo said. 'Keep an eye open for somewhere to moor. Thrupp's not far.'

A veteran waterman walking the towpath noticed Jo battling with the approach and climbed aboard to help. He jiggled the tiller a few times and the problem was solved.

'It's the cup on the skeg,' he said, as if that explained everything. 'The stock that's attached to the rudder must have come loose when you got stuck in the lock.'

Oh ha, she thought. She'd be a deadset legend up and down the canal by Monday. She thanked the man as he returned to dry land.

'There's a boat leaving,' Kim pointed. The bow of a blue vessel laden with bikes was edging into the waterway away about 100 metres ahead of them. 'The space looks right. Time to use your parallel parking skills, Jo.'

'Easy peasy.' Jo eased *Moriarty* into the gap with a deft touch of the throttle. Dugal jumped ashore and steadied the bow; Kim did the same with the stern. Three days on the water and they were a well-drilled crew. All near-disasters aside. Jo eased *Moriarty* to a stop with a few metres to spare from the next boat. They were bow to stern with an elegant green and gold vessel; the drawn curtains indicated it was probably unoccupied.

'This is a great spot,' Dugal said on his way to the cabin. 'There's a turnaround before the lift bridge, it's a short drive to Oxford and we can walk to the pub. Steph made a good choice.' He stepped into the cabin.

Kim leaned on the roof watching an elderly couple walk their spaniels along the path.

'I bet you are thinking of Sexy Rexy?' Jo sipped from her water bottle.

'Yeah. He'd love it here. Endless fields to run in. Lots of rabbits and foxes to chase.'

'Have you met your Rexy? One mad gallop and he'd be curled up in the saloon for the rest of the day, nudging your elbow to feed him treats.'

'True. And he's probably getting fat at Mum's. She can't say no to *her* darling boy.'

Dugal appeared in the hatch. 'Steph's parked at the pub just beyond the lift bridge. She says it's cosy and there's live folk music. Apparently they used to film a TV detective series there.'

'I do hope Steph is on expenses this weekend?' Jo said.

Half an hour later they were all ensconced in the pub, talking loudly to hear themselves over the fiddles and bodhran.

'I honestly do not know how you're all still alive,' Steph said. 'Mind you, I think it was Mac who jinxed your trip. He asked me on day one if Jo had sunk the boat yet.'

Jo shrugged off the hooting from her companions. Mac's ankles would be fleshy and weak when she returned to her death chariot in the studio.

'Have you heard anything from Hackett since he left your place?' Kim asked.

'Nothing but the note suggesting that for my safety I book into a hotel – on the company.' Steph waved the company plastic. 'I will spend that money on us instead. Another bottle and dinner for four?'

'Make that bottles,' said Jo.

CHAPTER 57

Morgan was peeved. He'd spent hours searching and was yet to find any boat of any kind linked to Sebastian. Unlike his visually chatty wife, the man had a tiny social media footprint. He updated his Facebook page six-monthly with photos of dinners out with his university friends.

'Damn, these guys need to get lives, Amy. They haven't grown beyond their quadruple sculling days.'

Morgan had searched Sebastian's client base again and found no expense claims for canal boat 'offices'. His personal emails were all still only to siblings and his parents, and his texts all work or family related.

Morgan stood and stretched. Oddly, he found himself more intrigued than annoyed. It was rare not to find a digital trail for such a large item.

'I'm guessing whoever asked Sebastian to look after the boat must have done so in person, which again makes it likely the vessel is moored nearby, probably within a mile of Thrupp. That's maybe 70 to 80 boats.'

Morgan stopped pacing. 'I might have to doorknock every boat, Amy. I suppose I could pretend to be doing a waterways survey. An ID would be easy to make and a check on overnight moorings and occupants would be plausible in summer.'

He'd need a good disguise. Morgan walked to the mirror in the bathroom, tapped his clean-shaven cheeks. Tinted glasses, fake beard, long hair and a hat should do it.

"Not even you would recognise me, Amy. I'll start early in the morning when people will still be drowsy from a night at the pub.'

Morgan sat down at his table and opened the box with the Sig Sauer. He planned to wait until dark then head for the fields between St Gile's and the Shipton Bridge. He'd never encountered late-night walkers there, away from the canal path.

His weapon test and target practice would be hushed by the suppressor. No one would hear a thing, especially if he also timed the gunshots with passing trains.

CHAPTER 58

Cabin fever defeated Hackett just after nine o'clock. A million books turned out not to be his thing at all, and simply congested the environment. He had to escape. The sun hadn't quite set but the foot traffic along the towpath was down to a trickle. The last wash from a passing boat had been two hours ago. He needed fresh air and a drink poured by someone else.

Light rain had been falling steadily for the past hour so he threw on Dugal's jacket, pulled up the hood, and headed outside. He still felt like a dork, but at least he looked like any walker by an English canal in stormy weather.

Common sense told him to walk away from Thrupp towards Shipton where there'd be fewer boats and people. Stupid bloody-mindedness made him turn towards the closer hamlet where two pubs offered respite from his claustrophobia. Pub closing was 11pm so he'd have time to enjoy an ale and the ambience of a cheery English pub. Not that he intended to talk to anyone; he just didn't want to feel alone.

He avoided the pub where he'd bumped into his grumpy son-in-law in case Sebastian was back there, maybe cast out by his angry wife. A few hundred metres later he entered a charming, rustic and noisy establishment.

Hackett found the guest coat rack inside the entrance, shrugged off his damp jacket and hung it on a peg. Nobody was likely to pinch it with the words TV Crew emblazoned on the back.

Bugger. How did I miss that yesterday?

The pub was crowded, convenient for blending in but a pain for expecting fast service. Hackett edged towards a corner, elbowing his way in behind a pear-shaped man whose giant bum was sprawled across two stools. His pint glass was almost empty, the barman approached.

'That's enough thanks, Derek. I'm off to brave the tempest outside.' He drained the dregs and pivoted to his right to stand. Hackett grabbed one of his stools as the other was claimed by an attractive brunette in her mid-40s. Hackett's type in a red dress but he didn't have time or the desire for seduction.

He ordered an Abbot Ale and closed his eyes in bliss as the first, second and third mouthfuls crossed his tastebuds. He glanced at the clock behind the bar and the beer turned acidic.

A security camera was staring right him in the face.

Fuck. Shit.

Would it be closed circuit, or could his stalker be snooping in on every camera in the bloody area and looking right back at him, right now.

Regardless of that possibily, every second Hackett sat there like a stunned mullet increased the risk of being seen. He slid off the stool to leave, then belligerence made him stop.

He picked up his glass and finished it the while looking down the barrel of the camera.

It was a *fuck you* to whenever the bastard found the footage.

Chapter 59

Memories of Morgan's basic weapons training came back as he crept through trees beside the railway. As a data expert he was mostly confined to a desk in the bowels of MI6 with the other tech moles. But the service was nothing if not generous in offering chances to learn extra skills. Morgan had expressed interest in going into the field some day, hence the basic training in martial arts and weapons. He suspected the programs were mostly designed to keep agents like him motivated for Queen and country.

He sloshed through the wet grass, gliding from tree to tree, firing a round at every third trunk. It felt good, powerful, the bullets striking with a satisfying thwhack. There was no muzzle flash and the rain meant he didn't have to wait for passing trains.

Morgan was counting the rounds; 10 fired, seven in the magazine, no sign of malfunction. He crept another three steps, sighted and fired, relishing the image of Mitch's face just before the killshot hit.

'I still plan to use the bow on your father, Amy,' Morgan said. 'Unless circumstances demand the gun for him too.'

Morgan crouched behind a tree, not far from first rail bridge across a branch of the Cherwell. He listened for late-night ramblers or boozers returning from the pub: nothing.

The first clip was empty now so he switched it for a new one and fired one shot to ensure it was still firing smoothly.

There was a footbridge to the north which crossed the main waterway where the narrowboats travelled. He ignored it and stayed in the treeline. He'd decided to check out the area around Thrupp again.

Morgan approached the second footbridge to Shipton, checked the area then crossed it and turned left. The trees were sparser as the tributary meandered towards the main river. Target practice was over for the night, he was now too close to the moored boats, so he tucked the gun into an inside jacket pocket.

The foliage was thick where the tributary turned left towards the hamlet. Morgan walked north to find easier access and spotted a gap after 20 metres.

A watery tinkle drew his attention to the canal.

Oh, my god, Amy!

Andrew Hackett was standing barely five metres from him; pissing into the canal in the rain.

Filthy prick. And stupid.

The green TV Crew jacket really was like a neon sign.

Dream come true, Amy. I swear I must have manifested him. But, this presents us with a dilemma.

Hackett was alone; and there was nobody else to witness him being marched away by a gunman. That, however, could change at any moment, and Morgan had no way to restrain him.

More importantly, he couldn't execute Plan A tonight; the church wasn't ready and the crossbow was at the cottage.

Morgan pulled out his gun. He should just shoot the bastard right here, right now. He could confront him on the path down there, and empty an entire magazine into his worthless body.

Man that's a long piss.

The urine stream was only now weakening.

Morgan had seconds to decide; shoot, capture or wait?

Regardless of the choice, he needed to be closer, ready to act when Hackett turned from the canal. Morgan kept his eyes and gun on Hackett as he stepped around the trees. He didn't see the discarded bicycle hidden in the grass until he stumbled on a wheel.

'Who's there?' Hackett start to turn.

Morgan thought he'd paused for a lifetime, until he realised he pulled the trigger seven times.

Chapter 60

Kim heard thumping as if from the bottom of a dusty well. Her throat was parched, tongue thick. The noise persisted, became more distinct.

'Go away!' It was Jo's hangover voice, answering for them both. Kim opened an eye; her friend lay on the opposite bed with a pillow over her head.

The thumping resumed in Kim's head – and on the cabin door.

'We're dying here. Piss off.'

'It's the police! Open up, please.'

'Shit!'

'Okay,' Kim said. 'Sorry. Just putting some clothes on.' She sat up, the blood didn't keep pace and she almost fell off the bed. 'Jeezus. I'm never going to drink again.'

She found a T-shirt and shorts. 'Are you decent enough for me to open the door?'

Jo threw back her sheet to reveal she was still fully clothed from the night before. 'At least I took my shoes off.' She swung her legs to the side.

The policeman knocked again.

'Yeah, yeah.' Jo stood, wobbled, sat down again. 'I'll wait here.'

Kim unlatched the door to a bearded officer in a navy-blue uniform and cap. Luckily his size blocked most of the harsh morning glare.

'Agh!'

The officer smirked. 'Big night out, ladies?'

'Yeah. Bit of a reunion at the pub down the canal.' Kim shielded her eyes with both hands. 'Is there a problem? I promise we didn't drink and drive. Or boat. To be honest, we barely walked. What can we do for you?'

'First up, if either of you is the skipper, I recommend you don't touch the engine or tiller for quite a few hours.'

Kim nodded and almost vomited. She swallowed the bile. 'We are responsible travellers, officer.'

'My name is Constable Viner. Do either of you, perchance, know anything about the body in the canal?'

'What?' Kim asked.

'Shit,' Jo added.

'How many passengers do you have on board?'

'Three,' said Jo. 'No, four last night.'

'Steph!' Kim called out. 'Are you guys both there?'

'Your knocking should've woken the dead,' Jo said. 'Oh sorry, bad choice of words. I'll go check if they're awake.' She walked gingerly to the closed door.

Kim turned to the copper, as her journalist brain emerged from the hangover fog. 'Is the body a man or a woman? Where was it found? Are there any injuries?'

Constable Viner raised an eyebrow, then ignored Kim as he took in a groggy Dugal in his underwear. 'What's going on?'

'There's a body in the canal.' Kim turned to the cop. 'Close to our boat?'

Viner nodded.

'Jeezus, Kim.' Dugal shook his head. 'The Cadaver Crew strikes again.'

The policeman's jaw dropped. One hand reached for his radio, the other rested on his baton. 'What does that mean?'

Kim raised her hands. 'No, no. It's a joke. We're a TV production crew. I'm a journo. He's a camera op. We've covered a few murder cases back in Australia. Our bosses gave us the nickname.'

Viner relaxed, although Kim noticed his hand remained close to his baton. She'd wondered how he'd actually use it against four people in a narrowboat.

Steph, already in jeans and a cotton top, trailed Jo into view.

'What's this about a body in the canal? Any suspicion of foul play?' Steph asked, also in full journo mode.

Jo snickered. 'We sound like a British TV drama.'

The officer was taking notes. 'Who do work for in Australia?'

'Channel 5 in Melbourne. They are on holidays,' Steph said, pointing to Kim and Jo. 'I'm the London correspondent. He is freelancing.'

Kim tried to retake control. 'What can you tell us about the body?'

Viner tried really hard not to laugh. 'Nothing, at this stage. But we may need to talk to you in more detail. Please stay on board while I make a call.'

They watched him step off the boat and pull a mobile from one of his many vest pockets.

'Why isn't he using his radio?' Kim whispered.

Viner walked futher away from the *Moriarty*.

'Let's go out for a stickybeak.' Jo led the way onto the cruiser stern, and a moment later the Cadaver Crew were leaning over the railing looking for a body.

Further down the towpath, about three boats away, they saw the police had set up a crime scene tent – around something.

'I'll get my camera,' said Dugal. 'Might be able to sell footage to a local station. Even if it's an accident.'

'*If?*' Jo snickered. 'Someone even drunker than us probably fell in the canal and couldn't get out.' She paled. 'Oh, now I feel terrible. Were they thrashing around out there and we didn't hear them?'

Dugal broke the mutual silent guilt session when he returned in shorts and a polo shirt with his mini camera and Steph's media pass. Any vision and sound he could get wouldn't be high quality but it would be from the heart of the story. The two of them set off along the path towards the police tent.

Kim took a breath, and turned away from Channel 5's foreign correspondent. Constable Viner stood with a foot resting on the gunwale of the next boat. Kim ducked inside, grabbed a pen and pad, and rushed forward. The outside door from the 'boudoir', such as it was, had been opened, probably by Steph to vent body and alcohol fumes. Kim sat out of sight and listened to the officer.

'It is a weird situation, Guv. A bullet-riddled body ends up close to the boat of a bunch of journos know as The Cadaver Crew.'

Kim wrote *bullet-riddled body* and *murder.*

'They have to be involved, but I'm not sure how.'
Wait, what? We're suspects? Why?

Viner said nothing for a minute, so Kim peeked to make sure he hadn't moved. He still had his size 13 boot on the beautiful green craft next to theirs. The owner of that boat wouldn't be happy if Mr Plod scratched the paintwork.

Kim noticed a curtain twitch, indicating someone there was watching and listening too.

'Okay, Guv. There are four of them; one male, three females.'

Why on earth would four hungover Australians be considered murder suspects in Oxfordshire? Kim wondered. Even drunk they'd have enough sense to move the damn boat.

Kim scurried back on deck at the stern, holding her notebook. Regardless of what the cop thought, she was a journalist on a story of a likely murder that now involved them.

Viner was back beside the *Moriarty*. 'What are those two doing down there?'

'Their jobs,' said Kim. 'We're news people. We have the right to make inquiries.'

'Not if you are the story, you don't.'

Jo snorted. 'How on earth are we the story, Officer?'

'We're the media, not killers, Constable Viner,' Kim said, more politely than Jo. 'Why do you think we're involved?'

Kim could tell Viner was torn between giving and getting information.

He sighed. 'There was a green jacket on the body.'

'It was raining last night.'

'It's branded.'

'With what?'

'It has *TV Crew* stencilled on the back.'

Kim felt a chill. 'And?'

'A Channel 5 logo on the front.'

'Oh fuck. Sorry, Officer,' Jo said, and then frowned at Kim. 'Who the hell could it be? We're all here.'

The penny dropped for both women.

'We might have an idea about the victim, Officer. Can you hang on a sec?' Kim said. She nodded at Jo, who stuck two fingers in her mouth and gave a piercing whistle. They both beckoned Steph and Dugal back to the *Moriarty*.

When they were close enough Kim said, 'Steph, how many Channel 5 jackets do you have at your apartment?'

She shrugged. 'One. It not like they're a fashion accessory.'

'Did you bring it with you?'

'No. I'm not– I wasn't working.'

'Did you bring Dugal's crew jacket like he asked?'

'No. I couldn't find it. Why?'

The Cadaver Crew looked at each other, at Steph, back to each other and then, like a well tuned choir they all said: 'Hackett.'

'Hackett. Who's that?' Viner asked.

'First, will you tell us whether the victim was a man or a woman?' Kim asked.

Viner sighed. 'A middle-aged man.'

Steph took control. 'You'd better come aboard again, Constable Viner. Have we got a story for you.'

Viner boarded the *Moriarty* and all five took places on the cruiser stern .

'We will happily tell you all we *might* know about who your victim might be, if you can guarantee some quid pro quo,' Kim began.

Viner shook his head. 'Sorry, I do not have the authority to guarantee anything. I can, however, put a good word in with my superiors.'

'Okay,' Kim said. 'Hackett, Andrew Hackett, is – maybe now *was* – Channel 5's chief financial officer in Melbourne. He was at my place a couple of days ago and it appears he borrowed a jacket. Hackett is, was, also a target of the same man who did the Hampstead shooting last week.'

Viner sat up straight in surprise. 'The Russian guy?'

'No, the victim wasn't Russian,' Kim said, as if *everyone* should know that. 'Neither is the shooter. In fact the damn Russians have nothing to do with any of this.'

'Whatever,' Viner said. 'It makes this a multi-force investigation. And it might explain the card. Which, admittedly, is why I was suspicious of you all."

Jo voiced the *Moriarty* crew's collective puzzlement. 'Card?'

Viner looked at Dugal. 'We found a sodden business card in the pocket, belonging to one Dugal Cameron, senior camera operator for *Melbourne Spotlight*.'

'Yep, that'd be me.'

'Constable Viner, you have a body and together we have already ruled out that the dead guy is not Dugal, even though the jacket seems to be his. Perhaps we can help you verify if that's our TV executive lying up there in your CSI tent.'

Viner shook his head vigorously. 'No way would any of you be allowed close to the deceased.'

'I understand,' said Kim. 'Our Australian cops usually take photos on their phones at crime scenes, you know, for reference during investigations. I'm sure you guys do the same.'

Viner rubbed his chin; Kim waited. Silence would work.

'Okay. Let me me call my boss. Confirming an identity quickly would be helpful.' Once again, he left the boat.

'Guys, guys,' Kim said quietly, full of inappropriate excitement.

'What what?' Jo whispered back.

'It has to be Hackett. The guy was shot.'

'How do you know?' Steph asked.

'I overheard Viner tell his Guv the body was *bullet-riddled*.'

'Shit,' Jo said.

'Understatement,' Steph said.

Dugal frowned. 'Poor Hackett.'

'Oh yeah,' Kim agreed. 'We are awful.'

'We are suspects,' Jo reminded them. 'Bloody idiot copper.'

'No we're not,' Kim stated.

'Oh yeah,' Steph threw her palms up. 'Let's hope they don't find out how much we all despised Andrew handsy Hackett. No one mention that, okay. The most important thing is to collect all the details we can, so we can do a live cross for 5 News and *Spotlight* asap.

Kim closed her eyes. She wanted to scream *this is my bloody story*.

Constable Viner reappeared with a smile. 'My Gov says I can't deliberately show you a photo of the victim,' he said quietly. 'However, if I happened to leave my phone on the seat while I'm taking all your names and details, including your mothers' maiden names, and what you called your first pets...'

He dropped his mobile next to Kim and took out his notebook.

'And we never reveal our sources,' Steph said.

Kim had seen several murder victims, most covered in blood. The image of this white face with dull, staring eyes made her gasp.

But the middle-aged man, wearing the Channel 5 crew jacket was not who she expected to see.

'That's not Hackett.'

She picked up Viner's phone and showed everyone, as he rolled his eyes.

'Who the hell is this?' she asked. 'And how did he get our Dugal's jacket?'

Chapter 61

Morgan felt numb; not an unexpected emotion after shooting a man, mid-turn, in the back *and* chest. Yet, it wasn't the murder that bothered him.

It was fact it was the wrong bloody man.

'We could've been celebrating, Amy.'

He held no sympathy for the innocent man he'd gunned down and sent pitching into the canal. It was the piddler's own fault Morgan had to shoot him.

'He saw the gun, Amy. I couldn't let him escape and call the police. They'd have swarmed the area within minutes.

'But now, fuck it, the whole of Thrupp and the waterway will be a busy homicide scene. Unless the body sank, or floated away before being discovered.'

It was eight hours since the event. Morgan had taken off, waded into a nearby tributary, and exited on a quiet section of the public walkway.

He'd wiped the Sig Sauer and suppressor down and hidden in a damaged grave at St Giles' Church. He didn't want to risk being caught with it, now it had been used in a homicide, but it was too early to dump permanently. He still had two bastards to kill.

Next had been the physical cleansing. His clothes went into the washing machine, and Morgan stood under a long, hot shower to remove any gunshot residue and canal mud. He didn't expect detectives to come knocking on his door, but it was better to be prepared.

'The bloody TV jacket will link the death of Mr Wrong Place Wrong Time to Mitch, especially with that pesky damn TV crew ramping up their theories. But the forensics should keep them wondering just how many weapons I have. They'll be thinking arsenal.'

Morgan made a pot of tea and two slices of toast and strawberry jam, and returned to his screens.

He still couldn't believe he'd fired so many times but realised he must still have been primed from his target shooting.

'Not very professional, Amy, I admit but the adrenalin was wild.'

He checked his newsfeeds. No ID on the Thrupp Canal Body as they were calling him. Police weren't even admitting it was a shooting yet.

'That's kinda weird, Amy.'

Morgan opened his Tara surveillance window. The only call of interest was to her mother last night, before the shooting.

Tara: Hey Mum. Now, don't tell me where you're staying.

Marianne: I won't, darling. Mitch ticked me off too, for talking on the phone about our, um, issues.

Tara: Yeah, I'm sorry, Mum. I didn't think this guy would really have the ability to capture every phone conversation. I thought only the government could do that.

Morgan smiled. 'Or people trained by the government.'

Tara: Let's meet tomorrow at the café we went to with the kids two weeks ago. I'll be there at 2pm.

Marianne: Good idea, darling. I'll call if I can't be *there*.

'Finally, these two are learning, Amy. And yet, finding the café will be as easy as checking Tara's credit card. We can get there before them and follow Mummy dearest straight back to Mitch.

CHAPTER 62

'I like Mondays, Steph.' Mac beamed at Curly Rogers who hovered over the speakerphone in *Spotlight*'s conference room. 'Walking in the door to another exclusive about our favourite story makes me smile.'

'He even shared a piece of his KitKat,' Curly said.

'Only coz I pinched it from Ciaran in News. Okay, Steph, what's the state of play.'

'Our police source says they've identified the victim. Malcolm Brenchley. He lived on the waterways, selling trinkets at village markets and from his boat. He was last seen at the other pub. As in, not the one we were getting hammered at, which was closer to our boat. They're only a few hundred metres apart.'

Mac chuckled. 'How did he end up dead instead of Hackett?'

'Obviously mistaken identity. Kim talked to some locals at the pub. Malcom had a reputation for light fingers, helping himself to anything not nailed down. We suspect he stole Hackett's – make that Dugal's – jacket, most likely from his pub because it was bucketing down last night.'

'That seems logical, which means Hackett is hiding somewhere in the area. Fancy having the balls to go for a drink when you're being hunted.'

'Balls? More like stupidity,' Steph laughed. 'We have discovered his daughter lives in a cottage on the canal.'

'Is Hackett there?'

'No. I checked before driving back to London. She was more polite than her mother, but gave me nothing. I don't think Hackett was inside, although I'm sure she knows where he is.'

'Pity she didn't trust you enough. It'd be good to get him on camera again. See if he's an emotional wreck, you know: How do you feel about yet another shooting, Andrew? Particularly as it seems this dead bloke was mistaken for you.'

Steph laughed. 'Is it wrong that none of us give a rat's arse about The Hatchet?'

'Terribly wrong,' Curly said. 'But, is it worth Kim or Jo hanging around the village–'

'Hamlet, Curly. It's tiny, only a few houses. It wouldn't even rate that honour without the pubs for the canal trade.'

'Okay. Are you saying it would be too obvious for them to follow the daughter?'

'Yep. They *could* moor the boat in front of her home and they might get lucky. But Jo said you'd have to pay to extend their rental.'

Mac snorted. 'She'll have me paying for the whole trip soon. I'll think about that. Any word from the cops about the killer?'

'No. And he is that now, isn't he,' Steph said. 'Until last night, as far as we know, Riley-Simon-Possible-Spy was simply an arsonist who'd viciously assaulted someone and failed as an assassin.

'And now he's a ghost again. Nobody reported anyone suspicious on the path last night. They've been taking the lousy pics of him to every boat. If they have any fresh info, they're not sharing. We were their first suspects. Can you imagine that?'

'Of course we can. You do know you've been initiated into the Cadaver Crew now. For goodness sake do not let the local cops know how unpopular Hackett is at Channel 5.'

Steph laughed. 'That's exactly what I said to the others. Right, it's getting late, and I've got lead stories for News and you guys to write. I'll send you a script in about an hour.'

'We'll look forward to it.'

Curly disconnected and made a note on his clipboard. 'A live cross to the canal would be good to follow her story. There could be developments.'

'I know.'

'I'm sure Steph would be happy to drive back to the thriving metropolis of Thrupp after a few hours sleep.'

'Yep.'

'But you don't want her to do that.'

'Nope.' Mac picked up his Collingwood mug and waved it at Carla. She smiled and took it through to the coffee machine.

'Have you already spoken to Kim?'

'Yep.'

Curly stood.

'Do you fancy the last KitKat?'

Curly snatched it. 'Thanks but I'm not telling Steph you've booked her rival for a live shot.'

'They're not rivals anymore, mate. They got pissed together last night, that's almost like true love.'

Curly shook his head. 'That's a bloke thing, Mac. It's a wonder they didn't accidentally-on-purpose shove each other into the canal.'

CHAPTER 63

Cabin fever was the only companion for Hackett on the *Booksman*. It was partially alleviated by whisky and a new respect for Ernest Hemingway; *For Whom the Bell Tolls* was holding his interest.

Hackett reached for his glass; it was empty. The Macallan bottle on the kitchen bench was a few fingers away from the same state. That was fine, plenty more in the pantry. He swayed as he stood, then steadied a thigh against the table and carefully poured a new measure. He slumped into the wingback without spilling any whisky but didn't pick up the novel.

The day had started with unexpected drama along the canal. He had been asleep until he felt a jolt to the boat. A peek through the front curtain revealed a large policeman resting a boot on his gunwale. That had been disconcerting. He jammed his phone back in a pocket and moved on. *Booksman* had been a convenient prop. Hackett half-expected a sharp knock on the door – but that didn't come until much later.

Somthing was obviously going on out there. The same cop was wandering back and forth, another two walked by, but whatever the cause it was beyond his limited view, and out of earshot.

He didn't dare join the curious busybodies who were passing with intent. He sat for a while near his open hatch and overheard talkthat one of the regular boat dwellers had drowned after a night at the pub. Some speculated he might have had a heart attack. Hackett hoped it was the prick who stole his jacket. He'd been soaked by the time he got back to the *Booksman*.

The police made two attempts to talk to him. Hackett assumed they were knocking at every boat along the canal, checking if anyone heard a drunk stumble past, or call for help from the water.

Hackett hadn't seen or heard anything, so he was not going to risk exposure, or his life, by talking to cops about something that wasn't his problem.

It meant he had to stay quiet all day. He locked himself in again and made sure the curtains were well drawn.

No one home here, Officer.

Hackett picked up the Hemingway and returned to the Spanish Civil War.

CHAPTER 64

'I want to start the live cross by walking along the path to our canal boat.' Kim gestured to *Moriarty* where a glum Dugal stood in the bow with Jo.

She was issuing the camera directions to a BBC crew from Oxford. Mac had organised a deal overnight – a free camera and soundman in exchange for a London exclusive on the canal murder. Kim's services were included in the negotiations. The broadcaster didn't know Kim would have paid for the opportunity to impress them.

'I'll stop on the grass between the boats.' Kim spread her arms. 'They're both beautiful craft, they'll make a nice backdrop for our Melbourne audience.'

Jonty, the camera operator, gave her a thumbs up. 'That works for us.' He pointed at the roof of *Moriarty*. 'A tracking shot of your walk from up there would awesome. But an extended monologue from above might look naff. A second camera would've been ideal.'

Kim looked up at Dugal; he shook his head. 'I checked – they don't have a tripod for the mini cam or a switcher to make it work.'

'How times change. You do recall Jo and I reported from a motorhome during a cyclone in New Zealand with just a smartphone and laptop?'

'Until the mountains collapsed around us.' Jo shivered.

'Yeah. I don't expect any dramas like that today.'

The rain had passed during the night, patches of blue reminded tourists it was supposed to be summer but the temperature barely nudged 20 degrees. There was no breeze to encourage Kim to restrain her shoulder length hair. She hadn't packed for a TV appearance. She was hoping a clean skirt and white blouse would be enough. She had no doubts about the story impact.

Detectives had so far been publically tight-lipped about the canal death. Radio stations and news websites were told a man had died overnight. There was no mention about him being shot or any connection to any other case.

Police wouldn't release the victim's name until relatives had been identified, but everyone on the canal knew who it was.

Kim watched Jonty and Asif set up lights and lay cables; they were grateful for a power source from the narrowboat. Dugal's professionalism outweighed his disappointment about not being involved; he was soon helping with the setup.

'Is *your* reporter likely to arrive before we do our program, Jonty?'

'She'd better. We have another story in Oxford an hour after you go to air.'

Kim willed the reporter to be on time. This was her own big opportunity; she didn't want it spoiled by conflicting schedules.

Asif attached a lapel microphone to Kim's blouse. 'Is that cotton?'

'Silk'

He raised an eyebrow. 'We shouldn't get any rustle. Best to check though. Can you go to your starting point?'

Kim walked to amidships of their elegant neighbour. *Moriarty* was special, but *Booksman* next door was in a class of its own. The curtain twitch Kim had seen earlier must have been her imagination. There had been no sign of life on board.

Kim straightened her skirt and blouse and waited for a cue from Jonty.

'Okay, going for a rehearsal, Kim, in three, two …' Jonty waved.

Kim started with her eyes on the path for the first two steps. 'Hello, I'm Kim Prescott reporting for *Spotlight* from the Oxford Canal for a camera and microphone check. Testing, one, two, three, four, five. I'll keep talking and talking until I reach this spot to continue the story.' She smiled at Jonty and Asif. 'How was that?'

'All good for me,' said Jonty. Asif gave a thumbs up and walked away with a phone to his ear. 'He's checking your control room in Melbourne is happy.' Jonty pulled off his headphones, stepped away from his camera and rolled his shoulders.

'Sorry we don't have a spare earpiece for you. We were a bit rushed; one of the equipment cases was left behind.'

'That's fine. I'll go on your cue. My producer won't worry about duration.'

'You were guarded with the information.' He grinned. 'I guess you know there's a producer sitting in our studios waiting to hear about the exclusive.'

'Oh, yes.' Kim matched his smile. 'I can't afford to have the BBC beat me to air. All will be revealed soon.'

Most of the story was already public knowledge – in Australia. Steph's new story led the evening News. That would have set the other media companies scrambling to match Channel 5. They would not have been given all the details.

Mac and Curly plotted an information drip feed for News and *Spotlight* to hold the audience through the most crucial ratings period. The canal live cross was mostly window dressing: *Spotlight* was live at a major crime scene – again. It would be a personal perspective their audiences loved.

Kim also understood her mentor was offering her an opportunity to impress a potential employer. Bless you Mac.

Andrew Hackett was gobsmacked. Kim bloody Prescott was about to do a live cross right outside his window. It was the familiar voice that dragged him from his book.

What the fuck was that about? Why the fuck was she even standing two metres from where he was.

Was she about to spring onto his boat and reveal his whereabouts?

Kim was about to report for *Spotlight*, that much he heard. But the rehearsal gave nothing away about the content and in a moment she was out of earshot. But it could only mean one thing. The only story Spotlight had an interest in on this side of the world was his story.

Had they found the shooter? Was it him who ended up dead in the canal last night? Had there been a shootout he'd completely missed?

'Two minutes, Kim.' Dugal had stepped in as floor manager.

He was greeted with a thumbs up. Kim knew he was happy to be involved. She patted her skirt for the 10th time and wriggled her shoulders to ensure the blouse looked right. They were habitual nervous tics before every television performance, live or recorded. It was good to feel the tingle again. This was more than being part of a big exclusive; it was a job interview.

'One minute, Kim.'

It was comforting to hear Dugal's voice, although it was unusual not hearing Curly or Richard Templeton in an earpiece prior to a live cross.

A professional broadcaster copes with the tech hiccups. You've got this.

The 30 and 10 second warnings followed. Then Dugal's visual cue. She lowered her eyes and walked.

> *'Thanks Richard. This is the path where the victim walked his final steps on Saturday. He had travelled it many times over the years. He sold his trinkets at village fairs and markets throughout Oxfordshire. He would often moor his boat in this tranquil hamlet and enjoy a few ales at the local pubs. Never a hint of any trouble. Never an indication his bullet-riddled body would be dumped into the waterway on a stormy summer night.*
>
> *'I've been travelling the canal over the past few days with Spotlight colleagues in this lovely vessel, the Moriarty. We're not sure if we were asleep when the victim went past. We hope we were still at the pub because it's too horrible to think of him being murdered a couple of boats away. There's always that nagging thought that we could have done something to stop it. Or help him.*
>
> *'We learned of the crime this morning when a policeman came knocking. Ironically, we briefly became suspects as the victim was wearing a Channel 5 rain jacket.*
>
> *'Naturally, Jo Trescowthick, Dugal Cameron, Stephanie Grant and I were shocked the victim might be a member of our media family. Sadly we assumed, wrongly as it turned*

out, that we knew exactly who the victim was. Fortunately, I was able to take advantage in a moment of police inattention to view a photo of the deceased. It cleared us of suspicion and put paid to our assumption, but created another mystery.

'Why was the victim wearing one of our crew jackets?

'You see, we thought the victim was Channel 5's chief financial officer, Andrew Hackett.

Spotlight viewers will know Mr Hackett has been the target of an extended vendetta. As we reported last week that vendetta came to England with the shooting in Hampstead of Mr Hackett's ex-bodyguard, Mitch Stevens.

Mr Stevens survived an attempt on his life but police have yet to capture the gunman.

'Mr Hackett has been in hiding. We now suspect he might be somewhere along the canals, in a cottage or narrowboat or a local hotel.

'We believe last night's shooting was a case of mistaken identity, and that Andrew Hackett was the intended target. It's looking fairly certain the victim took the crew jacket from the local pub, perhaps by accident, and that sadly resulted in his death.

'It's quite likely, in the darkness, the killer didn't know he was about to shoot the wrong man.

'Richard.'

Kim held her pose.

'We're clear Kim.' Dugal nodded his approval. 'You nailed it. Steph will be jealous.'

Kim glowed; she was back in action. Asif approached to help remove the lapel mic and transmitter. There was no sign of the BBC reporter, but she expected the interview would be with a hand-held mic.

'Hang on, Kim,' Jonty held a phone. 'Our reporter can't make it.' He continued to listen.

Kim was disappointed. She knew the BBC producer was watching the feed to Australia, but an interview on British television would look even better on her brag reel.

'Leave the mic, Asif. The studio wants you to do that again for our lunchtime news, Kim.' Jonty listened again then pocketed his phone.

'Just a couple of changes. Say Thanks Martin, make it yards not metres, and drop the *Spotlight* viewers reference, please.

'Oh, and our producer wants a chat when we've finished.' He smiled. 'Welcome to the Beeb.'

Hackett's hands shook as he poured a second pre-breakfast whisky. He'd opened the window and heard everything.

The killer had been here in tiny bloody Thrupp, walking the same towpath he had last night. Hackett had come within, what, the time it took to down a beer of being the dead man in the canal.

A coule of hours ago he was cursing the jacket thief and wishing him dead for being a thief.

Fuck, the bastard had actually died because he'd stolen the damn jacket. But not because he was a thief.

It could have been me. It was supoosed to be me.

Had the killer seen him via the camera in the pub? Or was everything that was happening to him just a rolling wave of coincidences?

And why did it feel like his own colleagues were gleefully shoving him out like a shag on a rock.

Perhaps he should he go to the cops now. It was obvious to the world he was a target for the deranged killer. Would they provide ptoection or a safe house. Probably not, why go to any expense to protect a foreigner? They might drive him to the airport and wish him a happy flight to Melbourne. He was rich, after all, why should British taxes pay for his protection?

CHAPTER 65

'You look pleased with yourself.' Jo handed Kim a coffee. They were sitting on the roof at the bow of *Moriarty*. 'And rightly so. They were two good crosses.'

Canal life continued around them: boats passed regularly, people walked the path, ducks scavenged for food. The oddity was the television crew packing away camera, lights, cables.

Kim was elated. She had flawlessly presented two news reports on an exclusive story to different media companies half a world apart.

'We're almost done, Kim.' Jonty called out. 'Charlotte has to get ready for the next bulletin. I gave her your number, so expect a call soon.' He waved and followed Asif down the path to their crew vehicle.

Jo admired Jonty as he walked away, then addressed Kim. 'Well done. A body is found almost under our boat – and you land a job at the BBC.'

Kim didn't know whether to laugh or grimace. Was it right to benefit from someone's misfortune? 'It's only a chat. We'll see what happens. It's still mid-summer – I wanted to go to Spain and Croatia before thinking of settling into a job.'

She ignored Jo's sceptical look and picked up her notebook. She hadn't shared all their knowledge with the BBC – or her former employers. There was the issue of Riley-Simon being a former spook. Pete Benson had given her contact details to his brother, so something might come of that. She was still a long way from confirming if the guy had been part of the security services. Jo must have read her mind.

'You didn't tell Steph about the spook angle, did you?'

'No. Pete gave *me* the tip to help get a foot in the door with a media outlet here. The question is how much do I tell the BBC?'

'Wait to see what they offer you, before you tell them any damn thing. They might take the lead and give it to one of their own.'

'Happens every day. No lead is sacred until you break the story.'

'Cute Jonty seems to think the interest in you is genuine. *What*?'

Kim smothered a laugh. 'You've got his number already?'

Jo grinned. 'Of course. I've only got a few more weeks before I'm back in the dungeon. He's coming down to London next week for dinner, a West End show, whatever.'

Kim waved to the skipper of a passing boat. She enjoyed the slow pace on the canal but the rush of a big story was addictive.

The sound of smashing glass made them both glance at the boat in front of them.

'I thought it was empty,' she whispered.

Kim nodded. 'I was sure I saw a curtain move while I was eavesdropping on Viner, but the police knocked several times and got no answer.'

'The owner might be deaf, or a hermit,' Jo said.

'Or a deaf hermit. Probably a lot of them around here,' Kim said. *Booksman*, however, did not look a hermit boat, whatever that might mean. It was clean as a whistle; everything glowed. There was no clutter on the exterior; no bicycles, pot plants or washing.

She somehow knew the owner wasn't a cliched recluse: grungy, old, cantankerous. So why would they be hiding? Unless the person on board wasn't the owner.

The answer stuck as her phone rang. She stared at the boat as she answered. 'Hello, Kim Prescott speaking.'

She thumped Jo on the thigh, pointed to their neighbour and mouthed one word: Hackett.

Jo's hand went to her mouth. She was bouncing.

'Hi, Kim, it's Charlotte Tanner at the BBC in Oxford.'

Kim had to put a restraining hand on her friend's leg.

'Hi, Charlotte.' Kim slid off the roof, and indicated Jo should follow her inside. She put her phone on speaker.

'They were a couple of great reports. Very professional and a huge boost for us. The cops have been tight-lipped. We had no idea there was a bigger mystery involved.'

'Oh yes, it's been quite the saga in Australia, this time around for about a month. But the whole story goes back six years, and another then three decades before that to European bus tour in the 1980s.'

"Really?'

'The body in the canal on Saturday night is the eighth connected to the case that we know about. Apart from Mitch Stevens in Hampstead, there's another two men who survived attacks – one from a crossbow; and who had a beer barrel smashed into his head.'

'My God! This is pure gold. We had no idea how big it was. We honestly thought the Hampstead thing was a Russian mafia hit. It's truly connected to last night?'

Kim gave Charlotte the cliff notes of the whole story leaving out spy theories.

'This is explosive, Kim. Much more complicated than we can ever present for our audience in a news story. I'll need to speak to my editor and London.' Charlotte cleared her throat. 'I am empowered to offer you some freelance work in a few weeks. We have two staff members going on maternity leave. But this is too spicy to leave you out there for other media to snap up. You're a good current affairs reporter and I'm sure working for the BBC would look great on your resume.'

'I'm definitely interested.' Kim did a fist pump. Jo grinned.

'Okay. I'll get back to you within an hour. Our original deal was for the use of our crew to share your story. I think our radio guys would like a report for lunchtime. They'll pay you too.'

'Sounds good to a traveller.'

'Please don't feel that you have to share everything with them.' Charlotte laughed. 'I can see a long format program in this material. My bosses need to discuss the right fit. I'm hoping you can maybe come into the studio tomorrow?'

'I'm keen, Charlotte. And I know how to protect a story from my own colleagues. It's a shark tank in Australian media too.'

Another hearty laugh from Charlotte. 'Does that mean you have more information?'

'I think I can conjure another exclusive – or two.' Kim glanced at Jo, then lifted her chin at the *Booksman*.

Jo nodded and grinned.

Chapter 66

'In breaking news, there's been a stunning twist in the case of the body found in the Oxford Canal. Police have confirmed the victim was shot in what they now believe to be a case of mistaken identity. An Australian television reporter has revealed her former Melbourne employer, Andrew Hackett, was the likely target. This report from Kim Prescott.'

Morgan gripped the cushion tighter. The reporter's every word pierced him like a stiletto; his second failure was being broadcast to the world. He had been expecting it, but it didn't soften the pain of letting Amy down again.

He was listening to Kim's radio report. She believed Hackett was having a sneaky ale at the pub, thinking he was off the radar, and someone stole his TV crew jacket.

He flung the cushion against the wall, wishing it was a plate. Or Kim Prescott.

He moved from the couch to his screens.

'Let's see if she did any TV for the BBC, Amy. And no doubt good old *Spotlight* will have a feature.'

He found Stephanie Grant's report and the cross to Kim the Channel 5 website. He frowned as Kim walked past the boat he'd admired the night he set up the cameras at Tara's. What a coincidence if Kim and her mates were travelling on *Booksman*.

'No, that's just window dressing, Amy. The reporter in the middle of the action. Pick something nice for the background.'

The report provided little comfort and no information about where Hackett might be. Morgan was back to square one; but with two hits, both botched. At least the canal man was dead, there was nobody to identify him.

'What will your father do now, Amy? Run or stay put?'

Morgan walked a circuit of the lounge.

'And what about Mitch Stevens? Can I take the risk of following Tara to the café meeting?

'Hackett *is* the priority. I don't believe he's left the county. And he won't be silly enough to go out for another beer. Probably thinks that's how I found him, on CCTV.'

That thought lifted Morgan's spirits.

'He's going to be jittery, Amy. He knows I'm close. He has to stay until the Paris trip, for which he'll need to surface to organise.

'I promise you, Amy, he won't get away next time. I will get him to St Brendans.'

CHAPTER 67

'Come on, Jo,' whispered Kim. 'You keep watch on the path while I flush him out.'

Kim stepped under the bow canopy of *Booksman*, then waited for a thumbs up from her friend. She hammered on the saloon door.

'Andrew, open up. We know you're hiding in there.'

Hackett had sabotaged her foreign correspondent plans; he was now fair game to advance her new reporting career.

There was no response, or sound from inside the cabin. Kim checked with Jo again. The path was still empty.

She knocked again. 'I can keep this up all day, Andrew. You know how persistent I am. And you're not my favourite person. What do I care if your killer walks past? We'll have a camera on standby.'

That was cruel. But necessary. Another two knocks; her knuckles were getting sore.

'The killer must know by now he got the wrong man. But he also knows you're here somewhere. And, no doubt, that your daughter is nearby.'

Kim knew she was being brutal. Hackett's ego would be battling with his fear and his anger. Which would trigger him?

She raised her fist again – as the door opened.

'Enough, you bitch!' Hackett hissed. 'Get in here before you get us all killed.'

Kim waved Jo to clamber aboard. Hackett shut the door behind them.

'Look out for glass on the floor. I couldn't clean it up while you were lounging around the back of your boat gloating like a peahen.' He gingerly stepped over the debris and retrieved a pan and brush from the kitchen.

'A peahen?' Kim said, as she checking out Hackett's lair. She'd seen five-star hotels that were less salubrious.

Jo nodded her approval too. 'If you fancy swapping boats, Andrew, I'll be happy to skipper this for a few weeks. Draw the killer away from you, so to speak.'

'How long have you been on board?' Kim asked, taking advantage that Hackett was still rattled.

'Three nights.' He dumped the broken glass in a bin.

'Who else knows you're here?'

'Sebastian – Tara's husband.' Hackett winced. 'And Tara. She caught me by surprise on the weekend. Wanted somewhere to stash my ex-wife and her boyfriend.'

'Is it their boat, or did Sebastian rent it for you?'

'It belongs to his uncle. He's on holiday in America.'

'So no card transactions, or paperwork to connect them or you to this boat.' Kim nodded. 'It was a good move.'

'Yes. It was perfect until you and your TV crew alerted half the world and then you almost smashed my door down.'

The familiar belligerence had returned; Hackett's ego needed to be punctured again.

'You were lucky to stay hidden this long. The killer obviously knows you're here.'

Kim watched Hackett bite back a retort. Good. Keep him on the back foot. 'How did his murder victim end up with Dugal's jacket?'

'Stole it from me.'

'After you pinched it from Dugal's cupboard,' said Jo.

'It was Channel 5 property. I needed it.'

'Then you lost it.' Jo wouldn't back down either. 'Why the hell were you in the pub?'

Hackett raised a defiant chin. 'I was going stir crazy.'

'After two days? Fuck, how did you cope during lockdown?'

'What are you going to do next?'

'I don't know because I've no idea if the psycho has left the area after another shooting fuck-up, or if he's hanging around waiting for me to raise my head like I'm in a game of Whack-a-Mole.'

'Okay. I have a solution that could help.'

Hackett looked dubious.

'The BBC are very keen on the story – and I need a new job. You're going to be my first exclusive interview.'

'Fuck off, Kim. I did an interview a few days ago for Stephanie and that didn't help one bit. No way. You won't be able to hide the fact I'm on a narrowboat.'

'True but he won't know what boat or where. You could be on the move for all he knows. Already long gone from Thrupp. We can even plant that seed.'

'An interview will to help both of you,' Jo said.

'How? The BBC will love Kim; the killer will know for sure I'm on a canal boat.'

'Among thousands of boats that are chugging all over England every day,' Kim stressed.

Hackett didn't respond; Kim took that as acceptance.

'Come on, Jo. I'll call the producer and see if they can get Jonty and Asif back here this afternoon.'

They headed for the bow door, without giving Hackett a chance to object. 'I'll knock quietly next time, Andrew. Make sure you let us in.'

As they clambered off the side Jo said, 'Did The Hatchet actually growl at you?',

'Both of us.' Kim led the way back into the *Moriarty*.

'So, my friend, what about *Spotlight*? Are you going to tell Mac and Curly you found Hackett?'

'I was going to call him after I spoke to Charlotte in Oxford. But I can't call or text them, or her. We have to presume all our phones are still compromised. Riley-Simon wormed his way into Channel 5. If I tell Mac I'm about to interview Hackett, he will pounce. We'll have to find another way to arrange things.' Kim stared at her phone which wasn't particularly acting like a smart device.

'Also, I bluffed Hackett to get the interview, but I don't want to risk getting him killed.'

'Don't worry,' Jo said. 'I have a solution.'

Dugal popped his head out of the cabin. 'Good, you're back. Can I get you coffees?'

Kim smiled. 'Yes, please. I'll have it white with a side order of your camera.'

Chapter 68

'Good old Collingwood forever,
They know how to play the game.
Side by side we stick together –'

'What the fuck is that noise?'

Mac snatched the phone, muted the footy club anthem ring tone and rolled to the side of the bed; not fast enough to avoid a push in the back that would have made 100,000 rabid fans roar at the MCG on grand final day.

'Sorry, darling. I'll take it downstairs.'

'Don't wake the kids.'

It was 2.10am, the number was unfamiliar. Most would suspect a scammer in Nigeria; Mac didn't hesitate to answer as he stepped outside the master bedroom in Beaumaris and headed for the kitchen.

'Hey, Boss.'

'Jo. Where are you? What's wrong?'

'Nothing. I'm in the pub.'

Mac rubbed a hand through his ragged ginger mane. 'Jeezus, Jo. I don't need to know you're celebrating Kim's new job in the middle of my night. You woke Kerrie. I'll be in the spare room for a week.'

'Don't be a sook. I'm ringing about something important.'

Mac grunted and opened the fridge door and found cold beef sausages on a plate.

'Okay, what's so crucial that you're ringing from a pub landline?' He took a bite and chewed. He'd thought the girls would wait until a civilised hour to ring. Jo had rung a mate who worked at her vet's surgery to call another random friend who then walked into Channel 5 and give Mac strict instructions about buying a pre-paid phone.'

'First, confirm that you paid for the phone with cash.'

'I couldn't get away from the office; I asked Kerrie to buy one on the way home from work. I told her not to use the card. Then I rang the number your mate gave me. As you know. What have you got that can't wait until morning?'

'An interview with The Hatchet from his new hideaway.'

'You little beauties! How did you find him?'

'Let's say that he was nearby.'

'So, the killer was on the right path, so to speak?'

'Yep.'

'What does Andrew have to say about the poor guy being the victim of mistaken identity?'

'Not much. I suspect Hackett reckons it was justice for having to walk home in the rain.'

'He's a callous one, our Hatchet. What did Kim get out of him?'

'Nothing much that's new for Australian audiences. He didn't want to talk about how he got to the hiding place, or where it is, naturally. But Kim guilted him on the fact that he's escaped two killers, and other people are dying because he's in hiding. That made him defensive; I would call it a combative interview. We should call him Boris – he's like a greased piglet.'

Mac laughed at the popular epithet for the former British PM. '

'I assume Kim did the interview for the BBC? International rights mean several local channels will get automatic access.'

Mac couldn't begrudge his star reporter, maybe former reporter, for angling for something good in a new market.

'Yes. But she's Kim and still loyal. She recorded a separate interview with Dugal's mini cam, and a microphone from the BBC crew. We'll drop you the footage. There's enough difference between the two to give you breaking news highlights.

'She naturally had to do a lot more background about Tugga's Mob for the BBC audience. The local producers are excited; they're talking about making a longer format program.'

'That's great news for Kim. When do I get my story?'

'Dugal hitched a ride with the BBC crew to Oxford, then caught a train to London. He'll have the vision done and dusted by now. It will beat you to work.'

'That's all worth being woken up in the middle of the night.' His stomach growled. He grabbed another sausage.

'I'm guessing this is going to cost me.'

'Yep. Let me add it up: one freelance reporter, a camera and operator, and one production manager – all at international rates.'

'But you work for me!'

'Do you want me to include the breaking-the-holiday rate?'

'No.'

'Okay. I estimate that will cost you two days rental on my narrow boat. I can't move it anyway.'

'Why not?'

'I'm losing my crew. Dugal is in London and the BBC wants Kim to hang around. I've got nobody to work the locks to get *Moriarty* back to its owner. Hackett said he'll be sneaking off to Paris in two or three days.'

'If the killer doesn't find him before then,' Mac said.

'Then you'll have a bigger story.'

'We so will.'

Jo snorted. 'Poor Hackett.'

'Have you seen Mitch Stevens or Hackett's ex-wife?'

'No. Should we? We have been on a canal boat remember.'

'And you've still managed to find everyone else. And another dead person.'

'True.'

'Anyway, apparently he's being discharged today, um, your Monday, and rumour has it they're heading Oxford way.'

'By rumour I assume you mean Ferdy Ackerman.'

'Of course. Curly reckons Mitch is sick of being stalked and might be making himself a tethered goat.'

'Why?'

'To draw out the killer.'

CHAPTER 69

The bowl of chicken tikka masala went cold on Morgan's lap as he watched Kim Prescott's BBC segment. The bitch had found Andrew Hackett again and used his clipped answers to deliver a concise summary of the saga to a new audience.

The murder on the canal was now firmly connected to eight deaths from New Zealand to Oxford. The Met police would be taking the whole interconnected story way more seriously now.

Morgan leaned closer to the screen. Hackett was subdued compared to his defiant display during the London interview with Stephanie Grant.

'Look at his eyes, Amy! He's stressed, probably drinking more than usual. Maybe struggling to sleep. That leads to rash decisions.'

Kim and her interviewee were below deck on an opulent canal boat. Naturally they never announced their location or the boat's name, and the engine was obviously running, so they *might* be on the move.

'Kim even said bon voyage and wished him a safe passage. He could be up in the Midlands, or somewhere along the Thames River or any*bloody*where.'

'But, while that suggestion clears her conscience, Amy, I think they're bluffing. He's not going anywhere. What's more he hasn't been anywhere. Look at those stuffed bookshelves: not your average paperbacks there. They are beautifully bound hardcovers. That's the collection of a true bibliophile.

'And what would that person call their narrowboat, Amy? They're on the sleek green and gold vessel I admired on the way to Tara's. Hackett has been hiding out on the *Booksman*.'

He stood and dumped his curry in the bin.'Your father is a sitting duck. The question now is: do I get the gun and shoot him on the boat, or take the risk of abducting him?

'Can we get what we've been dreaming about?'

Morgan's eyes misted. He wiped them with a shirtsleeve.

'Either way he needs to understand what he's done. The bastard needs to know everything, Amy.'

It was twilight; Morgan would have to wait another two hours to safely retrieve his pistol.

'Okay my love, unless we have no choice, I *will* get him to St Giles.'

Chapter 70

Kim and Jo had also watched her report on the BBC current affairs program, from the pub. The patrons were paying close attention, because it was one of theirs who'd died in the canal, but their gaze kept swivelling between the TV and the two Aussies.

Victor, one of the elderly barflies, had earlier loudly pointed them out. He'd seen Kim and the crew on the canal. Questions galore were fired at her after the program ended. Their quiet hamlet had turned into crime central and they wanted to know everything.

Except Victor, who said,'So eight bodies have been dumped in the canal then. That's bad for tourism.'

Kim's lone attempts to correct the record were overwhelmed by a debate on how the story might *attract* more tourists over the coming weeks.

Jo, meanwhile, was huddled with Jonty. The camera operator appeared equally smitten.

An incoming call from Charlotte gave Kim a chance to escape the throng. She waved her phone and stepped outside to hear.

'I trust you've seen our program, Kim. Your interview and background gave our viewers fabulous context for the Canal Killer.'

'Ha, so he's earned a catchy moniker already,' Kim laughed, as she wandered towards a low stone wall near the carpark entrance beside the pub. She sat down and took in the twilight view of the canal, where the water was still and reflecting a multitude of boat lights.

'One of the tabloids anointed him,' Charlotte said. 'It will do until we get a proper ID.'

Kim wondered if she should reveal Nathan's suspicion about Riley-Simon being a former spook. No. She had to track down Pete's brother first to try for some kind of confirmation. Even if it was just a rumour running through the intelligence services.

'I know you're supposed to be on a holiday, but can you stay in the area for us until at least Wednesday? We can find you accommodation if necessary.'

'Our narrowboat is fine, thanks Charlotte. My skipper has managed to squeeze the cost of a few days rental out of our – well, my former producer. And Channel 5's London correspondent and her cameraman will be back tomorrow. I'm surplus to *their* requirements, but free for anything you need to develop the story.'

'That's outstanding news. You've been setting the agenda – do you have any new angles in mind?'

A car approached from around the bend and Kim expected it to ease into the pub carpark. But the BMW sedan, travelling slowly, instead carried on to the end of the road where Kim knew there were some self-catering cottages and dozens of canal boats.

The car's occupants did not see her, which was lucky, because Kim saw them.

Tara Bancroft was driving: Marianne Hackett was in the front passenger seat; and Mitch Stevens was in the back.

'Kim? Are you still there?'

'Yes, Charlotte, sorry. I was thinking.' Kim smiled. 'And I might have a new lead to explore first thing in the morning.'

'You are the gift that keeps on giving, Ms Prescott. Jonty only lives a few miles away. I can send him early if you can confirm a story.'

'I can give him the heads-up, Charlotte. He's still at the pub with us.' Kim didn't elaborate on the likelihood the BBC camera operator might be sleeping much closer to the canal tonight.

'Excellent. We'll talk tomorrow.' Charlotte hung up.

As for the new lead, if Mitch Stevens refused to appear on camera, Kim would offer the possible spy connection. The BBC would surely have some contacts.

It was a ballsy move for Mitch to seek refuge here. Or was Curly right with his theory about Mitch wanting to lure Riley-Simon out?

Jo had shared that info over dinner, in between lusting after

Jonty. Kim had agreed the former SAS soldier would want to tackle the threat head-on.

Kim headed back inside, wondering if Mitch also had a covert squad of mates already in place here to provide backup. They *were* surveillance and camouflage experts, so there could be a platoon lurking in the hedges.

Regardless, Mitch's arrival here was promising. Once Kim found him, she could help announce his presence to the killer. If that was what he was up to.

She was about to open the pub door when the phone rang again. It was the *Spotlight* program theme.

Kim turned around and walked back to the carpark.

Chapter 71

Channel 5 production assistant, Carla Olson, was nursing a herbal tea as Pete Benson arrived in the dungeon. A steaming Collingwood mug sat in front of Mac's empty chair at the command post. It was rare for a reporter to beat the program producer into the office.

Pete eyed the coffee.

'I wouldn't touch that. Mac called while crossing Kingsway three minutes ago. He'll be here by 9.10.'

Pete shrugged, slung his bag on a desk and draped his suit jacket over a chair.

'I'll make you one.' Carla smiled and headed for the kitchen.

'Thanks, you are a treasure.'

Benson booted up his computer. He had returned late the night before with a cracker yarn from Mildura. He wanted to view Kenny's footage before the production meeting to verify his pitch for an end of bulletin feature: with an extra two minutes.

He checked his emails first. The single message was innocuous; a reminder that performance reviews were coming up. These personal assessments were so frequent these days it was like corporate spam.

But, the spelling of the name of the cheery human resources woman alerted Pete. Tracey spelt as Tracy, was the code for him to check a special number; one he couldn't use via the Channel 5 server, or his company phone.

Pete retrieved his personal mobile from his bag, accepted the coffee from Carla, and headed into the empty edit suite. This phone wasn't registered in his name, and he didn't even know who paid for the service. His brother Adrian had organised it before leaving for London, suggesting there might be situations where they could only communicate on the sly. They'd already done so a few times over the months; the last when Pete had told him about the possible secret agent link, and asked him to touch base with Kim.

Pete kept his eyes on the office and pressed the only number in the contact list. It was answered within 20 seconds.

"Well well, your mystery gunman has certainly upped the ante over here.' Adrian was not one for small talk.

'Yeah, and can you believe our very own Cadaver Crew were right in the middle of it.'

'The whole death by mistaken identity means you're in luck. The powers that be do not want a gunman wandering the canals looking for random prey.'

'But it *was* okay when he was after another Aussie, they didn't need to care about?' Pete said.

'Anyway, brother of mine, the back channels have been buzzing all day.'

'The tip was right – he's a spook?'

'I did not say that, *Peter*. And you'll never get any comment from anyone at MI6 about his previous employment. In the tech stroke early cyber arena.'

'Well thank you so much for not telling me that. Will you consider giving Kim a call?'

'Perhaps. In time.'

Pete noticed Mac had arrived and was waving at him with expansive gestures. Pete held up three fingers. 'Okay, bro. We'll talk soon. Time to let know Mac know Riley-Simon, as we've been calling this guy, is a double-oh gone troppo. Not that I heard that from anyone I know.'

Adrian laughed. 'Hang on, Pete; I haven't *not* shared the best stuff yet the MI bods wanted me to not share.'

'What?'

'Name and photo.'

'Fuck, bro! Why didn't you lead with that? Who is he? When do I get the picture?'

'Photo on the way. Not an official one because the source would be too obvious. His name is Morgan Handley. And he was booted from the service for being, well, a bit dangerous.'

Pete snorted. 'Isn't that a prerequisite for being a spy? Cold, calculating, deadly and mysterious.'

'But not reckless and delusional. Got the impression Handley is quite the sociopath.'

'What other impressions did they not give you?'

'Nothing,' Adrian said. 'But I followed up on his name. He did a computer science degree at Oxford, where his tutors considered him a genius. I'm betting that's what got him into Six.'

'That explains a lot.' Pete said. 'We knew he'd burrowed into our systems here; and hacked into the devices of everyone connected to Hackett.'

Pete's phone dinged. He opened the attachment.

Morgan Handley was a handsome guy in his mid-30s, with wavy, beach-blond hair. He looked more Aussie than English. 'When was it taken?'

'Three years ago at Athens Airport'

Pete whistled. 'You guys have a long reach. We knew he'd been in and out of New Zealand using his other IDs.'

'Righto. That's all I've got,' Adrian said. 'As I said, the back channels have been working overtime the past 24 hours. I will owe a shitload of favours. But everyone wants this guy stopped and you're the lucky reporter to set things in motion; with the name and photo given to you by an anonymous source.'

'Naturally. And thanks Adrian.'

Pete stared at the photo of Morgan Handley. He *could* walk out the door and delight his producer with an exclusive. He wouldn't have to reveal his source, but this scoop would confirm the rumours, accidentally started by him, that he had his own spook in the family. There was a much better option, even if it meant losing the exclusive.

He checked the edit suite phone; Kim was still on speed dial. He glanced at the row of international clocks on the wall. It was just before 9 pm in England. He pressed the number.

'Hello, Melbourne,' Kim said.

'Hello canal boat. Or pub. It's Pete here. I hear you've got both feet in the door at the Beeb already.'

'Oh yeah, mate. They're frothing about the Canal Killer and and finally lapping up the backstory.'

'Awesome. Now, I've just spoken with my contact in the services. He can't meet with you but – and I'm only giving you this to keep him one step from me – he says Nathan was right.'

'Wow,' Kim said. 'So Riley-Simon is/was a spy?'

'*Was* in their early cyber division. And his real name is Morgan Handley. I will send you a mugshot soon. I can't send it direct from my mobile because of the only name in my contacts; whom I do not want this psycho going after him.'

'Mate, you are my hero.'

Pete sighed. Kim would never give away an exclusive.

'Are you sure you don't want to break this yourself, tonight?

'We can share it, in a roundabout way. I will tell Mac I got this info from *you*. Then we can both make use of it.'

'Honestly Pete, I can't thank you enough.'

'Yeah well, this'll make Mac's day; and the BBC will love you. Talk soon.'

Pete transferred the photo of Morgan Handley to his private email folder. He used the terminal in the edit suite to dump it in a *Spotlight* program file, and sent copies to Mac and Curly. He sent the image separately to Kim. Then he slipped his phone into a pocket and exited the edit suite with a huge grin.

'Mac,' he said. 'Check your inbox. We have a name and mugshot for Hackett's vigilante. Riley-Simon – the most wanted man in two countries – is really Morgan Handley, ex-MI6 spy.'

Mac stood up. Sat down. Jiggled his mouse. Then roared with pleasure. 'How, where the hell did you get this, Pete?'

'Can't claim credit, Boss. Kim sent it to me because I'd given her the *possible* lead in the first place. Sorry, I told her last week I'd overhead Nathan saying something about Riley being a spy.'

Mac squinted at Pete. 'So you've both been holding out on me?'

'We wanted to confirm it, Boss'

'Yeah right,' Mac said. 'Righto, fill me in.'

Curly arrived mid-explanation so Pete had to start again.'

"Righto,' Mac finally said. 'Go write this up for the Morning News in an hour, and for *Spotlight* tonight, Pete. Two versions; you know the drill.'

Curly grinned at Mac. 'We are flush with good news today. We can combine this with a grab from Kim's interview with Hackett from his bolthole on the canal.'

'Indeed. Nice of her to share that with us, while keeping major secrets,' Mac said drily.

Chapter 72

A crowbar couldn't separate Jo and Jonty in their booth at the back of the bar. The'd barely touched their wine. Kim smirked. She was about to dash their hopes of a tryst on the *Moriarty*. Their boat was about to be become an impromptu newsroom.

'Hey guys, sorry to break up the huddle – but I've got important news.'

Jo frowned as Kim slid in beside them and lowered her voice.

'We have Riley-Simon-Spyface's real name; confirmation he was with MI6; and a better photo.'

Jonty was instantly all business. 'We need to get that on air. And we'll have to tell local police. How reliable is your source?'

'Rock solid. And I'm guessing the cops already know.'

'Great. I'll go get my camera from the van, and call Charlotte to see how she'll want to handle it. Are you up for an evening television cross? We can set it up for 9.45; 10 pm at the latest. Your boat, okay?'

'Absolutely.'

Jo's new beau kissed her on the cheek, said, 'To be continued, eh?' and headed oustide.

Jo's frown turned to a death glare. 'Brilliant. Couldn't this revelation have waited until morning?'

'Oh sure, just sit on it for 12 hours, Kim, while your best friend bonks a Pommy camera guy at the pointy end of the boat you're all sharing!'

Jo feigned a guilty expression. 'So, what's Simon's real name?'

'Riley's real name is Morgan Handley.' Kim showed her the photo that had come through from Pete while she was taking a quick pee on the way back to the table.

'That's a much better photo of Riley-Simon-Morgan,' Jo said. 'He is going to be so pissed off about being outed. Did you get this from Pete's brother? Did he finally ring?'

'Yes. No.' Kim shook her head. 'Info from the brother via Pete. And hopefully the photo will help the cops track him down before he makes another attempt on Hackett or Mitch. Speaking of the hunky bodyguard I have another surprise.'

'You are full of them tonight,' Jo said.

'Don't be a grouch. You'll have another chance with the spunky Jonty.'

Jo gave an expectant shrug.

'I saw Mitch Stevens drive past the pub.'

'When?'

'While I was talking to Charlotte and before Pete rang. Maybe 15 minutes ago. He was with Marianne and Tara.'

'That's risky. Do you think they were headed to Tara's?'

'Nope, opposite direction,' Kim pointed. 'I think it's a dead end; just a few cottages and more boats.'

'How freaky is that?' Jo said. '*Morgan*'s two targets might be moored within shouting distance of each other.'

'And Tara, at least, knows where her father is.'

'What are you going to do about them?'

'Nothing tonight.' Kim looked at her empty wine glass. No more alcohol; she had news reports to record, and a reputation to establish.

'We first need to focus on getting Morgan's name and photo broadcast as widely as possible. We can look for Mitch and Marianne tomorrow.'

Jo smiled. 'Good idea. And I think Jonty should base himself on our boat for the next few days – just in case there's a shootout on the canal for him to film.' She waved back at Jonty who was waving at them from the door.

'Yeah, right,' Kim said. 'Of course he should. Time to go to work.'

Chapter 73

The second bottle of Macallan was almost empty. Fuck Cedric; he could sue Hackett's estate for the $500. Or did he have time to consume the third bottle before departure – or death – beckoned?

Whisky had been Hackett's only company since resuming the hermit existence on *Booksman*. Kim and Jo had stayed clear, as agreed, after the interview. This vessel had to appear empty to anybody walking the towpath.

Hackett had not expected loneliness to weigh more heavily than the silence. He was seriously depressed. It wasn't like him. It must be the booze.

And a killer stalking you!

Even the financial news via his smartphone couldn't hold his interest. That in itself was telling. Making money was his prime reason for getting up every day. Had been since uni.

But he realised none of that mattered if he was gunned down by deranged pschyo lunatic. There would be no comfort in leaving large inheritances for his children. He was way too young for all his hard work and astute management to benefit others.

He snorted. Except Marianne. There was certainly nothing extra for her. She'd already squeezed him during the divorce despite her being the unfaithful spouse.

His own dalliance did not count. He'd had no intention of leaving Marianne for any of them.

And now the annoying drip-drip from the tap into the paper microwave packet he'd left in the sink *was driving him crazy*. He stomped into the kitchen before remembering movement like that might literally rock the boat. He vented his frustration by ripping the packet into pieces.

Hackett returned to the armchair and resumed his maudlin thoughts. Would Kim's interview work to throw his stalker off the scent?

The girls had only found him because he broke a tumbler. Otherwise, he'd be sitting in the dark going quietly mad without anyone – friend or foe – knowing, or caring, where he was.

Hackett found it strange to be on the back foot in negotiations, especially when it came to news and current affairs staff. Not that he had a say in what they covered. But he controlled the Channel 5 budgets and squeezing departmental balls was easy, and fun.

The 'content creators' would spend every cent the channel made if Hackett didn't keep a tight rein on them. His nickname as The Hatchet was well-earned. And he even liked it.

Fuck it. This is achieving nothing. He need to get out of here. He'd flirted with the idea of bribing Jo and Kim to let him travel with them. He knew the *Moriarty* had to be returned to Braunston soon, and that was kilometres north of Oxford. He could hide below deck and let them do the work.

He'd soon nixed the idea. He doubted he could tolerate a day, let alone three with the Channel 5 minions.

The walls were closing in. He'd reached the end. He would return to London in the morning. Or ask Tara to drive him to Manchester so he could catch a plane.

He emptied the last three fingers of whisky into his glass, downed a couple of sleeping tablets he'd found in Cedric's bathroom and threw himself on the unmade bunk in the stern.

Chapter 74

A power cable snaked from the pub across the carpark to the impromptu BBC studio space the team had set up outside. They'd decided against using the *Moriarty*'s interior.

Kim was buzzing. She'd enhanced her UK profile with another late news exclusive: the alleged Canal Killer's name and photo.

Jonty and Jo were busy packing the lights and camera back into his van, leaving Kim to field questions from the three drinkers, pints in hand, who'd watched her live cross.

'You're certain that's the prick who shot our Malcolm?'

'Allegedly, yes,' Kim said. 'A jury, as you know, will ultimately decide the truth of that which is why, guys, I stressed the police want to talk to him in relation to the shooting. Now, I'd better go help my colleagues pack up.'

Jo smirked as she joined them 'Are they asking for your autograph yet? You'll need an agent after the day you've had.'

'Are you offering?' Kim sat down on the van step just as her phone pinged. 'I expect mates rates.'

'Hollywood texting already?'

'Nathan,' Kim said, checking her watch. It was 9.15, which meant 10.15 tomorrow morning at home. 'Mac would've run a matching piece on the Channel 5 morning news.'

Kim hit the phone rather than text option for Nathan.

'Oh,' Jo said, oblivious. 'Jonty has been told they need the two of you for the breakfast news tomorrow. I suggested he stay on Moriarty tonight. I could charge the Beeb for his accommodation.'

Nathan Potter was greeted with loud laughter when he answered her call on the far side of the world.

Chapter 75

Morgan had stripped, cleaned and reassembled his Sig Sauer after retrieving the pistol and suppressor from the graveyard; and filled two magazines with 9mm rounds.

He and his weapon were ready for action.

Kim Prescott's latest news report had stirred both him up and then motivated him.

'I've been betrayed by the bastards at MI6, Amy. That is the only way she and her irritating cronies could have unmasked me. Not that it matters, the real me no longer exists anywhere else.

'This simply means we go tonight. Your father will die before sunrise'.

Morgan placed his weapon in the small daypack on the table, then added a roll of silver gaffer tape, six nylon cables, a lockpick gun, a tension tool, a coil of narrow nylon rope and a filthy rag.

It was well past midnight and cloudy. Morgan had already packed his clothes, computers and other gear into his car. When he left the cottage for the last time tonight, he'd never be back.

'Once I'm done with your father, we are out of here, Amy.'

The moment Hackett's body was found at the church, most likely first thing tomorrow, the cops would be swarming the district, searching every building.

'The police won't find us, Amy.' He ran his hand through his black hair, dyed that afternoon to match his next passport.

'Pick up the new car in Oxford at lunch time and head for the car ferry from Dover. We'll be in Southern France by Wednesday. Thursday at the latest. Once we hit Europe there'll be no hurry at all.

'Mitch Stevens can stew for a few months. Unless I find him on the boat with Hackett. Bloody unlikely given the whole fucking Marianne thing. But if he is there, I will shoot the fucker in the face before dragging Hackett, bound and gagged, back to the car.'

Morgan had no doubts Amy's father was on the *Booksman* and, contrary to Kim's attempt at misdirection, still moored in Thrupp.

He lovingly stroked the crossbow before taking it from its wall rack and putting it a canvas case along with two bolts.

Morgan would be so very close to Hackett when he fired. The man would be dead in a literal heartbeat – just as Amy intended.

He slung the bow case on one shoulder, his day pack on the other and let himself out of the cottage. His first destination was 400 yards across the fields, towards Thrupp, beyond the ruins of an Elizabethan manor house and into the grounds of the humble but centuries-old St Brendan's Church. The current minister was going to get a hell of a shock come morning.

Morgan opened the unlocked side door and stepped inside. He placed the crossbow, bolts and nylon rope behind the altar. He transferred the Sig to his inside coat pocket.

Next stop: Hackett's boat. He joined a narrow grassy tree-lined track for the 400-yard walk alongside an offshoot of the Cherwell Canal, where his unsuspecting quarry was hopefully sleeping. He made a beeline for the pedestrian bridge, then walked nonchalantly past the spot where he'd shot the man in Hackett's TV jacket.

Not that there was anyone around to see him.

'I'm going silent from here, Amy.' he whispered. 'I know you're with me.'

Morgan hugged the towpath shadows until he reached the *Booksman*, with its curtains drawn against the night, and prying eyes. He was pretty sure Hackett would be sleeping in the stern. In Kim's interview with him, he was sitting in a wingback chair beside a log burner in a timber and bookshelf-lined saloon. The chimney just above the bow's door confirmed the layout.

He slipped onto the front of the boat and inspected the door; it had a mortice lock, as suspected. Easy pickings; in theory.

He eased his pack off and took out the lockpick gun. It was efficient, but could be noisy as the trigger had to be pulled 12 to14 times to move the pins. He also had to insert a tension tool in the keyway to rotate the plug.

He felt no movement from inside *Booksman*, but took out his Sig and laid it on the ground within reach. He needed two hands for the lock. It took eight noisy seconds to open the lock.

Move! Move! Move! He felt Amy yelling at him.

He grabbed the Sig and was inside in another thee seconds. He closed the door behind him and was immediately assailed by the fug of body odour, booze and unwashed dishes.

Digital lights from a few kitchen appliances lit his way from stem to stern. Narrowboats were, after all, hallways with stuff in them.

He found Hackett in the crumple of a duvet on the bed in the stern; flat on his back and snoring like a congested frog.

Alcohol, or a sleeping tablet, Amy?

Morgan leaned closer and sniffed: whisky. He screwed his nose up. He took the dirty rag and gaffer tape from the pack, and ripped off length of the latter.

The he tapped Hackett's cheek with his gun.

'Wakey wakey, dickhead.'

The snoring stopped as Hackett's eyes snapped open almost as wide as his mouth. With his left hand Morgan shoved the rag in, and taped that mouth shut.

'You can die here right now – or plead for your life on my turf. Your choice.'

CHAPTER 76

Kim stared stupidly at the ceiling of the *Moriarty*. Sleep had taken a walk on the towpath without her, to escape the noisy amorous couple in the bow. They'd finally fallen silent, or asleep, but she was still wide-eyed.

She got up to get a drink and realised she could hear a different weird noise through the open window. It was a series of clicks like someone was using a ratchet.

She knew sound carried a long way over water, but this sounded very close; and who the hell would be racheting anything at this hour. She checked her watch; it was 2.22.

The closest boat was The Hatchet's and they were now stern to his bow. They'd turned their vessel around for the return journey, while they still had Dugal there to help.

The noise had stopped abruptly. Kim stepped quietly to the door of the cruiser stern. The top half was glass, covered by a curtain. Kim nudged it aside. She caught sight of the *Booksman*'s saloon door closing. Okay, maybe Hackett had slipped on deck for some fresh air.

Or – maybe someone else just boarded his damn boat.

The spine chill ran from her neck to her arse and back again. The Hatchet would no more be using a ratchet then singing karaoke Midnight Oil.

Was it Morgan? Was he about to kill Hackett? Kim's legs turned to jelly at the thought she might be responsible for leading the killer right... right... shit, right next door.

A gentle rocking of the boat indicated the lovers were back at it. Kim was torn about disturbing them. Her suspicion was as flimsy as her now damp T-shirt; she was suddenly sweating like her menopausal mother.

Shit. Concentrate.

Kim was about to disturb the love nest for some guidance when she saw a strangely-moving shadow emerging from the *Booksman*.

That's it. Kim dashed to the bow, whisper-shouted to Jo and Jonty to get the hell down the back with her coz there was *big trouble*, then dashed back again.

The weird weird shadow, now on the towpath, resolved into the shape of two men; one was being propelled forward, the other man held him by the scruff.

Her own fear and bad memories spiked – but didn't go off the charts.

Jo was suddenly, mercifully, at her back; Jonty right behind her still pulling his jocks up.

'What's going on?' her best friend in all the world whispered, laying a hand on her back. 'Mate, you are drenched.'

Kim nodded, mumbled 'bit stressed' then said more succinctly, 'I think Morgan just took Hackett off his boat. There,' she pointed.

All three could see two people walking oddly into the treeline just beyond where Malcolm Penney had been shot. Beyond that, they knew was a footbridge, walking paths, open fields and even a railway line.

'I have to follow them,' Kim said, like it was a sensible idea.

'You are bloody not,'

'I have to, Jo. What if it's my fault Morgan found him?'

'What if it is?' Jo demanded.

Kim started frantically dressing.

'Then we're coming too,' Jonty said. He ran back to the bow to grabbed his jeans and shirt, and everything Jo needed, despite her saying, 'We *are*?'

'No. I'm going alone. Jonty, you call the police, tell them the Canal Killer has abducted Hackett. I will follow them, and I'm going right now before I lose them.'

Kim finished lacing her runners. She grabbed her phone, dialled Jo, dropped the mobile in her jacket pocket, and shoved in her earbuds.

As she opened the door, she added, 'I will keep the line open to tell you where I'm going; where I am.'

Jo rolled her eyes and answered her phone. 'How will you know where you are?' she demanded.

Kim retrieved her phone and turned the volume down.

'You two follow me in the van. Somehow. And Jonty make sure your camera is ready. We want to ensure we get good vision if all this comes together at the OK Canal with Morgan, Hackett and the cops.'

'You are fucking insane, Kim.'

'Yes Jo, I believe I am.' She dramatically tapped the scar on her back for good luck.

The whole exchange had taken barely three minutes.

Kim sprinted along the towpath trying to make as little noise as possible while making up ground. There was no one ahead of her, so she left the path on a trail just beyond where she'd last seen the two men.

Morgan obviously had something more than outright murder planned for Hackett, or he would've killed him on the *Booksman*. Kim just had to make sure she didn't run right up their arses.

She crossed, very carefully, a footbridge then took to a grassy path running beside a small tributary of the main Cherwell Canal.

Why the hell was she doing this again? Last time she'd run around the countryside with a deranged killer on the loose, she'd been shot.

She whispered her location and direction to Jo.

'Okay, you loon. We're in the van, and Jonty has rung the cops and got Charlotte out of bed.'

'Think I've spotted them,' Kim said. 'If I don't answer you any time, it's coz I can't.'

She'd never been happier for an almost moon-free night, even if it made it difficult to to see. She'd only noticed movement ahead because Hackett was obviously struggling.

She followed them off the path and across a field, keeping low and as quiet as possible. About five minutes later, suddenly looming out of the dark like a gothic nightmare, came the outline of a building with a tower.

The sound of a door opening and closing, suggested Morgan had dragged Hackett into what turned out to be an old stone church with its own cemetery.

While still about 20 metres away, Kim whispered a description of the church to Jo.

Jonty said, 'Sounds like St Brendan's. We're halfway there. We'll update the police.'

Kim's heartrate spiked. The sensible thing to do now was wait for her friends. And the cops.

As she crept closer to the church, she questioned the whole idea of being sensible.

Chapter 77

'I swear I'm going to–' Jo snarled at Kim. There'd been no talk for a good two minutes which Jo knew meant her friend was doing something really dumb.

'Wait for us, please Kim. If you get shot again, I will kill you. We'll be there in– Jonty says five minutes.'

'I'm in the cemetery,' Kim whispered.

'Gah,' Jo exclaimed.

Kim had circled the church from a distance to confirm there were two entrances. Fear now outweighed daring, as she crouched behind a tombstone six metres from the wooden side door, which didn't look like it had been opened since Queen Victoria sat on the throne.

She wondered, nonetheless, how noisy it would be to open. Or, more importantly, how dangerous would it be.

Kim's heart was fairly hammering as she considered the risk to herself in trying to save the arsehole boss who derailed her career.

She approached the door to at least see if she could hear anything inside. She grasped the handle, turned it–

Damn, the bloody thing was unlocked.

Kim pushed the door ajar but stopped when she heard Riley-Simon-Morgan screaming at Hackett.

CHAPTER 78

Morgan was howling in rage. He wanted to smash something but Amy's father was already a bundle of flesh and bones at his feet. And Morgan had barely touched him.

The stupid bastard had slipped and smacked his head against the octagonal baptismal font.

The very same font where Morgan and Amy would've had their son baptised.

This was not the justice Amy demanded. Morgan booted Hackett in the back, no response. He walked around and kicked him in the guts, nothing. Blood dribbled from Hackett's cheek.

'I can't kill him like this, Amy. He must know who I am, and why I'm avenging you and–'

Morgan choked on the name that could never be mentioned without tears. He kicked Hackett again, in the chest.

Hacket responded with a grunt, then moaned and rolled onto his side.

Morgan ripped off the gaffer tape and unstuffed his mouth – wouldn't do to have him choke on his own vomit – then lifted the lid off the font and splashed holy water all over the stupid prick.

Hackett opened his eyes.

'About time, you bastard. We've been waiting too long.'

Hackett looked around, obviously wondering who the 'we' was.

'You won't find her. But she's here – in spirit.'

'Who?' The voice was croaky, scared.

'Your daughter – Amy. My lover. Your bodyguard turned her into my angel.' Morgan felt his eyes mist. The gun wavered.

Hackett scuttled backwards about six feet. Morgan grabbed him by the ankle and hauled him back. 'Don't even think about it.'

'You're a fucking lunatic.' Hackett lashed out with his feet, landing two kicks on Morgan's shin. He stopped moving the second Morgan put the muzzzle of the gun to his forehead.

'You. Are. Going. To. Die!'

The men stared eye to eye.

'But you will first listen to why you've been sentenced to death.'

'I didn't kill Amy,' Hackett said in desperation. 'I knew nothing about her until the night she tried to kill me. And Mitch shot her. He's the one you want.'

'Ever the fucking hero,' Morgan said.

'Did you hear that, Amy? Daddy is still not taking responsibility.'

'You're a craven coward, Andrew Hackett. It's beyond me how Amy could've been sired by a piece of shit like you.'

'I'm sorry Amy's dead. Truly. I would have supported her – if I'd known she even existed.'

'Just like you supported her mother, your girlfriend Judy, when she was drugged and raped by Tugga and his disgusting mates. What did you do then? Fuck nothing, You abandoned her without a backward glance.'

'*I didn't fucking know*,' Hackett shouted. 'Judy and I were over by then. I was with another girl. Aggh!'

Morgan had janmmed the barrel right between Hackett's eyes.

'Judy was pregnant with your child when she was assaulted by those animals.'

'Again, you lunatic, I did not know.

Morgan fought the urge to pull the trigger. Hackett couldn't die without knowing the full story.

'I need to calm myself, Amy. Get back on track. He's a dirtbag who must know the price we paid.'

He grabbed the nylon rope, dragged Hackett to his feet and onto a chair in front of the stone wall. He tied him to it using only one hand. The gun in his other did not leave Hackett's face.

Morgan's smile when he stepped back and moved behind the altar was snake-like. He was back in the zone

'Oh, fuck no!' Hackett's eyes were filled with horror.

'Fuck, yes.' Morgan walked slowly back to him, loaded crossbow blanced on his left arm. 'Rather appropriate, don't you think?

'I believe Amy pinned you to your back fence. They had to transport you to hospital with the bolt sticking through your shoulder, didn't they?'

Morgan cocked the crossbow. 'It should've wedged in your cold miserable heart.'

Hackett glared. 'You sick fucker.'

Morgan took aim. Hackett was barely two metres away. The bolt would still be accelerating as it tore though his body and rammed into the stone wall behind him.

'This is simply an eye for an eye, Andrew. You escaped Amy's retribution for failing her mother. But you won't escape my vengeance for Amy. And Benjamin.'

'Who the fuck is Benjamin? Is he some bastard son I'm supposed to have fathered? Great, blame me for everyone's fucking problems. Jeezus.'

Morgan sighted the crossbow. 'Benjamin was *my* son, Andrew. Amy's and mine. Your grandchild – until Amy was executed.'

Hackett's shoulders and head slumped. 'Oh, fuck.'

'He was going to be baptised here – like my father, and grandfather. And too many generations before them to count. Morgan almost twitched. Except me. I wasn't considered worthy of that honour, only being a stepson.'

Hackett let go a short laugh. 'What, so Benjamin being baptised here was going to be your redemption? Or a fuck you to your stepfather?'

'Do not talk about my son that way!'

The condemned man straightened. 'The police never said anything about Amy being pregnant.'

'It was in the autopsy report. I hacked into their files. Amy had no other lovers. He was to be my son. He would have been loved and cherished – not ignored.'

Hackett smirked. 'The police knew nothing about you at the time; otherwise you'd be in prison with her crazy Kiwi family. And there was no fucking baby, you deluded whackjob.'

'Shut up!'

'Fuck you. If you're going to kill me for some twisted fucking fantasy, I'm bloody well going to speak. Amy was only in Melbourne for a few weeks. If you ever fucked my daughter, at all, your sprog would've been a sexless tadpole when she died. You're fucking delusional.'

Morgan's lips pursed; he thrust forward with the crossbow. Hackett cringed but wasn't totally cowed; as if he'd accepted his fate.

'We've told him, Amy. He knows why. Time to die, Andrew Hack–'

A loud noise startled both men. Morgan realised the side door was ajar.'

Morgan moved slowly and quietly across the space to the door.

Chapter 79

Jo was sitting in the van with Jonty in the church carpark 10 metres from where her reckless friend was sticking her nose where it seriously did not belong.

She wanted to scream at Kim to get the fuck out of there, that armed police were on the way, but the stupid bitch had disconnected their call. Even Jo wasn't dumb enough to ring her back, in case she didn't have her phone on silent.

A light tap on her window nearly made her wet her pants. She wound it down to glare at the totally-camouflaged, in black from head to toe, SWAT-type guy who was probably not smiling at her right now.

Jo did not waste time, or mince words. She pointed at Kim and said, 'Can you go get my friend please before she gets herself shot again.'

'Can you confirm the shooter is inside?'

'Not 100 per cent. But Kim has been standing at that door for like 10 years, listening to *something*.'

A second commando appeared beside the first. 'Thermal imaging confirms two inside. One over there.'

'For goodness sake, Rambos – go get her out of there.'

CHAPTER 80

Kim's spidey senses overloaded in a millisecond: Morgan stopped talking mid-sentence; and a gloved hand covered her mouth as a very large man lifted her off the ground and backwards to the rear corner of the building. All while whispering, 'Don't struggle, you are safe.'

She then watched as a entire battalion of dark shapes moved into position near the door she'd been spying through only two seconds before.

'Stay put,' her alleged rescuer said, then followed his comrades into the church – all yelling stuff like: *'armed police; put the weapon down now*!'

'Stay put, be buggered,' Kim muttered and headed back to the door, her phone still recording everything, including shouts, thuds, sounds of fighting, and boots scrabbling on stone.

And fabulous video footage of two men wrestling Riley-Simon-Morgan to the flagstones.

The man was not going peacefully. 'Get off me, you bastards. He has to die. I have to avenge Amy. And my son.'

Two of the cops spotted Kim at the door but oddly did not chase her out.

Another two flipped Morgan onto his stomach and secured his hands and feet with flexi cuffs. The man who'd been tormenting Andrew Hackett for weeks was now bound at his victim's feet.

And The Hatchet was *still* complaining. 'You took your sweet time. I was seconds from being impaled by that bloody crossbow.'

'Oh for fuck's sake, Andrew,' Kim said. 'Shut up or I'll beg the these nice policemen to untie Morgan and let him finish the job'.

One of those nice policmen, possibly the same one who'd

grabbed her outside, approached her. Kim shoved her phone in her pocket. 'Not going to confiscate your phone, just want to ask you to stop filming us now please.'

'I'm a journalist caught in a big news story. I have a right to do my job. The police can't stop me doing that.'

'We're not actually police, Miss Prescott.'

'Oh. *Oh.*'

He tapped a thoat mic. 'Target secured. Hostage safe. What do you want us to do?'

'Armed response teams are about five minutes out.'

Kim recognised that Australian voice: Mitch Stevens. 'Make sure target can't escape and leave,' he said.

'You're soldiers,' Kim said. 'Mates of Mitch?'

'Sort of.' His accent was British. 'Off the record, and no further comment.'

'How did you find me? Us?'

'We've been monitoring your phone since your first news report about the guy in the canal.'

Kim grinned. 'Man, we have no privacy these days.'

The mysterious commando went back to Morgan to oversee the process of securing him to a nice sturdy church column. 'You're a lucky boy,' he told him. 'If we didn't have to cut and run, we'd take the time to turn you into pig tucker.'

One of the other not-policemen had untied Hackett. The fool was now getting right in Morgan's face, threatening to used the crossbow on *him*.

'Get back you idiot,' Kim's new friend said, 'Or we'll tie *you* to a pole too. This guy is restrained. You'll be the one locked up for years if the cops find him damaged, or dead when they get here.' He released the crossbow bolt and snapped it easily over his muscular thigh.

'Okay, lads, we are out of here.'

'Thanks for, um, everything," Kim said. 'Andrew, say thank you.'

The Hatchet was still silently glaring at Morgan.

'He's been through at least two ordeals,' she explained. 'He's going to need more therapy.'

Mitch's eight mates flowed out of the church like a well-oiled something.

Kim checked her phone; still recording. Well, only sound for that last exchange. Perhaps she could get more out of Morgan.

A clattering from behind announced the arrival of Jo and Jonty rushing in though the side door.

'Oh shit, Hatchet,' Jo shouted. 'What the hell are you doing?'

Kim turned back to find Andrew Hackett pointing a pistol at Morgan Handley.

'Wait, Andrew, you can't hurt him,' Kim said.

'Hurt him? I'm going to kill him.'

'As the other guy said, he's tied up. That's murder not self defence. The real police will be here any second. He'll go to prison. Don't be stupid.'

'For how long? Ten years? He's completely mad, Kim. He'll come after me again when he gets out. This is the only way. It has to end now.'

'Okay, Morgan will be dead,' Jo said. 'But you'll be the one who suffers in gaol.'

Morgan spoke, his voice raspy. 'Yeah, kill me, you go to prison. Let me live and I hunt you forever. Win-win for me.'

Hackett pushed the suppressor into Morgan's temple. 'Shut up. You don't decide anything anymore.'

He stepped back again, the gun steady. 'And I *won't* get charged with murder.' Hacket was addressing Kim now.

'I'll untie him afterwards and put the crossbow in his hand. I can say I grabbed the gun and shot him in self defence. We'll be the heroes, Kim. Those soldiers obviously don't want the glory, so they'll never contradict us.'

'What about *this* evidence?' Kim waved her phone, which was still recording.

Hackett's blood-streaked face went another shade of pale. 'How much?'

'Everything, Andrew. And, yes Morgan is delusional. I heard him talking to Amy before you came to. I know what this is all about; and what a prize coward you are. This stuff will put him away. And I will not lie for you.'

Hackett swivelled and trained the gun on Kim.

'Don't you fucking dare,' Jo shouted.

And then the real cops were invading the space, shouting: 'Armed police Drop the weapon. Drop the weapon. We will shoot.'

Kim, Jo and Jonty raised their arms in surrender.

Hackett stood there like a fool.

'Drop the weapon, sir.'

Kim glanced over her shoulder. 'It's okay. He's the kidnap victim. Some poachers helped us overpower the killer, before running off.'

'Don't care,' the lead cop said. 'Drop the damn weapon.'

Kim sensed that was Hackett's last chance. She turned back to the most dangerous man in the church. 'Andrew, please put the gun down. We're safe.'

Hackett nodded, dropped the gun to the floor, then stepped quickly and kicked Morgan in the groin.

CHAPTER 81

There was an eerie calm in the *Spotlight* office. The program was half an hour away, yet everything was under control, which unsettled Mac. Nervous energy fuelled news and current affairs so this quiet was strange indeed.

He was sitting at the command post in The Dungeon surveying his small kingdom. Curly sat opposite him, tidying a couple of introductions for Richard Templeton.

Carla delivered them a stubbie of beer each, without a word.

'Only a reporter takes a smartphone to a gun fight.' Mac said.

Curly laughed. 'Only our Kim tackles psychos with a smartphone, you mean. Twice now. And that's not counting The Hatchet as one of the crazy bastards. We better think of something soon, or she's never coming back.'

They had watched the compelling action-filled story Kim had filed for the BBC morning news three times already. The footage from inside the old church, including vision of Hackett and the no-longer elusive Morgan Handley, was rough and raw and rivetting. Her on-camera account of the night's adventure was measured and professional.

Mac was both proud and sad, because Curly was right: she might not come home.

Kim had generously shared the edited vision with Channel 5. They'd used some for the afternoon news, and Kenny was busy in Edit Suite 1 doing his dice and splice to put a package together for *Spotlight*.

Curly's script for Richard, and another live cross to Steph and Kim in Thrupp on Oxford – or wherever they were – would complete the best program they'd put together all year.

Mac's computer began singing with the tell-tale sound of a connecting Skype call. He hit the go button and – speak of the devil – Kim was grinning at him from the other side of the world.

More than grinning, she was almost beside herself.

Jo stuck her head in the frame too and waved. 'Have we got news for you,' she said.

'More news?' Mac asked, as Curly dragged his chair over.

'Weird news,' Kim said.

Mac waved his hands. 'Well, spill.'

'I just had a phone call from Nathan Potter. Apparently the usually so very secretive London spooks released Morgan's DNA to Victoria Police to assist in any outstanding cases he might be connected to.'

'Like the bashing of Brian Cowan,' Mac said.

Kim nodded. 'Yes. Only *Riley* left not a single trace of himself in Apollo Bay so they had nothing to compare it to, until–' she let things hang for–

'Kim,' Mac snapped. 'Quit fooling around.'

Kim and Jo were grinning like a pair of Chesire cats.

'Until they found a familial match to an old case.'

'Bloody hell,' Curly said. 'Do *not* tell us Morgan was Amy Stewart's sister. Ew.'

'Better than that.' Kim said. 'Morgan Handley is Tugga Tancred's son.'

There was dead silence on both sides of the world for five seconds then everyone started laughing.

'You are kidding,' Curly said.

'We kid you not,' Jo said. 'Morgan's mother must have been doing the cross Europe crawl at the same time as Tugga's bloody Mob.'

Mac eyes were wide. 'Kim, you absolutely must have a camera in The Hatchet's face when you tell him he was nearly killed by Tugga's son.'

'Oh yeah,' Kim grinned. 'And another in Morgan Handley's mug when we tell him he torched his inheritance in Apollo Bay.'

About the Author

Stephen Johnson is an Australian-born journalist, kayaker and motorhome traveller who now plots thrillers from his home on the Tamaki River in Auckland.

His debut novel, *Tugga's Mob*, was inspired by three seasons in Europe as a bus tour guide in the '80s. *Tugga's Mob* was a finalist in the 2020 Ngaio Marsh Awards for Best First Novel.

Boxed, the sequel, was set in the world of animal rights activism and the Melbourne media.

In *Kaikōura Rendezvous*, a cyclone, a down-on-his-luck fisherman and a TV reporter suffering PTSD from a bullet wound converge in New Zealand's South Island with deadly consequences.

Dead on Target is the fourth novel in the *Melbourne Spotlight* mystery series and is set in Australia and the UK.

The *Spotlight* TV crew also feature in *Dark Deeds Down Under 2*, a crime and thriller anthology edited by Craig Sisterson and also published by Clan Destine Press.

Stephen's self-published *Peace Stick* is a historical novel set behind the Iron Curtain during the 1962 Cuban Missile Crisis. It's based on a true story of innocence and hope as two East German schoolgirls deal with a world on the edge of a nuclear war.

And *No Repeats* is the first of an Auckland crime thriller series. Rebecca Cashmore's high-profile media and legal careers are threatened when her secret life implodes.

www.stephenjohnsonauthor.com

STEPHEN JOHNSON
TUGGA'S MOB

STEPHEN JOHNSON
BOXED

STEPHEN JOHNSON
KAIKŌURA RENDEZVOUS

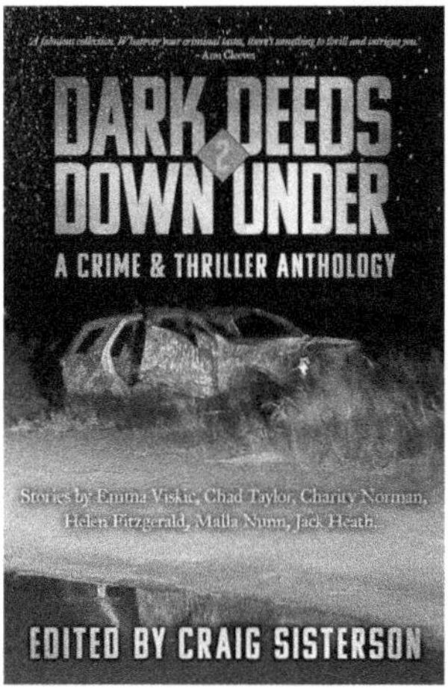
DARK DEEDS DOWN UNDER
A CRIME & THRILLER ANTHOLOGY
Stories by Emma Viskic, Chad Taylor, Charity Norman, Helen Fitzgerald, Malla Nunn, Jack Heath...
EDITED BY CRAIG SISTERSON